CHOCOLATE COVERD MURDER

"Tamzin, I need help," Lucy yelled. "Call 911."

There was no answering cry from Tamzin, which Lucy figured was typical. The woman was so self-absorbed, she was probably putting on fresh lip gloss and was too busy to make the call.

Lucy looked around the shop, past the tables stacked with blue-and-yellow boxes of chocolates and behind the counter, searching for the phone. It was then Lucy suddenly understood why Roger was so upset.

At first, she thought it was just some sort of promotion, a giant chocolate displayed on the marble table behind the counter.

A giant chocolate in the shape of a woman.

But when she took a closer look, she realized it was Tamzin.

Her body had been stretched out on the table and coated with chocolate.

Lucy ran out of the store and stood on the sidewalk, gasping for fresh air.

Tamzin was dead.

Somebody had killed her . . .

Books by Leslie Meier

Published by Kensington Publishing Corporation

A Lucy Stone Mystery

CHOCOLATE COVERED MURDER

LESLIE MEIER

KENSINGTON BOOKS
www.kensingtonbooks.com

KENSINGTON BOOKS are published by

Kensington Publishing Corp.
119 West 40th Street
New York, NY 10018

All Kensington titles, imprints and distributed lines are available at special quantity discounts for bulk purchases for sales promotion, premiums, fund-raising, educational, or institutional use. Special book excerpts or customized printings can also be created to fit specific needs. For details, write or phone the office of the Kensington Special Sales Manager: Attn. Special Sales Department, Kensington Publishing Corp., 119 West 40th Street, New York, NY 10018. Phone: 1-800-221-2647.

Kensington and the K logo Reg. U.S. Pat. & TM Off.

ISBN-13: 978-0-7582-2934-2
ISBN-10: 0-7582-2934-8

First hardcover printing: February 2012
First mass market printing: January 2013

10   9   8   7   6   5   4   3   2

Printed in the United States of America

For Abby

Chapter One

If the cold didn't kill her, the slippery ice on the sidewalk surely would, thought Lucy Stone as she stepped out of the overheated town hall basement meeting room into a frigid Monday afternoon. January was always cold in the little coastal town of Tinker's Cove, Maine, and this year was a record-breaker. The electronic sign on the bank across the street informed her it was five forty-five and nine, no, eight degrees. The temperature was falling fast and was predicted to sink below zero during the night.

Lucy hurried across the frozen parking lot as fast as she dared, mindful that a patch of ice could send her flying. Reaching the car, she made sure the heater was on high, and waited a few minutes for the engine to warm up. While she waited, she thought about the meeting she had just attended and how she would write it up for the local paper, the Tinker's Cove *Pennysaver*.

The topic under discussion was improving toilet facilities at the town beach and quite a crowd had turned out for the meeting. In her experience as a reporter, only dog hearings excited more interest than wastewater issues and this meeting had been no exception.

Of course, people had been complaining about the inadequate facilities for some time; a group of concerned citizens had even entered a float in the Fourth of July parade as a protest. The parade theme had been "From Sea to Shining Sea" and the float depicted the town beach strewn with sewage. The ensuing controversy had prompted the selectmen to address the issue, but there was little agreement on the solution. The budget-minded had favored continuing the present Porta-Potties, the cheapest option. Installing earth closets, the eco-friendly option, had brought out the tree-huggers; the business community, which depended on tourist dollars, had lobbied for conventional toilets, which would require digging a well and putting in an expensive septic system.

This was going to be fun to write up, she thought, as she shifted into drive and proceeded cautiously across the icy parking lot and onto the road. In addition to the cold, they had recently had a big snowfall, so the road was lined with high banks of plowed snow. It was hard to see around the piles of snow, so Lucy inched out into the road, hoping nothing was coming.

As she drove along Main Street, past the police station and clustered stores, past the Community Church with its tall steeple, she thought of possible opening sentences. She'd driven this route so often that her mind was wandering and she was halfway through her story when she cleared town and the landscape opened with harvested corn-fields on both sides of the road. The winter sunset was fabulous, the sky a blazing red that took her breath away. She couldn't take her eyes off the gorgeous color that filled the sky and was barely paying attention to the road when a large buck leaped over a snowdrift, landing right in front of her. She slammed on the brakes and skidded, hanging onto the steering wheel for dear life and praying she wouldn't hit the animal, when the car fishtailed and slammed into the snowbank on the opposite side of the road.

Heart pounding, she caught a glimpse of brown rump and white tail bounding unhurt across the field, and sent up a little prayer of thanks. Then she shifted into reverse, intending to back out onto the road. Pressing the accelerator, she heard the dismaying hum of spinning tires. Climbing out of the car, she found the front end deeply imbed-ded in the snow and the rear tires sunk up to the hubcaps in soft slush and realized she wasn't going to get out without help.

The sun was now falling below the horizon, the sky was a deep purple, and the road was deserted. She got back in the car and reached for her cell phone, remembering she hadn't charged it lately. Indeed, when she flipped it open, the screen blinked BATTERY LOW and immediately went dark. She was only a bit more than a mile from home, but in this frigid weather she didn't dare risk walk-ing. Her best option was to stay with the car and keep the engine running. Unfortunately, she'd been running close to empty for a day or two, too busy to stop and fill the tank.

It was just a matter of time, she told herself, before her husband, Bill, would wonder why she wasn't home and would come out looking for her. Or not. He might figure she was working late, covering an evening meeting, in which case they'd probably find her frozen body the next morning.

Perhaps she should write a note, letting her family know how much she loved them. Then again, she thought, perhaps not. What sort of family didn't come out and look for a missing member, especially on a night when the temperature was predicted to go below zero? She thought of Bill, who habitually watched the six o'clock news, and her teenage daughters, Sara and Zoe, probably texting their friends, all in the comfort of their cozy home on Red Top Road. Didn't they miss her? Weren't they worried? They'd be sorry, wouldn't they, when she was on the news tomorrow night. *Local woman freezes to death. Family in shock. "I should have known something was wrong," says grieving husband.*

A tap at the window startled her and she turned to see a smiling, bearded face she recognized as belonging to Max Fraser. She lowered the window.

"Looks like you could use a tow," he said.

"It was a deer," she said. "He jumped in the road and I swerved to avoid him."

"Doesn't look like the car's damaged," he said. "You were lucky."

"I'm lucky you came along," said Lucy. "I don't have much gas and my cell phone is dead."

"I'll have you out of here in no time," he said, signaling that she should close the window.

Max was as good as his word. In a matter of minutes, he had fastened a tow line from his huge silver pickup to her car. She felt a bump and heard a sudden groaning noise and all of a sudden her car popped out of the snowdrift. Max looked it over for damage and listened to make sure the engine was running okay, and when she offered to pay him for his trouble, he looked offended.

"Folks gotta help folks," he said. "Someday maybe you can help me, or pass it on. Help somebody else."

"I will," promised Lucy. "I certainly will."

Next morning, Lucy was writing her account of the meeting when Corney Clarke popped into the *Pennysaver* office, like a glowing ember leaping out of a crackling fire and onto the hearth. Her cheeks were red with the cold, her ski parka was bright orange, and her stamping feet sprayed bits of snow in all directions. "This is big, really big," she exclaimed, pulling off her shearling gloves.

Phyllis, the receptionist, peered over her harlequin reading glasses and cast a baleful glance at the melting puddle of snow. She drew her purple sweater across her ample bust and shivered. "Mind shutting the door? There's an awful draft."

"Oh, sorry," said Corney, pushing the door shut with difficulty and setting the old-fashioned wooden blinds rattling. "It's just I'm so excited about my big news." She paused, making sure she had the attention of Ted Stillings, the weekly paper's publisher, editor, and chief reporter.

"I'm listening," said Ted, leaning back in his swivel chair and propping his feet on the half-open file drawer of the sturdy oak roll-top desk he inherited from his grandfather, a legendary New England journalist. Like practically every man in town, he was dressed in a plaid shirt topped with a thick sweater, flannel-lined khaki pants, and duck boots.

Lucy typed the final period and turned around to face Corney. "This better be good," she said. Corney, an interior designer who wrote a monthly lifestyle column for *Maine House and Cottage* magazine, was always pitching stories, looking for free publicity.

"Oh, it is," said Corney. She took a deep breath and paused dramatically, then spoke. "Chanticleer Chocolate was voted 'Best Candy on the Coast.' "

It landed like a bombshell, and for a moment there was stunned silence in the newspaper office.

"You mean . . . ?" began Phyllis.

"What about . . . ?" murmured Ted.

"Talk about an upset!" exclaimed Lucy.

"That's right," Corney gave a self-satisfied nod. "It's the first time since the magazine began the Best of Maine poll that Fern's Famous Fudge hasn't won."

"Fern's Famous is an institution," said Phyllis.

Lucy nodded, thinking of the quaint little shop with the red-and-white-striped awning that had stood on Main Street in Tinker's Cove since, well, forever. The business was started by Fern Macdougal, who needed a source of income after her husband was killed in the Korean War. She started selling her homemade fudge through local shops, eventually buying her own place as the little business took off in the nineteen fifties when tourists began flocking to the Maine coast. Fern's Famous, with its big copper kettle and marble counters, was a must-see and nobody passed through town without picking up one of the red-and-white-striped boxes of fudge or saltwater taffy. Nowadays, Fern was in her nineties, but she still kept a sharp eye on the business, which was run by her daughter, Flora Riggs, who had added a catering service to the company, and her granddaughter, Dora Fraser, Max's ex-wife.

"Now, Ted," said Corney, turning to the reason for her visit. "You have to admit this is a big story. And it just happens to tie in very nicely with the Chamber of Commerce's *Love Is Best on the Coast* February travel promotion." Corney, as they all knew only too well, was chair of the Chamber's publicity committee.

"Whoa," said Ted, raising his hand. "February travel promotion? Are you crazy? This is Maine. I don't know if you've noticed, but there's two feet of snow on the ground, the temperature is fifteen degrees, and the forecast is for, surprise, more snow."

"Sleet," said Lucy. "We're supposed to have a warm spell. Global warming."

"Either way, snow or sleet," said Ted, "it's not exactly picnic weather."

"Maine is beautiful every time of year," said Corney, "but winter is my favorite time. The snow is so beautiful . . ."

"It's treacherous," said Lucy. "I barely made it home alive last night. If Max Fraser hadn't come along, I'd be headline news this morning. I got stuck in a snowdrift when a buck jumped in front of my car, out by those cornfields."

"There's a lot of deer out there," said Phyllis. "They eat the corn the harvester missed."

"You've got to be careful in the snow," said Corney, "but the town does an excellent job with the plowing. And you have to admit, on a day like today, when the sun makes the snow sparkle and the air is crisp, it's just a little bit of heaven here in Tinker's Cove."

Corney had a point, thought Lucy, thinking of her antique farmhouse on Red Top Road and how pretty it looked covered with snow, especially at night when the windows glowed with lamplight. Of course, the snow made it impossible to keep the house clean inside. Her daughters, Sara and Zoe, were constantly tracking in snow and mud, as did her husband, Bill. Even the dog added to the mess, rolling in the snow and shaking it off as soon as she came through the door. The kitchen floor was littered with boots and shoes; the coat rack was loaded with jackets and scarves and ski pants. Hats and mittens and gloves were spread on the old-fashioned radiators to dry.

It wasn't just the constant sweeping and tidying that got her down in winter, it was the way the house seemed to shrink in the bleak months after Christmas. The walls seemed to move in and the furniture grew larger. Every surface became cluttered with projects and busywork: the fishing reel

Bill was repairing, the scarf Sara was knitting for the high school Good Neighbor Club, Zoe's rock display for eighth-grade science.

Going out for a meal or a movie, even a shopping trip, was the obvious cure for cabin fever, but it wasn't easy. It took a lot of determination to get anywhere. First you had to layer on all those clothes, then you had to shovel your way to the car, which might or might not start. Once you were on the road, you had to be constantly vigilant, watching for slick spots and creeping slowly through intersections made blind by enormous piles of snow, and you had to remember to start braking well in advance of every stop sign. Once you reached your destination, you had to hunt for a plowed parking spot and then you had to watch your step when you got out of the car because the sidewalks, even when shoveled, soon became slick with ice.

None of that seemed to bother Corney, who was listing the advantages of winter. "Sleigh rides in the snowy woods," she said, prompting a snort from Phyllis.

"Endless shoveling," complained Ted. "Heart attacks—did you see the obits last week? Three old guys, in one week."

Corney ignored him. "We have all these romantic B&Bs with canopy beds and fireplaces. . . ."

"Fireplaces are awful messy. Wood chips, twigs, even leaves, and then there's the ashes. Filthy," said Phyllis. "And that stuff jams up the vacuum."

"Hot toddies and cocoa with tiny marshmallows," said Corney, as if she were raising the stakes in a poker game.

"The stink of wet wool," countered Lucy.

"Tree branches coated in ice, sparkling in the sun," said Corney, laying down a few more chips.

"Broken bones from falls on the icy sidewalks," said Ted. "The waiting time at the emergency room last week was three hours."

"We need to let the world know that Maine doesn't shut down in winter," declared Corney, ready to show her hand.

"It doesn't?" Lucy was skeptical.

"We have so much to offer," insisted Corney.

"Cabin fever. She's been cooped up too long and now she's hallucinating," said Ted.

"I'm sure that's it," said Lucy, laughing.

"Have your fun," said Corney, slipping off her fur-trimmed hood and giving her short, frosted blond hair a shake. "Let's face it: the economy sucks. Businesses are going bankrupt, people are losing their jobs, even their houses. Things are bad."

It was true, thought Lucy. Bill, a restoration carpenter, hadn't had a big job in over a year. He was making do, barely, with window replacements and repairs. Her oldest, her son, Toby, who was married and the father of little Patrick, now almost three, had become disillusioned with his prospects as a lobsterman and had taken out student loans to finish up the business degree he had abandoned. Even her oldest daughter, Elizabeth, who had landed a dream job with the Cavendish Hotel chain after graduating from college, was worried about looming layoffs.

"We have to do whatever we can to attract customers and get things rolling again," said Corney, "and that's what the *Love Is Best on the Coast* Valentine's Day promotion is designed to do." She smiled, as if explaining basic arithmetic to first graders. "Who cares if it's cold outside? That's better for business. The tourists will have nothing to do except shop and eat and drink. They'll have to spend money."

Ted was scratching his chin. "So what do you want? I can't write about Fern's Famous losing, they're one of my biggest advertisers."

"They didn't lose," said Corney, who always saw the glass as half full. "They came in second, just a hair behind Chanticleer. We have the two best candy shops in Maine right here in Tinker's Cove!"

"I suppose Lucy could do something with that," speculated Ted. "She can be pretty tactful, when she tries."

Lucy gave Ted a look. "Thanks for the vote of confidence."

"I know Lucy will do a great job." Corney turned her big blue eyes on Lucy. "You're going to love Trey Meacham. He's a fascinating guy, and a real visionary. Chanticleer Chocolate typifies the kind of success an enterprising entrepreneur can have in Maine. We're becoming a lot more sophisticated, it's not about whirligigs and fudge anymore. We have top-notch craftsmen and artists making beautiful things—oil paintings and handwoven shawls and burl bowls. And the local food movement is the next big thing: fudge and lobster rolls are great, but there are small breweries, artisanal bakeries, and farmers' markets with hydroponically grown vegetables, free-range chickens, grass-fed beef, all raised locally. That's the market that Trey has captured. His chocolates are very sophisti-cated, very unusual."

Phyllis raised one of the thin penciled lines that served as eyebrows. "I like fudge myself. With wal-nuts."

"I have absolutely nothing against fudge, espe-cially Fern's Famous Fudge. This is a win-win situa-tion. Two terrific candy shops. The old and the new. Something for everyone." Corney paused. "And believe me, Lucy, you're going to love Trey."

"I'm married," said Lucy. "I have four kids. I'm a grandma." She paused. "A young grandma."

"You're not blind, are you?"

Lucy laughed. "Not yet."

"Well, Trey is very easy on the eyes, and he's got an interesting story. He left a successful business career, got disillusioned with corporate life, and decided to break out on his own. It's been a little more than a year and he's already got several shops in prime spots on the coast. He's a market-ing genius. In fact, the Valentine's Day promotion was his idea. He says all the merchants in town need to work together to attract business. Compe-tition is out; cooperation is in. A rising tide raises all ships."

"Okay, you win," said Ted, holding his hands up in surrender. "I'm thinking we can maybe do a special advertising promo, a double spread, maybe even an entire special section, if there's enough interest."

"Now you're talking," said Corney. "The Cham-ber's going to have colorful cupid flags for partici-pating businesses, radio spots; we're hoping for some TV coverage. I've got an appointment at

NECN with the producer of *This Week in New England.*"

"Sounds good," said Ted. "Keep us posted."

"You know I will," said Corney, flashing a grin. With a wave, she was gone, leaving the door ajar, swinging in the wind.

Phyllis heaved herself to her feet with a big sigh and went around the reception counter, shaking her head as she struggled to shut the door. "You've got to get this door fixed, Ted, before I catch my death of cold."

"I know a terrific carpenter," said Lucy.

"Cash flow's a problem," said Ted. "Can we work out a barter deal?"

Lucy was intrigued; Bill had a lot of time on his hands these days. "What do you have in mind?"

"I have an old guitar. . . ."

"Absolutely not."

Ted was making a mental inventory of his possessions. "A typewriter?"

"Donate it to a museum," said Lucy, laughing.

"A frozen turkey? We didn't eat it at Christmas."

Lucy was tempted. "It's a start."

"I'm pretty sure Pam's got all the fixings: stuffing, cranberry sauce, canned yams."

"Throw in a bag of frozen shrimp and you've got a deal," said Lucy.

"You're a tough woman, Lucy."

"I've got hungry kids at home."

"How soon can we do this?" asked Phyllis, as a gust of wind rattled the door in its frame.

"I'll call him right now," said Lucy, reaching for the phone.

"Might as well set something up with the choco-

late guy, too," reminded Ted. "What's his name?
Meeker?"

"Meacham, Trey Meacham," said Lucy, as she
started dialing.

A sudden burst of static from the police scanner
on Ted's desk caught her attention and she
paused, finger in the air, waiting for it to clear.
The dispatcher's voice finally came through, or-
dering all rescue personnel to Blueberry Pond.

Lucy looked at Ted. "Are you going or should I?"

"You." He paused. "I'd go but I've got a phone
interview with the governor's wife in half an
hour."

"Really?" asked Lucy.

"Yeah. She's calling for a renewed effort in the
war on drugs."

"Stop the presses," said Lucy, sarcastically, as she
began pulling on her snow pants, boots, scarf,
jacket, hat, and gloves. She checked her bag and
made sure she had her camera and notebook, also
her car keys.

"You better hurry," said Ted. "You'll miss the
story."

"Yeah, well, I don't want to be a frostbite victim," said Lucy, stepping out and making sure the
door caught behind her.

A frigid blast of wind snapped her scarf against
her face and she pulled her hood up over her hat,
blinking back tears as she struggled across the
sidewalk to her car. Inside, the air was still and
cold, and she checked to make sure the heater was
set on high as she started the engine. While the
engine warmed up, she blew her nose and wiped
her eyes, then dug a tube of lip balm out of her

bag and smeared it on her lips. She flipped on her signal and cautiously pulled out into the snow-covered road.

The sun was bright and sparkling snow squalls filled the air as she drove down Main Street and out onto Route 1. There was little traffic, except for a police cruiser and an ambulance that passed her, lights flashing and sirens blaring. She followed them, eventually reaching the unpaved road leading to the pond, where a cluster of vehicles were scattered in the clearing that served as a parking area. She recognized Max's huge pickup among them, with his snowmobile in the back.

She turned the engine off, regretting the immediate loss of heat, and climbed out of the car into the icy blast blowing off the pond. She clutched her hood tight around her head and hurried down the path that had been trodden into the snow by booted feet. Ice fishing was a popular pastime this time of year, and several fishermen had even built shacks on the pond. Lucy had never quite understood the attraction of hanging out on treacherous ice waiting for a trap to spring, indicating a bite on the line, but then she didn't understand why people played golf, either.

Reaching the pond, she hesitated. She didn't like walking on ice; she didn't trust it. But there was a small group standing about a hundred feet from the shore, so it seemed safe enough. The temperature had been well below freezing since Christmas, she reminded herself, imagining the ice must be several feet thick. They used to cut huge chunks of ice from this pond, in the days before refrigeration. She'd seen photographs at the historical society of the ice cutters, with their horses and sledges loaded with enormous blocks of ice that were packed in straw and stored in ice houses until needed in summer.

The ice was slippery underfoot and she walked carefully, leaning forward and making sure to keep her hands free for balance, resisting the urge to stuff them in her pockets. Approaching the group, she spotted her friend, Officer Barney Culpepper, and quickened her pace. That was a mistake, as she ended up sliding into him and would have fallen if he hadn't grabbed her by the arm.

"Whoa, Lucy. Take it easy."

Barney was dressed for the weather in an over-sized, official blue snowsuit, his graying buzz cut concealed by a fur-lined hat that had flaps covering his ears. His eyes were watering, and his jowly cheeks were bright red, as was his nose.

"What's going on?" she asked.

"Somebody went through the ice."

"How can that be? It must be a couple of feet thick," she said, looking around at the little cluster of wooden fishing shacks.

"Dunno." Barney shrugged and wiped his eyes with a gloved hand. "Mebbe he made the hole too big, mebbe there's currents that make the ice thin in spots. I dunno. Seems like a terrible way to go."

There was a sudden surge of activity and Lucy pulled out her camera, thinking it wasn't going to be easy to get a photo in this weather, and with the group of rescuers and fishermen blocking her view. Then the crowd broke apart to make way for a stretcher and Lucy got a clear shot.

She yanked off her glove, stuffing it under her arm, and raised the camera to her eyes, automatically snapping several pictures of the blanketed victim. Then, when she'd lowered her camera, a stiff gust of wind lifted the blanket, revealing the drowned man's bearded face. Horrified, she recognized Max Fraser. Moving woodenly, she followed as the stretcher was carried to the waiting ambulance and was trundled inside. The doors were slammed shut and the ambulance took off, slowly, down the snowy track. There was no need to hurry.

Blinking back tears, Lucy turned to Barney. "Did you see what I saw?" she asked.

Chapter Two

"Yeah," said Barney, shaking his head sadly. "It was Max Fraser."

That was the trouble with living in a small town, thought Lucy. All the victims of horrible accidents were your neighbors and sometimes your friends, or your friends' kids. So were the petty criminals, for that matter. The police blotter, which was printed in the *Pennysaver* every week, was full of familiar names involved in minor tragedies: family quarrels that got out of control, drunk driving arrests, even petty thefts in these tough times. And drugs, always drugs—marijuana, OxyContin, and even heroin.

Of course, everyone knew Max. He was the divorced husband of Fern's granddaughter, Dora, and the father of their only child, Lily. But it wasn't simply the fact that she was acquainted with the victim and even owed him a debt of gratitude that was bothering Lucy.

"He was all tangled up in fishline," said Lucy. "And there was a lure . . ."

"A silver jigging spoon," said Barney.

"It was in his mouth," said Lucy. Max was gone, but she couldn't erase the image of the glittering silver lure dangling from his blue lips and nestled in his ice-coated beard. She remembered how glad she'd been to see his smiling face in her car window just last night.

"He was hooked like a walleye," said Barney. "What a way to go."

Lucy thought of Max's blue eyes, wide open and crusted with ice, and for a moment felt the earth spin beneath her.

"Whoa, there," said Barney, grabbing her arm and steadying her. She took a couple of deep breaths and focused on the snow-covered mountain rising behind the frozen pond, as if the picture-postcard scene could erase the gruesome image of Max's death mask from her mind.

"He probably didn't feel a thing," said one of the bystanders.

Lucy turned and recognized Tony Menard, who she'd interviewed last winter when he won the Lake Winnipesaukee ice fishing tournament in New Hampshire. He was a short, slight man with a French-Canadian accent.

"The cold? Is that what you mean?" asked Lucy.

"More like the booze," said Tony, with a knowing nod. "He must've been blind drunk, eh? To get tangled up like that in his own line."

Lucy knew that drinking often went right along with ice fishing. You had to keep warm somehow and alcohol gave the illusion of warmth, for a while, anyway. "Even so," she said, "how'd he manage to fall through the ice?" She waved her arm.

"Those shacks are standing, we're all out here. The ice must be a couple of feet thick."

Tony shrugged. "The current, maybe. You have to be careful and watch for thin spots."

"Snow ice," said Steve Houle, with a knowing nod toward the place where Max's body had been found. Lucy knew he was a volunteer fireman who organized the Toys for Tots campaign at Christmas. "See how it's white over there, not clear?"

Lucy looked and saw what he meant. "Yeah."

"Well, that happens when the ice melts and refreezes. It's not good."

Tony's head bobbed in agreement. "Punk ice. It's real dangerous."

"But wouldn't Max know about it?" asked Barney.

"Sure, but he could fish at night, and not see," said Tony. "Max was a big risk taker, no?"

"Yeah, his idea of testing ice was to zoom around the lake on his snowmobile," said Steve.

"You think it's down there?" asked Barney, pulling out his notebook. "Mebbe we should send in a diver."

"Could be," replied Tony, his voice rising on the last syllable. "He breaks through, tries to save himself, and his arms go ever' which way and somehow he gets tangled in his line. Could be."

"He wasn't on the snowmobile," said Lucy, remembering Max's competence as he towed her out of the snowdrift. "I saw it in his truck."

"He musta been blind drunk," said Steve.

"That, too," agreed Tony, shaking his head. "He was crazy."

"Yeah, like that old Steve Martin character," said Steve. "You know, the wild and crazy guy."

"That's him," said Tony. "Wild and crazy. We're gonna miss him."

The two drifted off to join their companions and Barney and Lucy headed back to shore together.

"Max was a good guy, and smart, too. Capable." She scowled. "I don't think this was an accident."

Barney gave her a sharp look. "The state police will handle the investigation. A lot depends on what the medical examiner finds."

Reaching shore, Lucy turned and looked out over the frozen lake, a white circle surrounded by bare trees and dark, pointed balsam firs. The place where Max fell through was a bluish patch, filled with bobbing chunks of ice; a handful of fishermen were gathered a respectful distance away. A column of smoke rose from one of the shacks, the metal smokestack glittering in the sunshine.

"It's a heck of a thing," said Barney, voicing her thoughts.

"Have you ever seen anything like that before?" asked Lucy. "I mean, with the fishing line and the lure."

Barney adjusted his thick navy-blue gloves and shook his head. "Can't say that I have."

"I don't buy the accident theory," she said. "It seems more like some sort of cruel joke."

Barney reached for her arm. "Lucy, don't go jumping to conclusions."

"I'm not," insisted Lucy. "But you have to admit it doesn't make sense. I interviewed Max last winter, when he won that snowmobile race. That race covers a thousand miles—you have to be a real survivor just to get to the finish line—and he won. I can't see how a man like that could get himself tangled up in fishline and fall through some punk ice."

Barney started walking toward his cruiser, parked like all the other rescue vehicles any which way in the clearing. "They said he drank a lot and I can tell you from experience that people can do some really weird stuff when they're drunk. And he had plenty of reason to drink lately."

"What do you mean?"

Barney rested his hip on the door of the cruiser, which sank a bit under his considerable weight, and looked her right in the eye. "This is off the record, right?"

"Sure," she said, always eager to get the inside scoop.

"He was having a run of bad luck. I happen to know 'cause he was involved in an altercation at the Quik-Stop, and I kept him overnight in the lockup at the station, just to dry out a bit. He was real chatty, like a lot of drunks, and was going on about how there wasn't any work and he needed money, his ex was after him. He also talked a lot about some woman. Tamzin this and Tamzin that. I didn't recognize the name, but he said she works at that new chocolate shop. He said she was trouble; everything was going fine until he met her." Barney paused, shaking his head. "It's always the same story with these guys; they're always blaming someone and it's usually a woman. You wouldn't believe how often I've heard it."

Lucy nodded. "Oh, yes, I would."

Barney opened the car door. "Remember what I said. Don't go jumping to conclusions." He paused a moment. "I've got some big news myself, but this is strictly off the record."

Lucy's eyebrows rose. "Sure."

"Eddie's coming home. Not just on leave, for good."

Lucy knew Barney's son, Eddie, was a marine and had served in both Iraq and Afghanistan. "That's wonderful news," she exclaimed. "I bet they'll have a parade."

Barney shook his head. "No way. Eddie doesn't want a big fuss."

Lucy thought she could understand. It must be hard to transition from war to peace, from the heat of battle to the chilly quiet of a Maine winter.

"Okay. We'll keep it off the record." Lucy squeezed his arm. "I'm really happy for you and Marge." She gave him a little salute and headed for her own car, her emotions in a tangle. What a day! Max dead and Eddie returning home. A loss and a gain, a minus and a plus. Life was crazy, she thought, noticing that the once sunny blue sky was gone; clouds had filled the sky and the temperature was dropping; Lucy's teeth were chattering when she got behind the wheel and started the car. She called Ted while she waited for the car to warm up and gave him the details of the story.

"Do you want me to come in and write it up?" she asked.

"You can do it tomorrow," he said. "Go on home. You must be frozen clear through."

"You know it," said Lucy, ending the call and dropping her cell phone in her purse. Her breath was fogging up the window and she wiped it with her gloved hand, then pulled off her gloves and held her bare hands over the heat vent, rubbing them together. It helped, but there was no remedy for her feet, which were blocks of ice inside her boots. Shivering, she shifted into drive and headed for home.

It wasn't just the cold, she realized. Her emotions were ragged. She didn't know Max well, but she'd liked him. He could have driven right on by when she was stuck in that snowdrift; he didn't have to stop and help her, but he did. In his way, he was a bit like Eddie, who had enlisted straight out of high school to fight terrorists. He wasn't the sort to turn away from a problem. If something needed doing, Max would do it. She remembered a microburst last summer that had knocked out power, including the town's single traffic light. Max had parked his truck and started directing traffic. They'd run a photo of him—standing in the middle of the street, soaking wet and wind-blown—on the front page.

Cold sleet was falling when Lucy pulled into the driveway of the old farmhouse on Red Top Road. The windows were golden, beacons in the darkening afternoon, as she hurried inside. A delicious spicy, beefy, tomato smell hit her as soon as she opened the door. Sara, bless the child, was standing at the stove, stirring up a big pot of chili.

"Oh, it's good to be home," she said, sinking into a chair and pulling off her boots so she could prop her cold feet on the radiator cover. "I was out in the cold for most of the day and I never warmed up."

"What happened?" asked Sara, tapping the spoon on the side of the Dutch oven. A high school senior, Sara was tall and slender, dressed in a stylish chunky sweater, skinny jeans, and UGG boots. Her blond hair shone in the lamplight.

"Max Fraser fell through the ice at the pond. He's dead."

Sara picked up the boots Lucy had dropped on the floor and placed them in a tray by the kitchen door, then helped her take off her jacket. "That's horrible," she said, gathering up Lucy's hat and gloves and scarf and tucking them in the jacket sleeve before hanging it up on a hook, along with the rest of the family's coats and jackets.

Lucy wiggled her toes, trying to coax some warm blood into her frozen feet. "It seems there's one every winter. I don't know why they keep going out on the ice. I don't trust it."

"Do you want some tea?" asked Sara.

"No, thanks. I shouldn't be sitting here like a lump, letting you do everything."

"Take it easy, supper's under control. Zoe made corn bread, the salad's chilling in the fridge. I just have to set the table."

"Well, in that case, you can pour me a glass of wine."

Lucy had that glass, and another, before the family gathered at the dining room table. Sara had set the table with red place mats and chunky pottery plates and bowls; the silverware gleamed in the candlelight.

The chili was delicious and Lucy had seconds; the corn bread was crispy around the edges and hot enough to melt the butter she slathered on with abandon. Even the salad was a treat, dressed up with goat cheese and nuts. It was all so delicious that it seemed a shame not to have another glass of wine, so Lucy did. She didn't want to think about the scene at the pond, she was concentrating on counting her blessings.

"That was some dinner," declared Bill, leaning back in his chair and rubbing his stomach. His beard was streaked with gray, as was his hair, but his stomach was still flat, a fact that irritated Lucy no end. Of course, her job was mostly sedentary, she reminded herself, while his involved physical labor that burned calories.

"I've got news," said Sara, putting down her fork. "Renee and I got jobs at Fern's Famous Fudge. I've got the paperwork for you to sign."

Lucy knew Renee La Chance, Sara's classmate who lived with her mom, Frankie, on nearby Prudence Path. "I hope it's not going to interfere with your school work," she said.

"It's only until Valentine's Day," said Sara.

"What are the hours?" asked Bill.

"After school and weekends."

"That sounds like a lot," said Lucy, wondering if the dinner had been part of a plan to gain her approval of the job.

"Please, Mom." Sara was on her feet, starting to clear the table. "Like I said, it's only a couple of weeks and I could really use the money. The senior trip is coming up and I don't want to have to ask you and Dad for money."

Zoe, an eighth grader, nodded soberly. "We know about the recession, you know."

"Let's not kid ourselves, Lucy," said Bill. "They've got a point. A little extra money wouldn't hurt."

"They're going to New York and I really want to go," said Sara, carrying the plates into the kitchen. She returned with steaming cups of hot coffee for her parents.

"The whole class is going," said Zoe, rising to help her sister finish clearing the table.

"I guess a job is okay, as long as your grades don't suffer," said Lucy.

"Thanks, Mom. You won't be sorry. I promise I'll study extra hard."

"I wish I could get a job, too," said Zoe. "I'm fourteen now. I'm old enough."

"A job's a big responsibility," said Bill. "And Dora might be a tough boss."

"It's going to be hard for her, losing Max," said Lucy. "I know they're divorced, but they loved each other once."

"She seemed real nice at the interview," said Sara.

"She can be sarcastic, she makes everything into a joke. She was behind that float last summer, the one with the diapers and toilet paper strewn on the beach," said Bill. "You might have to develop a thick skin if you're going to work for her."

For a second, Lucy thought of Max and the silver lure hooked through his lip.

"We could have Mexican sundaes for dessert,"

said Sara. "Dora gave me a jar of fudge sauce and we've got ice cream and peanuts."

"I guess Dora's not so bad after all," said Bill, grinning. "Do you want me to scoop?"

"It sounds like this job may be dangerous," said Lucy, sipping her coffee. "Dangerously fattening."

Chapter Three

Next morning, Lucy woke up knowing she was facing a busy morning. Deadline was at noon on Wednesday, and Ted's favorite maxim was, "It's a deadline, not a guideline." Much of the paper's content had already been written and edited and was ready to be sent electronically to the printer, but this week there were some last-minute news stories. Max Fraser's death was one; there were sure to be some late-breaking developments related to the drowning. And Lucy had an appointment with Trey Meacham at nine-thirty—it was the only time the chocolatier was free—which meant she had to write the story under pressure while the big old clock on the wall above Ted's roll-top desk ticked away the minutes to noon.

She had to get a move on, she decided, indulging in one final glorious stretch before getting out of bed. Bill's side of the bed was empty; he was already up. Lucy headed for the bathroom, passing through the upstairs hall. She could hear the girls' voices rising up the back stairs from the kitchen, telling each other to hurry, and then the slam of the door as they dashed for the school bus.

It was already past seven according to the watch she'd left on the bathroom vanity, so Lucy popped her vitamin, splashed some water on her face, smoothed on a dab of moisturizer, and ran a comb through her hair. Mindful of the interview, she took a few minutes to add a quick dab of mascara and a smear of lipstick.

Back in the bedroom, she pulled her favorite pair of jeans out of the closet. They were freshly washed, which was fortunate because she liked to look nice when she went out on interviews. And from what Corney said, it was worth looking nice for Trey Meacham—not that she wasn't happily married. She was. But there was something about meeting a reportedly good-looking man that seemed to require a bit of effort, an attempt to at least try to look good. As good as she could, considering she was in a hurry. So it was a very good thing that her favorite and best Calvins were clean.

Still in her nightgown, Lucy pulled on a pair of briefs and then stuck one foot into her jeans. She hopped a bit on that foot, sticking her other foot in the empty leg, and pulled them up over her bottom. Drawing the two sides together to fasten the waistband, she encountered a problem. What was the matter? She yanked her nightgown over her head and stood in front of the full-length mirror.

Goodness, when had that happened? She stood in shock, surveying the damage. A bulge of flesh, a roll, a muffin top, was spilling over the blue denim waistband, which was prevented from closing by a bulging, cotton-covered triangle of tummy. Guiltily, she remembered the seconds on chili, the three glasses of wine, the two pieces of buttery corn bread and, worst of all, the Mexican sundae.

It was clear she could not continue to eat like that, not if she ever wanted to wear these jeans again. It was time for action, so she threw herself flat on the bed and through sheer determination managed to button the jeans and zip them up. They'd stretch, she knew they would. If only she could get back up, onto her feet, despite her constricted middle.

Rolling onto her stomach, she used her arms to push herself off the bed, then marched stiffly over to her dresser, where she found a bra and a long, tummy-concealing sweater. The next challenge, she realized, was getting down the stairs.

"Are you all right?" asked Bill, as she shuffled into the kitchen.

"My jeans shrank in the wash," said Lucy, pouring herself a cup of coffee.

"Yeah, right," he said, laughing. "That's a good one."

"Are you saying I'm fat?" asked Lucy, turning to face him.

"No, no," said Bill, quickly backtracking. "You look great."

"I'm going on a diet," said Lucy glumly, seating herself with difficulty opposite him at the round golden oak kitchen table.

"I think we've all gained weight this winter," said Bill.

"You *do* think I'm fat!" exclaimed Lucy.

"Uh, is that the time?" Bill was on his feet, draining his coffee cup. "I've got to, uh, see somebody." He bent and kissed her on the top of her head. "Have a good day."

"I'm not counting on it," she said, sipping her coffee and watching him put on his outdoor clothes. Then he was gone, and she reluctantly went back upstairs to change into yesterday's comfortable, already stretched jeans.

Chanticleer Chocolate was just too cute, thought Lucy, steeling herself against temptation. The shop had a scalloped yellow awning and a handsome blue-and-yellow rooster on the sign that swung from a bracket over the door, and the mullioned windows were curtained with lace. Business must be good, thought Lucy, noticing a discreet HELP WANTED sign taped to the door.

Inside, a scattering of bistro tables were stacked with blue-and-yellow boxes containing three, six, nine, and twelve pieces of chocolate. An old-fashioned glass case containing trays of candies stood in front of the rear wall, beneath a large painting of the same rooster that was on the sign outside. Through a doorway behind the antique bronze cash register, Lucy caught a glimpse of a work area with a long, marble counter where, she assumed, the chocolates were made. The aroma of chocolate filled the air in the shop and Lucy reminded herself that smelling involved no calories and was almost as good as tasting, which did.

"Can I help you?" The speaker was a tall, slender woman with a remarkably large bust. Lucy didn't usually notice that particular feature, but there was really no avoiding it considering the woman's very low-cut black sweater dress. It was short and clingy, stopping some inches above the over-the-knee black stiletto boots that she was wearing.

"I'm Lucy Stone. I'm here to interview Trey Meacham."

"Right. I'm Tamzin Graves. I manage the shop," she said, with a toss of her long, wavy, bleached-blond hair. "Trey called, he's running a bit late, so maybe I can help you out and answer some questions."

She grinned apologetically and Lucy noticed some telltale crinkles on either side of her fire-engine-red lips, as well as a certain thinning of the skin beneath her heavily made-up eyes. Tamzin, she guessed, was well into her forties. Although, from a distance, you'd never know it.

"That would be great; I'm working on deadline," said Lucy, pulling her notebook out of her oversize handbag. "So I guess this is quite an honor, winning Best Candy on the Coast in the readers' poll."

Tamzin's bosom heaved with emotion and her hands fluttered, displaying impossibly long, painted nails. "It's fabulous! We had no idea! I mean, we consider these chocolates extraordinary, made with all natural ingredients and everything absolutely the finest, but still, you don't expect an honor like this, not in the first year, anyway."

"Right." Lucy was getting it all down. "And the chocolates are made right here, in the shop?"

"Oh, no. It's a quality control issue. Trey is a fanatic about quality. No, all the chocolates are made in an old sardine factory in Rockland. It's all been cleaned, with steam and everything, there's no trace of the sardines anymore." Tamzin giggled. "In fact, Trey got an award for creative repurposing of an existing industrial space—I think that's right—from Keep Maine Green."

"But it smells so chocolatey in here," said Lucy.

Tamzin's shoulders popped up. "It's phoney. Well, I mean, the chocolates themselves do have a scent, but we amplify it with a gizmo; it's in the corner. Every few seconds it squirts out a little puff of chocolate scent." She paused, obviously having second thoughts. "I think that's off the record, a trade secret."

"Are you giving away secrets?" Lucy jumped a bit at the booming male voice, and turned to meet the fortyish man entering the shop.

"Not at all, Trey." Tamzin was all aflutter and Lucy briefly wondered if she was having some sort of respiratory problem from the way her amazing chest was rising and falling.

The guy was handsome; Lucy had to admit Corney was right. He had streaky sandy hair that fell over his brow, liquid brown eyes a girl could drown in, a square jaw, and a firm handshake.

"Trey Meacham," he said, grabbing her hand. "You must be Lucy Stone."

"Right," said Lucy, somewhat dazed herself. "Tamzin was just telling me about your commitment to quality. Congratulations on the award."

"We're deeply honored," said Trey. His voice was deep and his tone serious. "It's kind of like hitting a home run the first time you come up to bat. I never expected to be so successful so soon, especially considering the economy. But chocolate, you know, is an affordable luxury. I think that's the secret. And people are weight conscious, too. That's why we package them this way—you can buy three in a box for fifteen dollars."

Lucy's jaw dropped. "Fifteen dollars for three?"

"A terrific little gift, an indulgence." He paused, registering her shock. "Think about it, what other luxury can you enjoy for fifteen bucks? Or as little as five, actually, because we sell them singly, too."

Lucy was thinking that a Snickers bar, her favorite, cost eighty-nine cents, but she didn't mention it.

"I can see you're not convinced," said Trey, throwing in a charming chuckle. "You'll have to try a couple."

He nodded at Tamzin and she withdrew a tray of chocolates from the case and set it on the counter, fluttering over it like a Tiffany salesman displaying an assortment of jewelry. The counter, Lucy realized, was lower than usual and gave Tamzin an ample opportunity to display her remarkable endowment.

"No, no," said Lucy. "I'm on a diet."

Trey's brows rose in astonishment. "You? But you don't need to lose an ounce!"

Lucy knew this was pure flattery, because she was dressed in a puffy quilted parka that entirely concealed her figure. "Swimsuit season's coming," she said.

"Swimsuits . . . that's a good one," said Trey, with a nod out the window at the snow that had begun to fall.

Following his gaze, Lucy noticed his car, parked

out front. It was an enormous green Range Rover, the current favorite gas-guzzling status symbol among the region's strivers and doers. She thought of Eddie, who'd risked life and limb in a war that was supposed to be about terrorism but just happened to be in a part of the world that contained enormous oil reserves.

"Really, you have to try them to appreciate the quality," said Trey, recapturing her attention.

"And the unique flavors," added Tamzin.

"That's right," agreed Trey. "And I'd like to mention especially that we're trying to overcome the male bias against chocolate."

"Chocolate's not just for the ladies," said Tamzin.

"Right. That's why we've got Mucho Macho. It's a manly blend with hints of beef jerky and German fingerling potato."

"In chocolate?" Lucy thought the mixture sounded repulsive.

Trey nodded. "Chocolate isn't just for sweets, you know. Think of chicken mole. In fact, we've got a chicken mole truffle."

"And lavender," said Tamzin. "So creamy and delicate. We call it Lovely Lavender."

Lucy was pretty sure she liked her lavender in a bar of soap. "Interesting," she said, suddenly remembering that time was fleeting and she had to meet a deadline. "Listen, I've got to wrap this up. Do you have a press release or something with the basic facts about the company?"

"Absolutely," said Trey, opening a slim leather portfolio and handing her a professionally produced PR packet.

"And I need a photo, too," she said, producing her camera.

Trey hopped around the counter and stood next to Tamzin, beneath the rooster. "Be sure to get Chanticleer," he said, grinning broadly. "Say chocolate!"

Lucy felt like groaning, but she snapped a couple of pictures instead.

"Well, thanks for everything. . . ."

"You can't leave without some chocolates," Trey said, grabbing one of the big boxes and forcing it into her hands. "Remember, a day without chocolate. . . ."

"Is a really crummy day," offered Tamzin.

"Well, yes," agreed Trey. "But I was going to say that a day without chocolate is like a day without sunshine."

"Oh, that's nice," Tamzin said, patting Trey's shoulder and straightening his collar. She turned slowly and regarded Lucy, obviously making some sort of connection. "Did you say your last name is Stone?"

"That's right," replied Lucy.

"Are you related to Bill Stone? The carpenter?"

It was an instinctive reaction, a tightening of the gut and an increased awareness, as if a predator was heard snapping a twig. "Sure, he's my husband," said Lucy.

"Well, he's a really nice guy," said Tamzin.

Lucy's jaw tightened. "I know," she said. "Thanks for the chocolate."

Making her way out of the shop she wondered how Tamzin knew Bill, and why he'd never mentioned her. Walking carefully down the icy side-walk to the *Pennysaver* office, she also wondered about the relationship between Trey and Tamzin. Was it purely business, or something more? And hadn't Barney said that Max was obsessed with Tamzin, repeating her name over and over when he spent the night in the town lockup? Lucy knew the speed with which news traveled in town; Tamzin must surely have heard of Max's death, but she hadn't seemed at all upset. Come to think of it, thought Lucy, pulling open the office door and setting the little bell to jangling, there hadn't seemed much of anything genuine about Tamzin, starting with her blond hair. And what about Trey? Wasn't he a bit too slick? Then again, she cautioned herself, she wasn't exactly Oprah or Barbara Walters herself, probing for shocking revelations. The interview was simply an opportunity for them to pitch their chocolates and her job was to write a flattering puff piece.

"Whatcha got there?" inquired Phyllis, pointing to the blue-and-yellow box.

"A small fortune in chocolate," said Lucy. "Want to try a Lovely Lavender, or a Mucho Macho?"

Ted was already opening the box. "Mucho Macho?"

"Beef jerky and some sort of potato."

Phyllis was studying the array of chocolates in their gold foil compartments, trying to match them to the pictures on the inside of the box top. "Pretty small if you ask me. I like something to chew on. A mouthful."

Lucy shrugged. "I'm on a diet."

"That one," Phyllis told Ted, pointing with a finger tipped in Midnite Blue, "is Mucho Macho."

"Here goes," he said, popping it into his mouth.

The two women watched closely to gauge his reaction.

"It's different," he said, after swallowing. "Okay. I'm not rushing over there to buy a box."

"Good thing, 'cause this box costs something like sixty bucks."

"Sixty bucks!" Ted was running his tongue around his mouth, trying to extract every bit of expensive flavor.

"Five bucks a pop. Trey says it's an affordable luxury."

"I've got to try one," said Phyllis, picking a chocolate with a bit of crystallized violet on top. "I'm going for Purple Passion." She popped it between her coral lips and closed her eyes, concentrating.

Lucy watched, amused, as Phyllis sucked and rolled the chocolate around in her mouth before swallowing and opening her eyes. "Well?" she asked.

"I guess I'm not a goor-met," admitted Phyllis, pronouncing the final *t*. "I like Fern's Famous dark chocolate with walnuts a lot better. And you can get a half-pound for six bucks—that's what I call affordable luxury."

Leaving the chocolates on Phyllis's counter, Lucy went to her desk and started fiddling with USB cables so she could upload the photos. "How long do you want this story?" she asked.

"I've only got room for ten inches—and don't forget to mention Fern's Famous," said Ted. The fax went into action and he stood over it, pulling out the sheets of paper as they appeared. "It's the ME's report," he said.

Lucy's hand was on the mouse but she paused, finger poised. "What does it say?"

Ted was scanning the tightly packed medical jargon, looking for something he understood. "Ah, here, conclusion. Death due to drowning, indicated by presence of water in the lungs. Contributing factors: high blood alcohol level and cranial bruising . . ."

"A blow to the head?" asked Lucy.

"Yeah, but the ME points out that there is no way of determining if the injury was the result of an attack by person or persons unknown or an accident."

All three fell silent, imagining Max Fraser's final moments. "I hope he went quickly, didn't feel any pain," said Phyllis.

"That's likely, considering his blood alcohol level," said Ted, "and the knock on his head."

"There's always at least one tragedy every winter," said Phyllis. "I hope this is the only one."

Lucy nodded. It was true. Winter brought its own seasonal perils: people fell through the ice on frozen ponds, cars crashed on slippery roads, houses burned down due to the improper use of electric heaters, furnaces backed up and entire families died in their sleep of carbon monoxide poisoning. You tried to be careful, but accidents happened. That was life. Now, even though the image filling her computer screen was of Tamzin and Trey in the chocolate shop, she wasn't seeing them. She was seeing Max Fraser's ice-crusted face and that glittering silver lure dangling from his blue lips. An accident? She didn't think so, although the police certainly would. She was beginning to think Max's death was the work of a killer with a warped sense of humor. And it was up to her, she realized, to make sure the killer was caught. Max had helped her and she'd promised to return the favor. It was a promise she meant to keep.

and that annoying silver line above her temples—
blue lines, in accord; but she didn't think worth
though the rather enormous scale she was beginning to feel. Miss one thousandth of a large
city's money, a sort of capital. Again it was up to
her, she realized, to make sure the letter was
caught that had helped her and she promised
to return the token if it was approved. She was at a
loss

Chapter Four

"Just black coffee for me," said Lucy.

Norine, the waitress at Jake's Donut Shop, crossed out the notation she'd started writing on her order pad. "No hash and two eggs sunnyside up with whole wheat toast?"

Lucy shook her head, mourning the loss of her usual Thursday morning feast. "I'm on a diet."

"And about time, too," said Sue, with a prim nod.

"Nonsense. You look great and breakfast is the most important meal of the day," urged Rachel Goodman, a firm believer in the benefits of three meals a day. "I'll have a cranberry muffin."

Norine was way ahead of her. "Two black coffees, two regular coffees, one cranberry muffin, and one crunchy yogurt. That about it?"

"That's it," said Pam Stillings, Ted's wife, who was a bit of a health nut and always had the yogurt topped with granola. She turned to Lucy. "Rachel's right. If you starve yourself, your metabolism shuts down and it takes longer to lose. Look at Sue." She smiled at the fourth member of the group, Sue Finch. "How do you think she survives on nothing but black coffee and red wine? She's got no metabolism at all."

"And if you ask me, the lack of nutrition is making her rather mean," said Rachel, unusually critical this morning.

"I eat." Sue tucked a lock of midnight black hair behind one ear. "I've found the perfect balance and I maintain it." She took a sip of coffee. "I simply don't see the point of eating calories I don't like, so I skip breakfast in favor of a glass of wine with dinner."

"More than one glass," sniffed Rachel. She'd majored in psychology at college, with a focus on addictive personalities.

"I had a cup of yogurt at home," said Lucy, sounding like a child announcing she'd tidied her room.

"Good girl." Pam nodded her approval and changed the subject, reporting on her work as a member of the Chamber of Commerce's publicity committee. "It looks like the *Love Is Best on the Coast* promo is really taking off." She paused, as Norine distributed the mismatched mugs that were a tradition at Jake's and filled them with coffee. "A lot of businesses are signing up."

"I suppose it's worth doing," said Lucy, in a doubtful tone. She was looking out the window at the frozen harbor and the parking lot littered with shrouded boats beneath a milk-white sky. Snow was falling but it wasn't serious, just what the TV weathermen called "ocean effect." It was funny, she thought, how you got to recognize different kinds of snow after you'd lived in Maine for a while. "I can't see why anybody would leave the comfort of hearth and home and spend a lot of money for this." She waved an arm at the bleak view, almost completely devoid of color.

"Are you kidding? Maine is beautiful in winter," declared Pam, as Norine set her bowl of granola-topped yogurt in front of her.

"I guess you've never been to the Bahamas," said Norine, sending a plate with a muffin sliding across the table to Rachel. "It's better in the Bahamas."

"No, no, no." Pam picked up her spoon. "It's best on the coast."

"You've been listening to Corney," said Lucy.

"That woman is trouble," said Sue, twisting her glossed lips into a scowl. "Somehow she convinced me to organize a Valentine dessert contest." She took a sip of coffee. "I'm counting on you all to enter."

"I'm awfully busy with the committee," said Pam. "I don't see how I'll have the time."

"Me, too," said Rachel, using her tongue to whisk a muffin crumb from her lip. "The Harbor Players are putting on A. R. Gurney's Love Letters and I'm directing."

"That's a first for you," crowed Lucy. "Congratulations."

"Yeah, I'm really enjoying it," said Rachel. "But the rehearsals are very time-consuming."

"That leaves you," said Sue, narrowing her eyes and pointing a perfectly manicured finger at Lucy.

Lucy shook her head. "I told you. I'm on a diet."

"You don't have to eat it," said Sue. "You just have to make it."

Lucy switched to Plan B. "I guess Sara and Zoe can whip something up." She drained her mug and signaled for a refill. "I bumped into Barney Culpepper the other day. He said Eddie's coming home. Permanently. He's done with the marines."

"That is a relief—now I won't have to worry about him." Rachel let out a big sigh. "They were so cute, weren't they? Those boys: Richie and Tim, Toby and Eddie. Remember how Eddie was the catcher, at Little League? That funny squat he had, with one leg stuck straight out?"

Pam nodded, smiling nostalgically. "They were so cute in those Cub Scout uniforms. Remember, Lucy?"

"I wish I could forget," said Lucy. "I was the den mother. They led me a merry chase. Those boys were a handful."

"They all turned out fine, though," said Pam. "My Tim's helping to rebuild New Orleans, Richie's going to make a big archaeological discovery. . . ."

Rachel smiled at the reference to her son. "We'll see."

"Oh, yes he is," said Pam. "Toby's a fine father. . . ."

"And someday he'll actually get that college degree," said Lucy, fretting about her son.

"He'll be a captain of industry," said Rachel. "And Eddie." She paused, thinking, while Norine refilled their mugs. "Do you think he'll become a cop like his dad?"

Lucy bit her lip. "You know, I think he may

need some time to figure out what he wants to do. I said the town would probably have a welcome home parade and Barney said he doesn't want a fuss."

Rachel's face clouded. "Oh, dear. I hope he doesn't have post-traumatic stress syndrome like so many returning vets."

"And I hope he gets started on something pretty quick," said Sue. "It's no good for these kids to hang around aimlessly. Before you know it, they're in the court report for drunk driving or drugs."

"I know," said Lucy, with a grim nod. "We got one at the paper yesterday and I had to format it. I was shocked at the number of drug cases."

Rachel shook her head. "It's an epidemic."

"Where does it all come from?" asked Sue.

"That's a good question," said Lucy, checking her watch. "Gosh, I can't believe the time. It's back to the salt mines for me. I've got a budget meeting at ten."

The ten o'clock news budget meeting had been Ted's idea and Lucy didn't like it much. Deadline was noon Wednesday and the paper came out on Thursday mornings, which meant she used to have all of Wednesday afternoon and Thursday morning free. It was valuable time she used to catch up with her friends and polish off some errands. But Ted had come back from a recent productivity seminar full of ideas, one of which was the budget meeting. Lucy thought the meeting was actually counterproductive—she'd often gathered valuable news tips as she went about town with her list of errands, crossing off grocery shopping at the IGA, vacuum cleaner bags at the hardware store, wine at the liquor store, and mailing bills at the post office. Ted didn't see it that way, however, and now she had to come in at ten instead of twelve-thirty on Thursdays. She didn't even pick up any extra pay; in fact, her salary didn't begin to cover the time she actually worked because she often stayed late at the office on the days the girls had after-school activities and needed a ride home.

The new system had only been in place for a couple of weeks and Lucy wasn't in a good mood when she got to the office. Ted, however, was bursting with ideas.

"Good, you're here," he announced, turning his desk chair around so it faced the room and pulling over two more chairs to form a circle. "We can get started. Phyllis, that means you, too. Put the phone on voice mail, please."

Giving him an evil look, Phyllis punched a few buttons before pushing her chair back and getting to her feet. She hated leaving her comfortable area behind the reception counter, where her chair was just right and items like her enormous pump bottle of Jergens lotion and a big box of tissues were at hand, along with a photo of her husband. She perched uneasily on the chair Ted indicated, then shoved it aside and went back to her desk, wheeling her preferred chair across the office and seating herself.

Lucy was already in place, wrestling with the problem of Sara's job at Fern's Famous, which meant she would need a ride home at five-thirty.

"Let's begin," said Ted, rubbing his hands together. "Lucy, you have the usual selectmen's meeting. I'll take the school committee and the conservation committee, that should be a hot one because of the proposed toilets at the town beach."

"About time," said Phyllis. "Those Porta-Potties stink."

"APTC wants those ecological earth closets, composting toilets," said Ted. "They're up in arms over a septic system so close to the cove."

"That's not news," said Lucy, who knew the letters stood for the Association for the Preservation of Tinker's Cove. "They're always up in arms."

"I'll follow up on the Max Fraser investigation," said Ted, consulting his notebook.

Lucy started to protest but he brushed her objections aside. "I've got something else in mind for you, Lucy." He turned to Phyllis. "You handle the events calendar. Is there anything I should be aware of?"

Phyllis gave him a look. "How the heck am I supposed to know? It's only Thursday, I haven't even started."

"Oh." Ted looked disconcerted. "When you file the press releases, don't you read them?"

Phyllis sighed. "No. I don't have time. I scan them for the date, that's all. So I can file them."

"Well, in the future, perhaps you could just look them over and make copies for me of the important ones," suggested Ted.

Phyllis heaved her bust, a gesture that usually boded trouble, and Lucy pressed her lips together, trying not to smile. "I told you. I don't have time to read them or decide which is important. How do I know, anyway? Is a bake sale important? What about a roast beef dinner at the VFW? How do I decide?"

Ted wasn't about to give up. "Well, a production by the Harbor Players would be more important than a bake sale, for example."

Phyllis smiled in triumph. She knew she had him. "Just you try explaining that to the Junior Women's Club. They think their annual bake sale should be a first-page story."

"Right," said Ted, studying his list. "Moving along, we're going to do a special supplement for the *Love Is Best on the Coast* weekend. There will be special rates for advertisers, an events calendar, and a story. That's where you come in, Lucy. I want a big feature on a couple, an older couple, who've made love last. Don't be afraid to pull out all the stops—I want this to be over-the-top romantic."

"Like one of the fiftieth-anniversary couples?" They often ran stories about such couples, usually accompanied by then and now photos. "The Crabtrees were in the paper last week."

Phyllis was chuckling. "You mean the Crabbytrees? They were duking it out at the Quik-Stop the other day."

"Definitely not the Crabtrees," said Ted. "We want a cute, loving couple, not the Bickersons. Maybe even an old couple who fell for each other years ago but married other people, but then their spouses died and they found each other again. They reconnected." Ted was beaming, he really liked this idea.

Lucy didn't. "How in heck am I supposed to find this adorable couple?"

Ted shrugged. "Ask around. You'll turn up something, you always do."

Lucy chewed her lip thoughtfully, trying to come up with a suitable couple and, much to her surprise, coming up with a few names that she scribbled down.

"That's it, ladies," said Ted, with a satisfied nod. "I think we made some good progress this morning."

"Hold on," said Lucy, remembering the conversation at Jake's. "I'd like to do something about illegal drugs and youth. Have you seen the court report lately? There's a big uptick. We could follow up on your interview with the governor's wife."

Ted shook his head. "Trust me, Lucy. That's too big for us. We don't have the manpower or budget to do an investigative report like that." Before Lucy could protest, he swiveled his chair around and reached for the phone on his desk.

Disappointed, Lucy shoved her chair under her desk and stood, tapping her fingers on the chair back. She didn't want to write puff pieces, she wanted to tackle important issues, but she knew that Ted was struggling to keep the paper afloat. Maybe he was right to focus on promoting business, at least for now. She pulled out her chair and sat down, studying her list of loving couples.

She'd jotted down a few notes when Phyllis's husband, Wilf, came in, holding the door for Ted, who was leaving. Wilf was the mail carrier and he set the day's delivery, bound with a rubber band, on the counter. "Hi, sunshine," he said, with a wink.

Phyllis blushed and smiled at her husband as if they were still honeymooners. "Hi, yourself."

Too bad she couldn't write about them, thought Lucy, but she knew Ted would never go for it. He'd cite journalistic ethics, conflict of interest, or something. Lucy didn't buy it. She figured he just wanted to make her job harder.

"Hi, Wilf," she said, glancing at her list. "You know everybody in town, right?"

"And their dirty secrets," he said. "Only the trash haulers know more about folks than me."

"You're just the man I want," declared Lucy, explaining her assignment to him. "So tell me, do you think the Wilkersons, over there on Bridge Street, would be good subjects?" The Wilkersons had recently announced their fiftieth wedding anniversary and had even renewed their vows.

"I can't really say—people's mail is confidential. Postal regulations."

"How about a yes or no answer?"

"Okay. No to the Wilkersons."

"But why? They're so cute."

"Like I said, I can't elaborate. Regulations. But trust me. You don't want to look foolish, now."

"Okay." Lucy crossed the Wilkersons off her list. "What about the MacDonalds? The people with the farm stand."

Wilf shifted his weight from one sturdily booted foot to the other. "Don't think so."

"Oh." Lucy crossed off another name. That left her with the Sturtevants.

"Oh, gosh, no!" exclaimed Wilf, vehemently.

"What? They seem very happy," said Lucy, who often saw them walking their dog, an aged schnauzer.

"Too happy, if you ask me," said Wilf, with a leer.

"You can't make an expression like that without telling us more," said Lucy.

"That's right," added Phyllis. "Besides, you know you'll tell me later and I'll tell Lucy, so you might as well tell us both now and get it over with."

"Well," Wilf began, in a low voice, "they get a lot of mail in plain brown wrappers, if you know what I mean. And you didn't hear it from me."

"Eeuw," groaned Phyllis. "He's eighty if he's a day."

"And she's got more whiskers than that dog," said Lucy, crossing off the last name on her list.

The fax machine was whirring when Wilf left and Lucy got up to get the message, which she figured was one of the lunch menus that arrived around this time every morning. Instead, she found that the funeral home had sent Max Fraser's obituary.

It was written in the usual flowery style, announcing that "Maxwell Fraser has passed over to that distant blessed shore where he will be joyously reunited with his mother Andrea and father Phil, Gramps and Gran, Uncle Harry and Auntie Maude."

Taking it back to her desk, she passed the stack of new papers, with her photo of the rescuers carrying the stretcher with Max's body on the front page. She hoped he was enjoying the family reunion, but, personally, she had her doubts. She figured Max would rather be zooming from cloud to cloud on his snowmobile.

She started typing the text, editing as she went. When she finished removing all the hyperbole and religious references, she was left with two short sentences. She had to have more so she reluctantly reached for the phone to call Max's ex-wife, Dora. Dora had just answered when Bill arrived, toolbox in hand, to fix the door.

"I'm so sorry to bother you at such a difficult time," she began, after identifying herself, "but I need some information for Max's obituary."

"It's no bother, heck, I oughta be glad he's gone, right?" Dora sniffed. "That man was nothing but trouble."

Lucy knew Dora had a reputation for cracking jokes so she wasn't surprised at Dora's glib comment. There was something in Dora's voice, though, that gave her pause.

"I know you were divorced," said Lucy.

"Right. Seven years ago. But I couldn't get rid of him. He kept turning up, like a bad penny. Worse than that. Like one of those coins you've got in your purse that you can't quite tell what the hell it is, it's all stuck with candy wrapper or something. Could be a penny, maybe a dime. You know you should get rid of it, but how?" She sighed. "That was Max."

Lucy found herself nodding in agreement. "Do you happen to know his mother's maiden name? The funeral home left it out."

"Gooch."

Lucy wasn't sure if this was a joke or not. "Really?"

"Yeah." Dora giggled. "She was a Gooch from Gilead."

Lucy suspected Dora was a bit hysterical and decided she better wrap the interview up. "What about Max's education?"

"He graduated from Tinker's Cove High, did a year in Orono at the university." She snorted. "He flunked out, of course. I used to tell him he majored in partying."

"He was quite the sportsman," prompted Lucy.

"If you call drinking a sport," said Dora.

Okay, thought Lucy, we won't go there. "One child, Lily, right?"

Dora's voice softened. "Lily, yeah. Max got one thing right."

"What about clubs he belonged to? Church?"

"Rod and Gun, o'course. That's all, I think."

"Awards?"

"Well, he won that snowmobile race, practically bankrupted himself doing it." Dora paused and Lucy heard her sniffling. "But if you ask me, I don't think his death was any accident. Max was smart about some things. He knew how to take care of himself."

"Do you think he was murdered?" asked Lucy. Bill, who was removing the pins from the door hinges, paused and gave her a look.

"I . . . I . . . I don't know what to think." And with that, Dora sobbed and hung up, leaving Lucy confused and wondering what she meant. She'd said she was glad Max was finally out of her life for good, but Lucy wasn't convinced. There'd been something in her voice that indicated real sorrow.

"You're awful quiet all of a sudden," commented Phyllis, who was filing press releases by date in an accordion file.

Bill was hanging a tarp over the empty door-frame in a feeble effort to keep out the cold while he planed the door. "I don't want you getting involved, Lucy," he said. "You better leave this up to the police. If Max was murdered, that means the killer could be right here in town. You don't want to get tangled up with any murderer."

"Of course not," said Lucy, deciding she could use some fresh air. "How about some hot coffee?" she asked. When Bill and Phyllis jumped at her offer, she got up and grabbed her anorak. Once she got outside, however, she had second thoughts. The snow was continuing to drift down and the sidewalk was slippery underfoot. She needed to move, though, so she started off in the direction of Jake's. Normally she would drive even that short distance, but walking would burn a few calories and clean out her lungs. If the sun came out, she'd get a bit of vitamin D, but a glance at the cloud-covered sky made that a dim possibility. But most of all she wanted to think over what Dora had said.

Max knew how to take care of himself.

He sure did, thought Lucy, walking past the hardware store with its display of snow shovels in the window. And he'd been ice fishing on Blueberry Pond for years. He would certainly know where the soft tricky spots were. The ME said he'd gotten a knock on the head. How did that happen? Did he slip and fall, hitting his head? She supposed it was possible, but she doubted it. She'd seen the careful, deliberate way Max had worked to free her car and remembered how he'd checked it over, making sure it hadn't been damaged. The more she thought about it, she decided as she reached Jake's, the more likely it seemed that Max's death was no accident.

She was just leaving the café with her cardboard tray of coffees, one regular for Bill, one black with skim for Phyllis, and plain black for herself, when she met Frankie La Chance on the sidewalk. Frankie lived with her daughter, Sara's friend Renee, on Prudence Path, off Red Top Road near the Stones' house.

"Lucy! I've been meaning to call you," exclaimed Frankie, in her charming French accent.

"Same here," said Lucy. "I understand Renee is working at Fern's Famous along with my Sara."

"Which means they will need rides," said Frankie. "I am hoping we can carpool. What do you think?"

"You're a lifesaver," said Lucy. "What is your schedule like?"

"It's all over the place, but I can commit to Monday, Wednesday, and Friday."

"That gives me Tuesday, Thursday, and Saturday," said Lucy. "Not good, but better than every day."

"Good." Frankie nodded. "I must run. I've got a couple who want to buy a house."

"Good for you!" exclaimed Lucy, who knew Frankie was a real estate agent. "Does this mean the market is turning around?"

"I wish," moaned Frankie. "They're older, a retired couple, I think they have money. Very cultured, they talk about art and music. Awfully particular. I've showed them a lot of places already, but nothing has been quite right. They have excellent taste; they're staying at the Queen Vic while they look."

Frankie started to go but Lucy caught her arm. "I have to write a story about an older couple who've made love last—do you think they'd be good subjects?"

Frankie broke into a broad grin. "Absolutely!"

"You say they're at the Queen Vic?"

"Yes. Roger and Helen Faircloth are their names. You can say I suggested them to you."

"Thanks," said Lucy, vowing to call them as soon as she got back to the office.

The heavy blue tarp was still hanging in the doorway when she arrived, as Bill had set the door on sawhorses and was working away at it with a plane. Phyllis, who was bundled up in her winter coat, took the hot cup gratefully, and so did Bill.

"I'm almost finished," he said, taking a long swallow and setting his cup aside.

"Can I help?" asked Lucy.

"Nope," he said, running the plane over the edge of the door a few more times and then re-hanging it on its hinges. He pushed it shut, and the latch clicked easily. "All done."

"Good work," said Lucy, seating herself at her desk and sipping her coffee. "What are you doing next?"

Bill had settled in Ted's chair, enjoying his coffee break. "I'm going to see about a job on Parallel Street, a bathroom remodel. What about you?"

"I've got to set up some interviews," said Lucy. "And I've got to pick up Sara and Renee."

Bill nodded and began packing up his tools.

When he was gone, Lucy reached for the phone

and called the Queen Victoria Inn. Helen Faircloth did indeed sound quite charming on the
phone, but she and her husband were not available this afternoon or Friday since they would be
house hunting. Lucy set up an appointment for
Saturday afternoon, at the inn. Then she got to
work on the birth announcements, one of the
paper's most popular features, noticing a decided
uptick in the number of unmarried parents. She
sent an e-mail to Ted, suggesting they do a feature
story on the trend, and at five o'clock she left for
the day, heading over to Fern's Famous to pick up
Sara and Renee.

Parking in front of the fudge shop, she had a
clear view through the plate glass windows. There
was no sign of Sara or Renee, who she guessed
must be busy in a back room, but she saw Lily, Max
and Dora's daughter, standing by the cash register,
staring off into the distance. Then she turned and
smiled and Lucy saw the girls, pulling on their
jackets and coming toward the door, so she gave a
quick honk to let them know she was waiting.

"How'd it go?" she asked, as they piled into
the car.

"We got to make fudge," said Sara. "It's easy."

"We can eat as much as we want," said Renee.

"Better watch that," advised Lucy. "It's very fattening." She pulled out into the road. "Did I see
Lily working there?"

"Yeah," said Sara.

"I thought she was at college in Rhode Island,"
said Lucy. "Did she come home because of her
dad's death?"

"She's taking a semester off," said Renee. "She

wanted to go back, but her parents weren't able to manage the tuition so she's working and saving."

Lucy sometimes thought she could drive the route home blindfolded, she'd done it so many times, so her mind was free to ponder this new information, wondering how Max's death would change Lily's situation. There might be a small estate; nobody died absolutely penniless. There might be a life insurance policy, a bit of property, even a stamp or coin collection. But even if Max didn't leave much behind, Lily would qualify for more financial aid now that she was fatherless and would probably be able to resume her education.

Lucy knew that money, especially the lack of it, was a frequent bone of contention between divorced couples. She'd never seen Max's name on the lists of deadbeat dads that the paper received from time to time, but Barney had said he was worried about money that night he'd spent in the lockup. No wonder; the recession was hitting lots of people, and Max was probably no exception. But if Max suddenly had had a reduced income, it could mean that he was worth more dead than he was alive. And that, she thought, as she braked for a stop sign, was a dangerous situation to be in.

Chapter Five

The Queen Victoria Inn was a survivor from an earlier, more gracious time, when the wives and children of prosperous Boston and New York businessmen would spend the entire summer at the coast, enjoying the cooling breezes and languid atmosphere. Back then the rocking chairs on the front porch would be filled with gossiping matrons, fanning themselves and keeping an eye out for their children's matrimonial prospects. Those days were gone and now most of the guests could manage to get away from their high-pressure jobs for only a weekend and spent much of their vacation barking orders into cell phones or pecking away at laptop computers.

The Faircloths were different, Lucy discovered, when she met them in the inn's spacious dining room for afternoon tea on Saturday. Unlike the handful of others scattered at the cloth-covered tables, they weren't hunched over any electronic devices whatsoever. They were simply sitting and chatting and obviously enjoying each other's company.

"Hi! I'm Lucy," she said, joining them.

Roger Faircloth immediately leaped to his feet and pulled out a chair for her. He was tall and moved easily despite his age, which Lucy guessed must be close to seventy. His abundant hair was snow white, his face was tanned, and he was beautifully dressed in gray flannel slacks, tasseled loafers, and a camel cloth blazer. His blue oxford-cloth shirt was topped with a jaunty striped bow tie.

"Thank you," murmured Lucy as she lowered herself onto the chair Roger slid beneath her. She wasn't used to this sort of treatment and was frankly relieved when she found she'd succeeded in connecting with the moving chair.

"Allow me to introduce my wife, Helen," he said, taking his seat and signaling to the waitress.

"I'm so pleased to meet you," said Helen, who was every bit as good-looking as her husband. Her shoulder-length blond pageboy was streaked with gray, but her subtly made-up face exhibited only a few well-moisturized lines. She was wearing a blue twinset, which matched her eyes, a pearl necklace, and a tailored pair of slacks. A rather large diamond glittered on her finger, along with a broad gold wedding band.

"Well, I'm very grateful to you for agreeing to this interview. Tea is on me, of course," said Lucy, eager to get that detail out of the way.

"Absolutely not," said Roger, as the waitress, Caitlin Eldredge, appeared to request their preferences. Roger chose a hearty Lapsang souchong, but Helen and Lucy opted for Earl Grey. Moments later, Caitlin arrived with a steaming silver pot for each of them as well as a tiered silver stand containing scones, assorted cakes, and tiny sandwiches.

"Please, help yourself," invited Helen. "A young person like you must have a hearty appetite."

"Not so young," replied Lucy, "and I'm trying to lose a few pounds."

"It's a struggle, isn't it?" agreed Helen. She turned to her husband with a twinkle in her eye. "I'm afraid you're going to have to eat for both of us."

"I'll do what I can," he said, piling the little triangular sandwiches on his plate.

"Roger can eat as much as he wants and never gains a pound," said Helen. "It's so unfair."

"My husband, too," said Lucy, opening her notebook. "I understand you're here in town looking for a house."

"Yes," said Roger, polishing off a salmon sandwich and reaching for another. "We definitely are. Tinker's Cove is a beautiful town and we think, no, we *know* it will suit us perfectly."

"What prompted the move?" asked Lucy.

"Oh, we've lived in Connecticut for most of our marriage, that's over forty years."

"Remarkable," said Lucy.

"Not so remarkable. It's easy to stay married when you're in love," said Roger, beaming across the table at Helen. "She's every bit as pretty as the day I married her."

"Oh, Roger," protested Helen, her cheeks turning pink. "You're embarrassing me." She turned back to Lucy. "Isn't he impossible?"

"I think you're fortunate to have such a loving

relationship," said Lucy, feeling she was in danger of losing control of the interview. "So why did you leave Connecticut?"

"Oh, our house burned down," said Helen, with a little shrug.

"That's right," agreed Roger, buttering a scone. "Total loss."

"Oh, my goodness." Lucy was shocked. "That's terrible."

"When life hands you lemons, you make lemonade," said Helen, brightly. "We decided to look at it as an opportunity. When you've lost everything, you see, at first it's very terrible. You're shocked. The photos, the artwork, the antiques, all turned to ashes."

"We were quite serious collectors," said Roger. "We had an early Warhol, a Basquiat. . . ."

"I never liked those much, dear. It was the Wyeths I hated to lose," said Helen.

"For me, it was the antiques. That Goddard highboy. . . ."

"Brown University had just made inquiries, too. They wanted to buy it."

"Buy it!" hooted Roger. "They wanted us to leave it to them."

"Doesn't matter now," said Helen, with a sad smile. "It's gone." She took a deep breath and straightened her back, taking a sip of tea. "It's all gone, but we decided not to look at it as a loss but to move on. We'd always wanted to live on the coast—I just love Maine, you see. And if I can't have a Wyeth landscape on my wall, I can have one right outside my window."

"That's a wonderful attitude," said Lucy. "Can you tell me how you met?"

"I was in London, modeling," said Helen. "It was the Swinging Sixties."

"I wasn't swinging, I was at the London School of Economics. I call it the Slogging Sixties."

"We met on a double-decker bus," said Helen. "The bus swerved 'round a corner and I lost my balance. I landed right in his lap!"

"Talk about luck! This beautiful girl lands in my lap. I took it as a sign that she was meant for me." Roger finished off his scone and reached for a tiny square of chocolate cake.

"So you married and came back to the U.S. and settled in Connecticut?" asked Lucy.

"More or less," agreed Roger.

"Any children?" asked Lucy.

Helen shook her head sadly. "It just never happened, it's my one regret."

Roger was looking over the remaining cakes, deciding between a lemon curd tart and a mocha mini-cupcake. "I know you feel that way," admitted Roger. "But I think—no, I know—we were spared a lot of heartache. Think of the Westons."

Helen turned to Lucy, her blue eyes brimming over. "Their daughter was killed in a car crash."

"And even when there aren't any tragedies, children do tend to test a marriage," said Roger, choosing the mini-cupcake.

Helen dabbed at her eyes with a lace-trimmed handkerchief. "We've had good times, haven't we, Roger?"

"You betcha," said Roger, reaching across the

table and covering her small pink hand with his larger speckled one. "It's like that old song: 'I Got You, Babe.' "

"You certainly do," said Helen, leaning toward him and smiling.

The two remained gazing into each other's eyes until Caitlin returned. "How's everything?" she asked.

"Just lovely," said Helen.

"Good, I'll be back with the check," said Caitlin.

Lucy reached for her bag. "This is on my expense account," said Lucy. "I can't thank you enough. . . ."

"Nonsense." Roger's voice was firm. "Call me old-fashioned but I couldn't let a lady pay for me. Besides, I'm the one who ate all the food!"

When Caitlin returned, Roger snatched the little plastic folder from her. "I'll just sign," he said. "We're guests here."

Caitlin pressed her lips together and leaned forward, whispering in Roger's ear. Suddenly Roger's face flushed beet red. "That's absurd. I never heard of anything like that. What sort of establishment is this?"

"I'm just following orders," she said, looking extremely uncomfortable.

"I'm sure it's a misunderstanding," said Roger, scribbling on the bill and snapping the folder shut. "Here you go. I'll take it up with the management later."

Caitlin shook her head, refusing to take the folder. "Cash only, those were my instructions."

"Can't you see I have guests," protested Roger. "I'll take it up with the manager later." He practically tossed the folder at her. "Now off you go, like a good girl."

Caught off balance, Caitlin snatched the folder out of the air and walked off, scowling.

"I'm so sorry about that," said Roger, turning to Lucy. "I don't know where they get their help these days."

"From right here in town," said Lucy, who sympathized with Caitlin's predicament and hoped she wouldn't get in trouble. "She's in my daughter's class at school."

"Well, I'm afraid she's going to learn a hard lesson. There's no tip for that girl."

"It wasn't her fault, Roger," said Helen. "It's just a misunderstanding. I'm sure you can straighten it out with the manager." She paused, beaming at him. "You always do."

Roger turned to Lucy. "You know what they say: Behind every successful man there's a good woman. I don't know what I'd do without my Helen. I don't deserve her."

"Of course you do, Roger. It's I who don't deserve you."

"No, dear, you are the glue that holds us together."

"No, Roger. You are. It's your strength. I'd be lost without you."

"And I without you."

Time for me to get lost, thought Lucy, feeling as if she'd eaten too many sweets. Which was funny, when you came to think of it, because all she'd had was tea. Plain tea with no sugar.

* * *

Back home, Lucy checked the mailbox that stood out by the road and found a couple of bills, a flyer from the hardware store, and a thick envelope like a wedding invitation. Intrigued, she opened it and found an engraved card from the Chamber of Commerce inviting her to the Hearts on Fire Ball scheduled for Valentine's weekend at the VFW hall. The part about the VFW hall was a bit discouraging, but the event was black-tie optional, which made her heart beat a little faster, imagining how handsome Bill would look in a tux. And she couldn't remember the last time she'd had a reason to wear anything dressier than a pair of slacks and a nice sweater.

Hurrying into the house, she debated how best to approach the subject with Bill, who declared himself allergic to neckties. A rented tux was a lot dressier than the all-purpose blue blazer he wore, most often with an open-necked shirt, when a jacket was absolutely necessary.

Lucy paused in the kitchen to slip off her boots and hang up her jacket, taking a moment to neaten up the coat rack. Why couldn't Bill and the girls manage to use the little loops for hanging that were sewn into their jackets? Instead, they tossed them on the row of hooks any old way, piling them one on top of the other until the whole mess slid off onto the floor. Catching herself in a negative train of thought, she resolved to try to think more positively, like Helen Faircloth. There was nothing she could do about winter, the weather was out of her control. She could control her thoughts, however, by concentrating on the positive aspects of the season. Like the ball.

The TV was on in the family room; Lucy could hear bursts of sound that indicated a sporting event of some kind. Maybe Bill would like a snack, she thought, popping into the powder room and applying a fresh coat of lipstick and a squirt of cologne. Thus armed, she advanced into the family room where she found her husband in his usual chair, a big old recliner, slapping his knee.

"A three-pointer," he declared. "You shoulda seen it. Right across the court. Wait, hold on, they're replaying it."

Trapped, Lucy perched on the sectional and watched as an abnormally tall man with many tattoos seemed to launch a basketball with an effortless flick of his wrist that sent it sailing from one end of the court to the other and right through the hoop.

"Amazing," she said.

"And they said he wasn't worth sixty million dollars," scoffed Bill.

"Fools," said Lucy, thinking to herself that nobody on God's green earth deserved sixty million dollars, not when other people were hungry and homeless.

"That's the quarter," said Bill, as a buzzer sounded.

Remembering her mission, Lucy jumped up. "Can I get you something? A beer? Would you like me to throw some popcorn in the microwave? There's a mini-pizza in the freezer I could heat up for you."

Bill looked at her suspiciously. "Did you smash up the car?"

"No. What makes you think that?"

"Dunno. You're not usually this nice. Are the

girls okay?" He paused. "Don't tell me Sara's in trouble. Or Zoe?"

"Don't be ridiculous," said Lucy. "The girls are fine. And so is the car."

"Well, you obviously want something. What is it?"

Lucy plopped herself in his lap, giving him the full benefit of her cologne. "Don't I smell good?"

"You always smell good," he said, nuzzling her neck.

Lucy stroked his beard, noticing the gray. "You know what holiday is coming up?"

"Mother's Day?" he teased.

"No." She nibbled his ear. "Valentine's Day."

"Funny you should mention it. I noticed a bunch of red hearts in the windows at Fern's Famous."

For a moment, Lucy wondered if he'd also noticed something at Chanticleer Chocolate, or rather, someone, but pushed the thought from her mind. "No chocolate for me," said Lucy. "I'm on a diet."

You had to hand it to Bill, he could be amazingly prescient. "So what do you have in mind, *sweetheart?*"

Lucy handed him the invitation.

"A ball?"

"Wouldn't it be fun to get dressed up and dance? We could dance the night away."

Bill shrugged. "The VFW does a pretty decent prime rib."

"I could wear something with a low neck," she murmured in his ear. "And I haven't seen you in a tux since our wedding."

A shudder seemed to run through Bill's body. "A tux?"

Lucy knew the value of a strategic retreat. "It's optional." She sighed. "Of course, I'd look pretty silly all dolled up in lace and black satin if you're not dressed up, too."

"We'll see," he said.

"You mean we can go?"

"Yeah," said Bill, as she bounced in his lap and gave him a big hug.

"You can pick up the tickets at the Seamen's Bank," said Lucy, hopping off his lap. "Do you want popcorn or pizza?"

"Just a beer," he said, turning the volume up with the remote. "Whaddya mean, I can buy the tickets?"

"Well, it's ten dollars cheaper for men."

"Isn't that discrimination?" he asked, grinning. "I'm surprised your feminist ire isn't aroused."

"Sometimes even a feminist has to be practical," said Lucy, heading for the kitchen. "I think they want to encourage men to attend."

When she returned, Bill was frowning. "The Celts are behind," he muttered, taking the bottle of Sam Adams. "It's barely a minute into the second quarter and they're trailing by five points."

"Sixty million dollars isn't what it used to be," she said.

"You're telling me. The guy's a bum."

Lucy wanted to wrap things up before she started cooking dinner. "So you'll get the tickets?"

"I'll go, I'll think about the tux, but I'm not buying the tickets."

Lucy plunked herself down on the sectional and grabbed a magazine off the coffee table. "You're being ridiculous, you know," she said, flipping through the ads for beauty products and designer handbags.

"I hate writing checks," he said, groaning as a ball bounced off the rim.

"They take cash, even credit cards," said Lucy.

"Banks have weird hours." Bill leaned forward in his chair. "Damn."

Lucy knew it was counterproductive but she couldn't stop herself from arguing. "So it's okay for me to rearrange my schedule, but not for you?"

"I work hard," he snapped. "The least you can do is be supportive."

Lucy couldn't believe what she was hearing. "Like I don't work hard, too?"

"Yeah!" he exclaimed, as a ball made it through the hoop. "You have a part-time job, Luce. It's not the same thing as being the breadwinner."

Lucy threw down the magazine. "Men are so self-centered!" she declared, grabbing another.

"Hey, I'm a good guy," he protested. "I said I'd take you to that ball, didn't I?"

Lucy stared at the black-and-white photo of a nearly naked man and woman entwined in a steamy embrace on a beach; they appeared to be coated in baby oil.

"A funny thing happened when I was doing an interview at Chanticleer Chocolate. The woman who works there, Tamzin, asked about you."

"Did she?" Bill was staring at the TV, where two commentators in blue blazers were recapping a play. "I helped Max put in the shelves in the storeroom."

"You never mentioned it," said Lucy.

A commercial for an erectile dysfunction drug was playing on the TV; a man and woman were sitting in separate bathtubs, outdoors. "Who does that?" asked Bill, incredulous.

"Dora said Max was nothing but trouble. . . ."

Bill was flipping channels, pausing at a golf match. "You can say that again," said Bill. "He never paid me for that job." He was staring at the parched Arizona landscape that filled the screen. "Look at that, must be eighty degrees at least."

"How much did he owe you?" asked Lucy.

"We agreed on five hundred dollars, but I haven't seen a cent—and I'm not the only one he stiffed."

"Who else?" asked Lucy.

"Just about everybody," said Bill, watching as Phil Mickelson made a putt. "Nice."

"If he owed a lot of people money, a lot of people had a motive to kill him, didn't they?"

Bill looked at her. "I don't follow you. What would killing him accomplish? You still wouldn't get your money back."

"You'd get revenge," said Lucy.

"Pretty cold comfort, if you ask me," said Bill, draining the bottle of beer and switching off the TV. "What do you say to a 'matinee,' before the girls come home?"

Lucy was caught by surprise; she was wondering who else Max might have stiffed. "Now?"

He grinned wickedly. "Yeah, now. Like in that commercial. We can be spontaneous, right? And I don't need any pills, either."

Spontaneity didn't appeal to Lucy, who was newly self-conscious about her body, thinking of the tummy bulge she'd noticed the other day. "I feel fat," she said.

"Don't be silly," said Bill, taking her hand and drawing her into an embrace. "I love you just the way you are. You're perfect."

Lucy felt her resistance crumbling as he wrapped his arms around her.

"A little bit of extra flesh is sexy," he murmured, whispering into her ear.

Lucy felt as if she'd been slapped and pulled away. "I've got to start supper," she snapped, marching into the kitchen.

"What? What did I say?" demanded Bill.

Lucy grabbed a couple of onions and began chopping, furiously smacking the knife against the cutting board. How on earth did the Faircloths do it, she wondered, as her eyes filled with tears. It was the onions, she told herself. Onions always made her cry.

Chapter Six

Sunday morning, when the breakfast dishes were all cleared away and the dishwasher was humming, Lucy sat down at the round golden oak table with the newspapers. Bill was outside splitting wood, and the girls had gone over to Prudence Path to babysit little Patrick while Toby and Molly went to a christening.

Lucy always read the *Boston Sunday Globe* first, starting with the colorful magazine. She was turning the pages slowly, savoring this bit of quiet time, pausing to admire a mouth-watering photo of a red velvet layer cake. Perfect, she thought. Just the thing to make for the dessert contest.

Flipping the page over, she eagerly read the recipe but didn't find it all that appealing. It called for too much sugar—two cups—and two whole sticks of butter, as well as an awful lot of red food coloring. It also called for the addition of vinegar, which made the whole thing sound more like a science experiment than a cake.

No, red velvet wasn't the way to go. Maybe cupcakes, she thought. They were all the rage. Maybe she could work up a cupcake with a gooey chocolate surprise filling and a ganache topping. That sounded yummy, but she'd never had much luck getting ganache to set and she couldn't enter cupcakes with runny icing. And she had no idea how to get that chocolate filling inside the cupcake. Did you bake it in? Was there some sort of magic process involved like the Denver Chocolate Pudding in her Fanny Farmer cookbook that she sometimes made as a special treat?

Another specialty was the clafouti she often made in summer, when cherries and blueberries were in season. She'd found the recipe in her Julia Child cookbook and it was surprisingly simple. It was the only recipe in that book that she actually made. She was wondering if she could figure out a way to make a chocolate clafouti, perhaps with frozen raspberries. That would be really good, and original. She suspected all she'd have to do would be to add some cocoa powder to the recipe, but how much? Chances of getting it right the first time seemed slim—and would it also need a chocolate sauce? She rather thought it might, which made the project seem awfully ambitious.

She was leafing through her Paula Deen cookbook when she heard someone tapping at the kitchen door. Libby, never a very good guard dog, was giving mixed messages, simultaneously growling and wagging her tail, when Lucy opened the door. Discovering it was Frankie, the dog erupted into a joyful dance of greeting.

"Down," said Lucy firmly, pointing to the dog's bed.

The Lab settled down with a big sigh and Lucy took Frankie's coat. "Want some coffee? It's nice and hot."

"Sure," said Frankie, slipping into a chair. "I can't stay long, I've got another appointment with the Faircloths. I've been showing them everything from here to Portland and back."

"I meant to thank you for telling me about them," said Lucy, pouring two mugs and bringing them over to the table. "They are every bit as cute as you said and I got a great interview."

Frankie sipped at her coffee. "I'm getting a bit sick of them, to tell the truth. Talk about picky!" She shrugged philosophically. "Of course, when you're spending the kind of money they are, I guess you can be picky. They have a lot of art and antiques and they want a house that will showcase their collections."

Lucy was puzzled. "I thought they lost everything in a house fire."

"You're right," said Frankie, knitting her brows. "I guess some of their stuff was saved—they must have it in storage." She wrapped her hands around the mug. "Actually, I was wondering about the couple at Chanticleer Chocolate. Do you think they're looking for a house?"

"You mean Trey and Tamzin? I don't think they're a couple," said Lucy. "Where did you get that idea?"

Frankie took a sip of coffee. "I saw them outside the store. They were arguing; I guess that's why I thought they were a couple." She giggled. "Maybe it's just their names. Trey and Tamzin. They sound like a couple, no?"

Lucy smiled. "I don't know much about Trey, but I do know that Tamzin is very flirtatious. She flaunts her assets, if you know what I mean."

Frankie's eyebrows went up. "Really?"

"Tight dresses, very low necklines, thigh-high boots. Stilettos."

"Not chic," said Frankie, who favored tailored pantsuits enlivened with colorful scarves.

"That's one way of putting it," said Lucy. "She's certainly not subtle. She's got 'em and she flaunts 'em."

"It's better to leave some things to the imagination," said Frankie, with a sly smile. "But as far as you know, Trey doesn't have a family?"

There was something in her expression that made Lucy wonder if Frankie was interested in Trey for herself. If so, she thought, she wasn't the only one. "I don't think so, but I don't really know," said Lucy. "I know Corney said she finds him very attractive."

"Oh, Corney, she goes after all the single men, but she never catches one," said Frankie, looking at her watch and getting up. "I can't be late for the Faircloths. Roger gets very annoyed."

"He seems so formal, old-fashioned even," said Lucy, getting up and taking Frankie's coat off the hook where she'd hung it.

"He's very easygoing—as long as he's getting his way," said Frankie, pulling the coat over her shoulders and buttoning it. "But I told him, I can only give them the morning. I must go to the funeral this afternoon."

"I'll see you there, then," said Lucy, opening the door.

Funerals were always a big draw in Tinker's Cove, especially if there was reason to believe the sad observance would be followed by a generous spread. It was no surprise that Max's funeral, actually a memorial service since Max had been cremated, attracted a large crowd. Lucy figured most of the mourners were looking forward to the buffet lunch from Fern's Famous, which had a highly popular catering service run by Flora, as well as the candy business.

Lucy, who was sitting beside Bill in the crowded Community Church, was finding it difficult to concentrate on the eulogy as her thoughts kept straying to Flora's curried chicken puffs and beef satay. They also did a really tasty Greek spinach pie and truly amazing Swedish meatballs that Bill couldn't resist, and neither could she. Faced with all that delicious food, she knew she had to have a plan, so she intended to follow the suggestion in an article she'd read recently that advised limiting yourself to a single bite of high-calorie foods. "The second bite will taste just like the first," the author claimed.

Lucy was soon checking out the congregation, trying to judge the size of their appetites. The fishing crowd were undoubtedly big eaters and she hoped Flora had taken that into account. She was mulling over the best strategy for attacking the buffet, vowing to load her plate with crudités rather than cheese cubes, when the minister intoned the final benediction. Everyone stood as the chief mourners exited the front pew and began walking down the aisle. First went Lily, accompanied by her mother; she was holding tightly to Dora's hand. Flora walked behind them, beside Fern, who refused her daughter's offer of a supportive arm despite her advanced age.

Lucy was struck by the image this family of women presented: four generations, obviously sharing the same gene pool, all dressed similarly in black. Lily, the youngest with her fresh complexion and long blond hair and her mother, Dora, with her frosted bob. Flora, in her sixties, with salt-and-pepper hair, bore the same lines on her face as her mother, only less deeply etched. Fern was the smallest of the four, and the oldest, but was clearly the respected head of the family. Watching them, it occurred to Lucy that they made a complete unit in themselves and she wondered if there had ever really been a place for Max. How did he fit in with this tightly knit group?

The four women were followed by a scattering of Gooches from Gilead; at least Lucy supposed that's who they were. Max's parents had died years before and he was an only child, so she assumed these mourners were a loosely related collection of cousins, aunts, and uncles. They didn't have the same sense of unity about them that the four women had; they didn't resemble each other but came in a variety of shapes and sizes. A gawky, red-haired kid slouched along beside a very short, very fat woman who might or might not be his mother, a stocky man with a gray beard accompanied an attractive woman with streaked blond hair, a young man with a studious air and wire-rimmed glasses followed behind them.

The center aisle soon filled with people moving slowly toward the exit and Lucy was about to join them when Bill caught her arm. "Let's go out the side door," he said, whispering in her ear. "We don't want to be at the end of the procession."

Apparently Bill had also been thinking hard about the best strategy for getting first dibs on the buffet and was planning an end run around the crowd. The reception would take place at the Macdougal family homestead, a huge old Victorian that had been completely renovated and now sported an authentically gaudy paint job of brown, cream and red. Lucy remembered how the house had looked when she first moved to Tinker's Cove; it had been practically bare of paint then and the sagging porch roof was held up with a couple of two by fours propped against cement blocks. That was before Fern's Famous had become the successful business it was today, of course.

Lucy and Bill weren't the only ones who'd avoided the crush at the church door. They found quite a number of people were already helping themselves to the buffet when they arrived, which Lucy thought was pretty rude. They should have waited for the reception line to form and murmured the usual platitudes to the grieving family before stuffing their faces, which would have been the proper thing to do. She noticed with alarm that the curried chicken puffs were disappearing fast, however, so Lucy decided there was nothing to do but abandon her principles. She did it reluctantly, fully aware that her extremely proper mother was probably spinning in her grave as she loaded her plate, careful to take only one of everything. Even so, the plate was filling up fast.

"Great food, but you can always count on Fern's Famous," said Corney, joining Lucy and Bill on the padded window seat in the bay window. Like Lucy and Bill, she was holding a plate piled high with finger food. "I don't know what it is about buffets, but I always eat too much."

"I think we'll have a light supper," said Lucy, talking with her mouth full. "Is that okay with you, Bill?"

"Mmph," said Bill, apparently in agreement.

"I'm feeling full and we haven't even gotten to the dessert table yet," confessed Lucy.

"Don't skip the desserts," advised Corney. "They've got something new—a Black Forest cake with brandy-cherry filling. It's absolutely delicious."

Lucy was surprised since she knew Corney was perpetually on a diet and avoided desserts. Come to think of it, she realized with a guilty pang, she was on a diet herself and had no business eating any dessert. "Maybe Bill can give me a bite of his," she said. "I'm trying to lose a few pounds."

"I normally don't eat sweets but that cake is worth the calories," said Corney. "Besides, when a guy takes you to dinner he doesn't want to hear you complaining about the calories. He wants to see you enjoy yourself."

"So you had the cake on a date?" said Lucy, picking up Corney's hint.

As she guessed, Corney couldn't wait to tell her all about it. "Trey took me out last night. We had a lovely meal at the Queen Vic—they get their desserts from Fern's Famous, you know."

"That does sound nice," said Lucy, noticing that Bill was wandering toward a group of men clustered in a corner. "Did you have a good time?"

"I did. Trey is everything a girl could want. Tall, handsome, wealthy. And he's fun, he's got a great sense of humor."

"Sounds like you're smitten. Has he asked you out again?"

"That's the thing," said Corney, scowling. "I'm not sure whether it was a real date or a business dinner. He spent an awful lot of time talking about his plans to expand the business and how the Chamber could help."

"That's tricky," said Lucy.

"You said it. I don't quite know how to play it. I called to thank him. I didn't want him to think I was chasing him, but I wanted to let him know I'm available and I really like him." Corney's face fell and she looked down at her empty plate. "He didn't suggest a second date. In fact, all he wanted to talk about was some kind of special chocolate that's going to revolutionize the confectionary business." She sighed. "I now know a lot more than I ever wanted to about chocolate."

"Bummer," said Lucy, chewing a meatball. "What's his relationship with Tamzin? Are they a couple?"

"I'm not sure." Corney lowered her voice. "It would explain why he doesn't fire her. Have you seen the way she dresses? That woman is sooo un-professional."

"Men like that sort of thing," said Lucy, as a sudden silence fell in the room. All heads had turned toward the door where Dora and her family were entering; each woman was carrying a flower arrangement they'd brought from the church. A few friends rushed over to take the flowers and help them with their coats, and the noise level rose again.

The reception line formed and Lucy and Bill took their places along with everyone else, shuffling slowly along. Lucy wasn't sure what to say under the circumstances. "I'm sorry for your loss," was okay for Lily, but not quite the thing for Dora. "Terrific party, great food," came to mind and Lucy giggled, which made people look at her. When her turn finally came, she murmured something about a terrible loss, we'll all miss him, and was promptly passed along from Dora to Lily and then to Fern and Flora.

Duty done, Lucy and Bill made their way through the crowded rooms to the little study off the hall where they'd left their coats. Lucy's good black pants were feeling uncomfortably tight as she made her way to the door, and her conscience wasn't about to let her forget she'd overindulged. That Black Forest cake was every bit as good as Corney said, even though she'd only had a few bites, but she'd been unable to resist the mini-cupcakes with lemon filling and buttercream icing topped with coconut. All that delicious food made her sleepy and she was yawning and buttoning her good black coat when Fern herself approached her with a foil-covered plate.

"Lucy, I wonder if you'd do me a favor?" she said, placing a blue-veined hand on Lucy's sleeve. Her voice, usually firm and authoritative, was a bit quavery today and she looked tired.

"Whatever you want," said Lucy.

"You know my friend, Julia. . . ."

Lucy knew Fern was one of the few people in town who dared to call Miss Tilley by her first name. Of course, they had probably been school-mates well before World War II. "I'm sure she would have come if she were able," said Lucy.

"Yes, she's getting over the flu. I absolutely forbade her to come," said Fern, with a flash of her usual bossiness. "But I put together a little plate for her and I wonder if you could deliver it for me."

"Sure," said Lucy, taking the foil-covered dish. "I'm sure she'll appreciate it."

"I happen to know she loves my Boston cream pie, so I gave her a big piece, and some other things, too."

"I'll take it right over," promised Lucy, making eye contact with Bill who gave an approving nod.

"It will be your good deed for the day," said Fern, patting her hand.

It was only a short drive to Miss Tilley's old Cape-style house and the car didn't have time to warm up. Bill stayed outside, keeping the engine running, while Lucy dashed up the path. She was chilled clear through when she knocked on the door, which was opened by Rachel.

"What are you doing here on Sunday?" Lucy asked, stepping inside.

"I was on my way home from the play rehearsal and thought I'd stop by and check on Miss T," said Rachel. "She's had a touch of the flu."

The house was wonderfully warm and cozy. Miss Tilley kept a fire going all winter in the ancient keeping-room hearth that had once served for both heating and cooking. Nowadays, of course, the fireplace was supplemented with heat from a modern furnace and cooking took place in the kitchen ell that was added on sometime in the 1920s.

The house was generously furnished with antiques and Lucy always felt as if she were stepping back in time when she visited her old friend. Miss Tilley was sitting in her usual Boston rocker today, with a colorful crocheted afghan covering her knees. Cleopatra, her Siamese cat, was seated on her lap, a softly purring sphinx.

"How are you?" asked Lucy. "I hear you had the flu."

"Nonsense. It was nothing more than a head cold, but everyone made such a fuss I didn't dare show my face at the funeral."

"Your friend Fern sent along some Boston cream pie," said Lucy, handing her the dish.

Miss Tilley promptly lifted the foil and examined the cake, smacking her lips. "I'll have that for my supper," she said.

"You'll have chicken soup for supper," said Rachel, taking the plate and carrying it into the kitchen. "There's a pot all ready for you on the stove. You just have to heat it up."

"I'd rather have pie," said Miss Tilley.

"If you finish all your soup, you can have some for dessert." Rachel raised an eyebrow. "And don't think you can put the soup down the drain. I'll know."

Miss Tilley shifted in her chair, a guilty expression on her face. "I'm not a child, you know."

"Then stop acting like one," snapped Rachel.

"My goodness," said Lucy. "It seems you two need a break."

"You said it," said Rachel, laughing as she seated herself on the sofa. "We are turning into a pair of bickering biddies."

Miss Tilley smiled and stroked the cat. "I don't know what I'd do without Rachel. I'd be in a pretty pickle, I'm sure."

"It's not easy keeping you on the straight and narrow," said Rachel, smiling fondly at her old friend. She'd started visiting regularly after Miss Tilley had an automobile accident years ago and now she was officially certified by the town council on aging as a home helper and even received a small stipend for her efforts.

"I would have liked to have gone to the funeral," said Miss Tilley. "For Fern. There aren't many of us old-timers left, you know, and she was so fond of Max."

"Was she upset about the divorce?" asked Lucy, perching on the sofa.

"She certainly didn't approve, divorce isn't something one approves of. But having said that, I don't think she was terribly surprised when the marriage didn't work out. She was never in favor of Max and Dora getting married; that was Flora's idea."

Lucy was puzzled. "How was it Flora's idea? Wasn't it up to Max and Dora?"

Miss Tilley pursed her lips. "Max had gone away, he wasn't the sort you could tie down. I remember him when he was a little boy, he'd come into the library and take out all sorts of adventure books. He read about all the explorers and astronauts and deep-sea divers. He wanted to see the world, he told me, and when he got out of high school he started traveling. I used to get postcards from him now and then. He went all over and somewhere he learned how to surf and he started competing and winning, too. There was quite a fuss about him when he came home for a visit, articles in the newspaper and all that. He was quite the hero, and Dora was his girl."

"And they decided to get married?" asked Lucy.

"Oh, no. He was only here for a short while before he had to leave for some surfing contest in Mexico or somewhere."

Lucy was puzzled. "So Dora followed him?"

"No. It was Flora."

"But she's old enough to be his mother."

"Oh, she wasn't interested in him for herself," said Miss Tilley, with a flap of her age-spotted hand. "It turned out he'd gotten Dora in the family way and Flora went down to wherever he was and made him understand his responsibility. She dragged him back and got them married before either of them knew what had happened. Fern told me she didn't think it was a good idea to force a marriage like that and it turned out she was right because the marriage didn't last." Miss Tilley's voice was fading and Lucy suspected she was growing tired. "And now poor Max is gone and he was much too young."

"Perhaps it was better that way," said Rachel, in a thoughtful voice. "I don't think he would have wanted to grow old."

"It's certainly not for everyone," said Miss Tilley, slapping her lap and causing the cat to leap onto the rug, where she began grooming herself.

"I've got to go," said Lucy, getting to her feet. "Bill's waiting for me outside. He's probably having a fit."

"I'd like to see that!" said Miss Tilley, giving her a little wave.

"Oh, no, you wouldn't," said Lucy, bending to give her a peck on the cheek. "Mind Rachel and eat your soup."

"I'll consider it," said Miss Tilley.

Chapter Seven

A few weeks later, the Tuesday before Valentine's Day, it was only ten o'clock and Lucy was starving. She'd had a piece of toast (whole wheat with a tiny sliver of butter) and a sixty-calorie pot of light yogurt for breakfast. Along with a glass of orange juice and black coffee, she figured it totaled about three hundred calories, which was apparently not enough to sustain life in Maine in February.

Her strict diet had resulted in the loss of six pounds, and her jeans were fitting better, but all she could think of as she made her way down Main Street was a big bowl of hot oatmeal, studded with raisins, sprinkled with sugar, and covered with cream. It hung before her eyes like a mirage in the desert, but she was about as far from any desert as a human being could be. Tinker's Cove in February was cold and wet and anybody with any sense was staying indoors, where it was warm and dry. Which was not possible for her because she was working on a man-in-the-street feature about Valentine's Day.

"What are your plans for Valentine's Day?" was the question she was supposed to ask five people. The replies would run in this week's paper along with head shots of the people she interviewed. It was a cute idea and the sort of thing she normally liked to do. The only problem was she couldn't find one person, much less five, and she was cold and wet and hungry.

Deciding to try the post office, she trudged down the empty street, sloshing through slush and telling herself the cold, damp mist that hung in the air was good for her complexion. She was just passing Chanticleer Chocolate when a huge SUV pulled up to the curb and Brad Cashman jumped out.

Brad was her neighbor. He lived on Prudence Path with his wife, Chris, who was Sue's partner in Little Prodigies Child Care Center.

"Hi!" she said, greeting him with a big smile. "Got a minute?"

Chris smiled back and cocked a wary eyebrow. "Maybe."

"I'm doing one of those man-in-the-street things, and I could really use some help. Just one quick question and a photo. Okay?"

Brad zipped his jacket, which had been open, and stuck his hands in his pocket. "Shoot."

"Say cheese." Lucy snapped the photo. "What are your plans for Valentine's Day?" she asked, pulling out her notebook and opening it to a fresh page.

"Funny you should ask," he said, nodding at the

store. "I'm on my way right now to buy chocolates for my three beautiful ladies."

"That would be your wife, Chris, and the twins?"

"Pear and Apple," he said. "I can't leave them out."

"How old are they now?"

"Old enough to know about chocolate," said Brad, turning up his collar and moving toward the store. "See you around, Lucy."

"Thanks," she said, as he opened the door and vanished inside.

One down, four to go, thought Lucy, continuing down the street. She was just passing the police station when she spotted her friend, Barney, about to get into his cruiser. She couldn't help envying his official winter gear, the insulated blue all-in-one that covered him from chin to ankles, plus his fur-lined hat and sturdy boots.

"Barney!" she called, running to catch him.

"Hey, Lucy," he replied, turning to greet her. "What's up?"

"Got a moment for a man-in-the-street question? I just want to know what your plans are for Valentine's Day. Are you getting something for Marge?"

"Sure am. I always get her a big bunch of pink roses."

"Not red?" asked Lucy, snapping his photo.

"She doesn't like red. She likes pink."

"Because of the breast cancer?" Lucy knew Barney's wife, Marge, was a breast cancer survivor and pink was the color associated with efforts to raise money for a cure.

Barney's bulldog face crumpled, which Lucy

knew was an indication of deep thought. "I don't think so. I think she just likes pink roses."

"Pink roses are lovely," said Lucy, writing it all down. "She's a lucky lady."

"No, Lucy." Barney was shaking his head. "I'm the lucky one. I don't deserve a wife like Marge."

"She must be thrilled to have Eddie home, safe and sound."

To her surprise, Barney's thoughtful expression deepened. "You know how it is with kids—you never stop worrying."

"I saw him at the Quik-Stop," continued Lucy. "He looks so handsome and fit."

"I'm just glad he's got all his arms and legs," said Barney. "A lot of these kids coming home are missing 'em."

"How's his mental outlook?" asked Lucy.

Barney shrugged. "It's hard to tell. He doesn't say much."

Barney looked so worried that Lucy didn't know what to say and resorted to the usual cliché. "It's a big adjustment, it's bound to take time." She noticed Barney's eyes following Max's old pickup, driven by Lily with Eddie in the passenger seat.

"Are they dating?" she asked.

Barney shrugged. "Don't ask me. He doesn't tell me anything."

Par for the course, thought Lucy, remembering how sullen and uncommunicative Toby had been before he met Molly.

"She's a nice girl," said Lucy. "He could do worse. Which reminds me, how's the investigation going?"

Barney looked confused. "What investigation?"

"Max Fraser, of course."

"Oh, that," he said, adjusting his gloves. "That's over and done. The guy drank too much and got himself in a pickle. The surprise is it didn't happen sooner."

Lucy shivered, which was her usual reaction whenever she thought of Max drowning in the freezing pond water. "There must have been some sort of follow-up. The ME's report said he had been knocked on the head."

Barney shifted from foot to foot. "Yeah, but he said there was no way of telling if it was intentional or accidental."

"Which left it open for an investigation," said Lucy.

Barney sighed. "We questioned a few people, didn't come up with anything suspicious. The last person who admits seeing him alive is Dora, his ex, but she says that was in the evening, well before he went through the ice."

"Where did she see him?" asked Lucy.

"At home. She says she was having trouble with her car and he stopped by to take a look and see if he could help."

Lucy nodded. "He was like that, he got me out of a fix when I got stuck in a snowbank."

"Problem is, he never did look at the car. She admitted they got in a fight; she wanted money for Lily's schooling. Last she saw him, he was driving off in a huff."

"Bill says Max was up against it lately and owed a lot of people money. That could be a motive for murder."

"If you're saying Max had a lot of enemies, I'd

say that's a lot of hooey. Like I said, he drank too much and got careless. We found an empty bottle of Southern Comfort in his truck." He paused, making eye contact. "And if he did have a falling out with somebody, and I'm not saying he did, well that somebody isn't anybody you want to tangle with, Lucy. You'd better stick to asking folks how they're going to celebrate Valentine's Day."

"Point taken," said Lucy, her teeth chattering. The mist was beginning to solidify, turning to sleet. "Have a good day."

"You, too, Lucy." Barney opened the door of his cruiser and Lucy dashed across the street to the liquor store.

Stepping inside, she gave a little shake.

"Pretty nasty out there," said the clerk, a fellow in his forties with oversize eyeglasses and a shock of graying hair that fell over his forehead. "What can I do for you?"

"I'm Lucy Stone, with the *Pennysaver.* I'm interviewing people about their plans for Valentine's Day."

"You want to know how I'm going to celebrate?" he asked, with a grin.

"If you don't mind." Lucy produced her camera. "And I have to take your picture, too."

He shrugged. "Well, as you might expect, I'm going to bring home a nice bottle of champagne and drink it with my wife."

"Say bubbles," said Lucy, snapping his photo. "What's your name?"

"Cliff Sandstrom."

"Any particular brand?" asked Lucy, noticing a

display of Southern Comfort bottles by the cash register.

Cliff grimaced. "I wish I could go for the Veuve Clicquot but I think it's going to be Freixenet this year," he said. "Business is down, due to the economy."

"You'd think people would drink more, to forget their troubles."

"Oh, they do, but they buy the cheap stuff. Not much profit in that."

"Ahh." Lucy pointed at the Southern Comfort. "Do you sell a lot of that stuff? I drank it in college once and got really sick."

"Sportsmen like it. They say it helps them stay warm. Especially the ice fishermen."

"I heard Max Fraser liked a nip."

"Yeah." Cliff nodded sadly. "He was in here the afternoon before he died. He always took a bottle along when he went ice fishing."

"Was he a problem drinker?" asked Lucy.

"Let's say he was a regular customer," said Cliff. "Not one of my best customers, if that answers your question."

Lucy thanked him and turned to go, noticing that the liquor store was directly opposite Chanticleer Chocolate. Turning back to Cliff, she grabbed a bargain bottle of chardonnay and set it on the counter. "Is this stuff any good?"

"We sell a lot of it," said Cliff, ringing it up. "That's four ninety-nine."

Lucy handed him a five. "How's the new chocolate shop doing?" she asked. "They won the 'Best on the Coast' poll, you know."

"I saw that." He handed her a penny, which she put in the dish by the cash register. "We lost out to the Wine Warehouse in the outlet mall."

"Sometimes I think those polls are rigged to favor big advertisers," said Lucy.

"It wouldn't surprise me, though I gotta say there's a steady traffic across the way."

"Well, Valentine's Day is coming."

"It's a funny thing," he said with a leer. "The customers sure tend to linger, especially the guys."

"Maybe they can't make up their minds," said Lucy. "The flavors are quite unique and Tamzin tends to go into detail, explaining them all."

"That must be it," said Cliff, chuckling.

Leaving the store with her purchase tucked under her arm, Lucy decided to stop in at Chanticleer Chocolate for a chat with Tamzin. The feature was a good excuse and she was sure Tamzin would jump at the chance for some free publicity.

Lucy looked both ways before crossing the street from habit, but she really didn't need to bother; there was no traffic on Main Street today. The road was beginning to fill with an inch or two of slushy sleet and she was grateful for her duck boots with their waterproof rubber bottoms.

A couple of musical chimes rang out when she opened the door, a marked improvement over the jangly bell at the *Pennysaver*. The shop was dimly lit with mood lighting and carefully placed monopoints that highlighted the boxes of chocolates arranged on little tables, but there was enough light for Lucy to see that Tamzin and Brad Cashman were standing very close. So close, in fact, that Lucy was certain she'd interrupted an embrace.

"Uh, two small boxes of strawberry blasts for the twins . . . ," he said, stepping away from Tamzin.

"*Bebe* or *petite?*" asked Tamzin, in a cool, professional voice.

"Bay-bay," said Brad. "And a *grande* for my wife."

"Assorted flavors?"

"Yeah," he said, avoiding making eye contact with Lucy.

Tamzin floated about the shop in her black boots with killer heels, gathering up the various boxes of chocolates, which she placed on the counter. Then, leaning over to display her décolletage, she began wrapping each box with the shop's trademark paper. It was a lengthy process involving a great deal of folding and tying, which took much longer than necessary due to the flirtatious chatter she was making.

While she waited her turn, Lucy began to understand why customers, especially male customers, tended to spend a lot of time at the shop. Finally, Tamzin was bending down, yet again, giving Brad a generous view of her bosom as she reached for a chic little shopping bag. Slipping the wrapped chocolates inside, she slid it toward him. "That will be ninety-six thirty," she said, with a big smile.

Lucy's eyes grew wide as she watched Brad hand over his credit card; she couldn't imagine anybody spending that much on chocolates. Goodness' sakes, a bag of premium dark chocolates only cost three ninety-nine at the IGA.

Then, giving her a quick smile, Brad hurried out the door and Tamzin greeted Lucy with a big smile. "What can I get you? A little extravagance for yourself? A gift?"

"Actually, I'm working," said Lucy, explaining her mission. Tamzin was agreeable and posed for a photo, then told Lucy she had no special plans for Valentine's Day but was hoping that would change.

"I'd hate to spend Valentine's Day all by myself," she said, with a little pout, and Lucy remembered Barney saying that Max had been obsessed with Tamzin.

"I suppose you miss Max quite a lot," said Lucy.

Tamzin lowered herself onto a tall stool and hooked her heels over the bottom rung; she looked like she were about to break into song in a nightclub. "We had some fun," she said, with a shrug, "but that was all. It was nothing serious."

"But a death like that affects us all. And besides, there aren't that many available men in a town like Tinker's Cove."

Tamzin's eyes sparkled. "They're all available, honey."

Lucy was shocked at her bluntness, but had to concede she had a point. "I suppose they are," she said, deciding she'd better make one thing very clear. "Except for my husband. He's definitely off limits." She smiled when she said it, but it was a warning, a preemptive strike.

Not that Tamzin noticed; she was lost in her own thoughts. "Come to think of it, I was going to call you. About your daughter, Zoe. Trey has given the okay for her to work here after school."

Lucy knew Zoe was eager to make some extra money, but she didn't know she'd gone so far as to apply at Chanticleer. She wasn't at all sure Zoe was mature enough to handle a job in addition to school, and furthermore, she was uneasy about letting her work with Tamzin. The woman was hardly a good influence. Lucy didn't like the way she dressed and she sure didn't like her attitude toward men, especially married men.

"I'm not sure Zoe has time for a job, and besides, she's just turned fourteen," said Lucy, hedging until she had a chance to talk with her daughter.

"Oh, she's already said she'd take the job. I texted her first thing this morning. She's going to start today, after school."

Lucy felt the blood rushing to her cheeks. She was furious about being sidestepped this way. Tamzin had no business getting a commitment from Zoe before she checked with her parents. After raising four kids, Lucy knew her rights and responsibilities as a parent and she wasn't about to relinquish them.

"She can't start today," said Lucy, narrowing her eyes. "Zoe's not sixteen, she needs a work permit from the Superintendent of Schools and it takes a few days to get it."

Tamzin rolled her eyes. "Are you kidding me?"

"No." Lucy looked her in the eye. "The child labor laws are quite clear and I will report any violations."

"Okay," said Tamzin, reaching for her phone, "but Trey's not going to like this."

"Then he can hire somebody else," said Lucy, turning on her heels and pushing the door open. This time she found the little musical chimes really irritating.

Chapter Eight

Lucy was so furious with Tamzin that she didn't even notice the sleet and slush as she marched back to the *Pennysaver* office. She plunked herself down in her chair and reached for the mouse, then proceeded to strip off her winter clothing, feeling unusually warm as she clicked away, Googling Tamzin Graves.

"Did you put the heat up?" she asked Phyllis, who was regarding her with amusement.

"I would if I could, but you know as well as I do that Ted freaks out if the thermostat is a hair above sixty-five," she replied.

Lucy shrugged and stared at the screen, but the only thing that turned up was an announcement that ran in the Portland paper a few years ago reporting that Tamzin had achieved black belt status in tae kwon do at the Maine Martial Arts Academy.

"Typical," snarled Lucy.

"What's got into you?" asked Phyllis.

"That witch at Chanticleer Chocolate, and witch isn't the word I want to use," said Lucy, scowling at the computer screen.

"But it rhymes with witch, right?" asked Phyllis, chuckling.

"You said it." Lucy swung around in her office chair and faced Phyllis. "She hired Zoe behind my back, never even mentioned a work permit. She wanted Zoe to start this afternoon."

Just then Lucy's cell phone rang and she began digging in her purse for it. After a few more rings, she dumped the entire contents on her desk and snatched it up. "Zoe! I thought you might be calling."

"Mom, I can't believe you did this to me!"

Zoe's voice was so loud that Phyllis could hear her right across the room.

"I did what I thought best," said Lucy.

"And now I'm out of a job!"

Phyllis had turned back to her computer, but Lucy knew she was listening to every word.

"They were taking advantage of you," said Lucy. "You need my permission to work and I'm not going to let you work illegally. These laws are there for a reason. It's easy for employers to take advantage of underage workers."

"Mom, it's a chocolate shop, not some sweatshop."

"Then I don't see what the problem is. They can file the paperwork. . . ."

"Then you mean I can work there?"

Too late, Lucy saw she'd stumbled into a trap. "I guess so. If the permit's approved," she said, reluctantly. It wasn't really the work permit that was the issue, it was Tamzin. She really didn't want her daughter anywhere near the woman.

"You're the best, Mom. Tamzin's pretty sure they can have everything in order by tomorrow afternoon. She says Trey knows somebody in the Superintendent's office."

"Oh, great," said Lucy, with a noticeable lack of enthusiasm.

Looking over at Phyllis, she saw her shoulders shaking with laughter.

"It's not funny," said Lucy, flipping the phone shut.

"I know," said Phyllis. "It was just your expression. You looked so pissed."

"I've been advised not to play poker," said Lucy, already calling Sue. "Have you got a minute?" she asked, knowing that Sue was working and the needs of the kids at Little Prodigies took precedence. "Can you talk?"

Getting an affirmative, she continued, in a whisper. "I was over at Chanticleer Chocolate and I saw Brad Cashman in a, well, compromising situation."

"Hmmm," said Sue. "I'll have to check the invoice." A few moments later, she was back on the phone. "I'm in my office. Exactly how compromising was the situation?"

"I'm not sure," admitted Lucy. "I think I caught them kissing. They sort of jumped apart when I went into the shop."

"I've heard she's a real flirt."

"That's an understatement. She actually told me she thinks all men are available."

"They probably are," said Sue.

"How can you think that?" Lucy was shocked. "Does Chris seem upset or worried?"

"No. She's the same as always."

"Maybe she doesn't know," said Lucy. "Or maybe it's just the way Tamzin treats every man who comes in the shop. I saw her wrap a box of chocolates and it was about as subtle as a pole dance." She paused. "Maybe you can give Chris a heads-up."

"This is awkward—I'll have to think about it. I don't want to cause a problem if there's nothing there, if it's just a little flirting," said Sue.

"If she knows there's a potential problem she can take action," said Lucy. "She can cook his favorite dinner and wear a sexy nightie to bed."

"You think it's that simple?" Sue sounded amused.

Lucy bit her lip. In her experience, men were that simple. She and Bill had been married for over twenty-five years and there hadn't been much that a meat loaf dinner and a scented candle in the bedroom couldn't fix, but maybe she was just lucky. "It's worth a try," she said.

"I guess I can send up a test balloon and see if she's worried," said Sue.

"That's a good idea—but you better be careful. Use tact."

"Of course," said Sue, sounding a bit miffed. "By the way, have you been thinking about the dessert contest? It's just around the corner. Have you come up with any ideas?"

"Not really. Besides, I'm on a diet."

"And I told you to make a diet dessert," said Sue. "There's plenty of recipes on the Internet."

Lucy heard a distant childish wail. "Gotta go," said Sue.

Lucy sat for a minute, holding her phone and scowling. Things were not going well. She sighed and looked out the window. It wasn't an inspiring sight. The street was filled with filthy snow, the sky was gray, it was so dark, in fact, that the street lights were still on and it was almost noon. She was thinking that if she had a gun she'd probably shoot herself, when she noticed Bill's red pickup truck going down the street. Impulsively, she punched in his cell phone number.

"Hey," he said.

"I saw you driving by."

"I'm done for the day. I thought I'd head home and have some lunch."

"Want some company?"

"Sure."

When Lucy got home, she found Bill was already heating up a can of soup on the stove and mixing up some tuna salad for sandwiches. A bowl of chips was on the table and she took one, then remembered her diet and put it back. "I hate myself," she said, collapsing in a chair.

"It's that sort of day," said Bill, unwrapping a loaf of bread. "Do you want a whole sandwich or a half?"

Despite herself, Lucy was smiling. "I can't believe you remembered."

"What? I noticed you've been skipping seconds and desserts and only been eating half-sandwiches lately."

She stood behind him, resting her cheek on his

back and slipping her arms around his waist. "I've been trying to exercise, but it's hard this time of year."

Bill was about to pull some slices of bread out of the plastic bag but stopped. "I know how you can get some exercise," he said, with a wink.

"I might not have the right clothes, or the right equipment," said Lucy.

"Don't worry," said Bill, turning off the stove and taking her hand. "You don't need any clothes—and I happen to know you've got the right equipment."

"Oo-oh," said Lucy, following as he drew her upstairs.

An hour or so later, Lucy found her mood was much improved as she finished her one-hundred-calorie bowl of soup and half-sandwich lunch. "I'm not happy about Zoe working at Chanticleer Chocolate," she told Bill, putting down her soup spoon. "I don't think Tamzin is a good influence."

Bill grinned at her. "What have you heard?"

"It isn't what I've heard—it's what I saw. I caught her in a compromising position with one of our upstanding citizens."

"As long as he was upstanding, I don't see the problem." He smiled at her. "Come to think of it, you're no stranger to compromising positions."

Lucy still felt warm all over. "We're married."

"Good thing," said Bill, scratching Libby behind her ears. The dog was hoping a few leftover scraps might come her way. "Otherwise what we just did would be very wrong."

"I'm no prude . . . ," began Lucy.

"I'll say," said Bill, with a leer.

"That woman's trouble and I don't want Zoe around her."

"From what I've heard, she's pretty harmless," said Bill, clearing the table and carrying the dishes over to the dishwasher. "You can't blame a fellow for looking, especially when you consider what most of the wives around here look like. Even if they've got nice figures, they hide them in baggy sweatpants. They don't even try to look good."

"That's no excuse for infidelity," said Lucy.

Bill closed the dishwasher door and leaned against it, crossing his arms. "She puts on a good show, but from what I've heard that's as far as it goes."

"What about Max? I heard they were seeing each other." Lucy gave him a look. "I bet you didn't know she's got a black belt in tae kwon do, did you?"

Bill rolled his eyes and grinned. "Don't tell me you think she's some sort of black widow killer?"

"I wouldn't be surprised. She's certainly able to overpower a man, especially a drunk one. And she seems to be morally challenged. Look at the way she went behind our backs to hire Zoe."

"That's hardly the same thing as committing murder. Besides, I don't think Max was interested in Tamzin. I heard he and Dora were seeing a lot of each other."

Libby gave a little yip, and Bill looked out the window as the mailman drove up to their box. "Mail's here."

Lucy watched as he went down the driveway,

without his coat. Men were so silly. And blind. Didn't he see it? If Max had left Tamzin and gone back to Dora, Tamzin would have been hurt and angry. Maybe even angry enough to kill him.

That afternoon, instead of simply parking out front and waiting for Sara and Renee, Lucy went inside Fern's Famous, hoping to have a word with Dora about Max. The police might consider his death an accident, but she wasn't satisfied and she knew Dora had her suspicions, too. But instead of Dora, she found Flora behind the cash register. Her salt and pepper hair was cut in a neat bob, gold granny glasses perched on her nose, and she was wearing a red-and-white-striped smock with the Fern's Famous logo embroidered on the pocket. Her complexion was fresh and smooth, belying her sixty-odd years, and Lucy wondered if chocolate had something to do with it. Dark chocolate, anyway, was supposed to promote good health.

"The girls'll be out in a minute," she said, with a little nod. "Dora's got them packing up Valentine's Day orders."

"I'm not in a hurry," said Lucy, glancing around the shop. Unlike Chanticleer Chocolate, with its mood lighting and artful displays, Fern's was bright and white and the trays of fudge were kept free of contamination in a huge glass case. The atmosphere was almost clinical, and a vintage poster with two apple-cheeked children and a smiling Holstein nibbling a daisy declared, WE USE ONLY THE PUREST FARM-FRESH INGREDIENTS.

"Sara's a good worker," said Flora, pulling out a

tray of penuche and realigning the little cubes with a gloved hand.

"That's nice to hear," said Lucy. "How's Dora doing?"

"About like you'd expect, I guess," said Flora. "Lily's the one I'm worried about. She really misses her dad. They spent a lot of time together."

"I didn't know that," said Lucy. "I guess I thought she'd be closer to her mom."

Flora slid the tray back in place. "Oh, she is. They had shared custody, so she spent time with both of them. I don't approve of divorce, but I have to say they were very amicable. They got along better after the divorce, really, and I have to give Max credit for being an excellent father. He taught Lily to fish and hunt and ski, turned her into a real outdoors person."

Lucy thought of the beautiful, ethereal girl she'd seen in the shop so often. "She looks so fragile," she said.

Flora laughed. "That fragile creature is a hell of a shot. We've been eating venison all winter, thanks to her. And she didn't just shoot it. Max made sure she hung it and dressed it proper."

Lucy figured her own girls' reaction to a job like that would be a big *Eeeuw.*

"She's a good cook, too," continued Flora. "Not only killed the beast but cooked it, too. Ragout, she calls it, but I think it's just a fancy word for stew."

"I saw her with Eddie Culpepper—do you think they're serious?"

"I hope not. She's way too young for that,"

snapped Flora, looking up as Renee and Sara came through the door from the rear of the shop. "Well, here're your girls. See you tomorrow."

For some reason that Lucy couldn't understand, Flora's words sent the two girls into paroxysms of laughter.

"What's so funny?" asked Lucy, as they all got into the car.

"Nothing," said Sara, giggling as she fastened her seat belt.

"Flora said you were packing up mail orders," said Lucy, starting the car and switching on the headlights. "Was it interesting?"

The girls didn't answer but started laughing again. Something was screamingly funny and Lucy couldn't help wishing she was in on the joke.

Chapter Nine

Sociologists estimate that forty to fifty percent of American marriages end in divorce and the numbers are even higher for second (sixty-seven percent) and third (seventy-four percent) marriages. Even couples who stay together tend to drift apart, according to a recent survey by the Association of Retired Citizens (ARC), which reported a marked decrease in romance among couples age sixty and older. Some lucky couples, however, defy the odds. Take, for example, Helen and Roger Faircloth, who insist they are still in love after more than forty years of marriage.

Interviewed recently at the Queen Victoria Inn, where the couple is staying while house-hunting in the area, Mr. Faircloth declared, "It's easy to stay married when you're in love." Beaming at his wife, he added, "She's every bit as pretty as the day I married her."

The couple met in London on a double-decker bus in the Swinging Sixties. Mrs. Faircloth was pursuing a modeling career and Roger was a student at the London School of Economics. In the years since. . . .

Lucy flipped through the notes she had taken during her interview with the Faircloths but found them surprisingly thin. She should have written the story up immediately after talking with them, but she'd procrastinated, aware that the deadline for the *Love Is Best on the Coast* supplement was weeks away. Now it was Wednesday, deadline day, the story was finally due, and she couldn't remember what happened between their fabled meeting in London and the Connecticut house fire that prompted their decision to relocate to the Maine coast.

"If I can't have a Wyeth landscape on my wall, I can have one right outside my window." That was a great quote from Helen, and Lucy certainly planned to use it in her story, but where were the hard facts? What sort of career did Roger have? He certainly didn't spend forty years gazing at his beloved, like some lovesick swain.

And what about Helen? Did she continue to model? Lucy knew they didn't have any children; it was their "one regret," according to Helen. So what did she do for all those years besides dust the antiques and cook gourmet dinners for Roger? They said they'd collected art and antiques, they'd referred to a Goddard highboy, paintings by Warhol and Basquiat, all gone in the fire. "When life hands you lemons, you make lemonade." That's what Helen had said in a remarkable display of resiliency.

Lucy considered. They were resilient. Maybe she could do something with that. A quote from a marriage counselor would fill some space, she thought, but she still had a huge hole in the middle of her story. There was no way of getting around it, she had to call the Faircloths for more information. She knew they were still in town, she'd seen them just the other day, walking hand in hand on Main Street.

When she got Roger on his cell phone, he apologized profusely but said it wasn't a good time to talk.

"This will only take a minute," Lucy pleaded, glancing across the office at Ted, who was hunched forward, peering at his computer screen and pounding away on his keyboard. "I'm on deadline. If you could just tell me a little about your career. . . ."

"Sorry. It's really impossible. I must go, I'm in the middle of a meeting with my realtor."

"I see. I'm sorry to interrupt," said Lucy, ending the call.

"That's no way for a reporter to talk," snapped Ted, glaring at her from his desk. "Call him back. Say the phone died and cut you off."

Lucy remembered the set of Roger's jaw at the Queen Victoria Inn; there was no way she was going to badger him. "He won't answer," said Lucy. "He's in a meeting."

"I need that story, I've got twenty inches to fill," said Ted.

"I know, I know." Lucy was already dialing one of her sources, a marriage counselor she'd quoted before. When she got through with him, however, she had only added an inch or two to the story. Maybe Frankie could help her out, she thought, dialing the real estate office. The phone was ringing when Lucy remembered Roger had said he was in a meeting with his realtor.

Much to her surprise, Frankie answered.

"Hi, it's Lucy. I'm sorry if this is a bad time."

"No, it's fine," said Frankie. "I was just working on some comps—but I'm glad you called. I've got a showing later. Can you pick up the girls?"

Sure, no problem," said Lucy. "So the meeting with the Faircloths is over?"

"What meeting?"

"I just spoke with Roger and he said he was in a meeting with his realtor."

"Well he wasn't meeting with me," said Frankie, "and he better not be meeting with any other realtor, because I have a signed contract with him."

"Maybe I misunderstood," said Lucy, who was pretty sure she hadn't. "You know how I'm writing about them and their amazing love story? Well, I've kind of run into a wall and I'm hoping you can help me out."

"Sure," said Frankie. "What do you need?"

"Some background. Roger's career, for example. Stuff like that."

There was a long pause before Frankie spoke. "Sorry, but all I know is that they used to live in Connecticut and their house burned down. I guess some stuff was saved because they're always saying they need room for the Duncan Phyfe sideboard and debating where they can hang the large Max Bohm seascape to best advantage." She sighed. "To tell the truth, I'm getting a little tired of the Faircloths. I have shown them every house in five towns and nothing is quite right. I told them maybe they should build, but they say they want to move into something right away, they don't want to wait a year while a house is built."

Lucy knew when she was beat. "Can you give me some warm and fuzzy quotes about how they are still in love?"

"Of course," said Frankie, "just give me a moment."

Lucy was listening to Frankie and typing in her flattering description of the Faircloths' relationship when she remembered that little awkward scene about paying the bill at the Queen Victoria Inn. When she'd finished, she found herself asking Frankie if she thought the couple were genuine.

"What do you mean?" asked Frankie.

"I don't know. They just seem a bit off. When we had tea at the Queen Vic, the waitress asked Roger to pay cash, something about his credit being cut off. And now, all of a sudden, he doesn't want to talk to me. It just makes me wonder."

"That's the trouble with being a reporter," said Frankie. "You don't trust anybody." She paused. "But they have left the Queen Vic, they said it wasn't quite up to their standards. They've moved to the Salt Aire."

"Oh," said Lucy, impressed. She knew the Salt Aire Resort and Spa was strictly top-of-the-line, the most luxurious—and most expensive—hotel in Tinker's Cove. "I guess I do have a suspicious mind, but it did seem odd for this guy who's got such very expensive tastes to argue over a restaurant tab."

"That's how the very rich are, Lucy," said Frankie. "Especially the ones with old money. They pinch every penny."

Lucy thought of some of the summer people

who occupied the big shingled "cottages" on Shore Road—they ran up big bills at shops in town and were slow to pay. It was a common complaint among the local merchants. "I'm sure you're right," said Lucy. "Thanks for the quote."

"Uh, Lucy, talk about trust, I got a real unpleasant surprise last weekend."

"What happened?"

"I was doing an open house—they're an older couple, desperate to sell because he's got cancer and isn't expected to live long and she can't keep up the big old place on her own. You probably know them, the Potters."

"Oh, yeah. They've got that nice colonial on School Street."

"It's a steal. Needs a little work but a bargain for the right buyer. And they're such a nice couple, I really want to help them out and get it sold."

Lucy was wondering where this was going. Was it just a sales pitch? "Yeah, well, I'll keep it in mind." Then a thought came to her. "You know Eddie Culpepper is back and he might be looking for an investment. . . ."

"That's the weird thing, Lucy. He came, along with Lily Fraser."

Ah, young love, thought Lucy. It was enough to warm the cockles of your heart. "I guess they're getting serious."

"I'm not so sure that's a good thing. When the Potters came home, they discovered his Oxy-Contin had been stolen, right out of the medicine cabinet."

Lucy's jaw dropped. "You don't think Eddie and Lily took it?"

"I don't know what to think," said Frankie. "I blame myself. I should have told the Potters to take the meds with them, it just slipped my mind." She paused. "And I should have kept a closer eye on those kids. I got distracted, an old client of mine came in and we got chatting. I think that's when it happened, Eddie and Lily were upstairs by themselves."

"Are you sure?"

"No, I'm not sure," admitted Frankie. "But I've been wracking my brain and that's the only time I think it could have happened. The bottle was in the upstairs bathroom medicine cabinet and they were the only people who were up there without me."

Lucy had a terrible sinking feeling. "Did you report it?"

"We had to; OxyContin is a controlled substance and Mr. Potter needed to get a new prescription. But I didn't name Eddie and Lily and I noticed they didn't sign in. The officer said it happens all the time. Kids steal drugs from their parents, home health aides steal from their patients, staff members steal from hospitals and pharmacies. And then there's the phony prescriptions, the people who go to a bunch of doctors and get multiple prescriptions."

Lucy had no idea. "For this OxyContin?"

"Yeah. Either they're hooked themselves, or they sell it. A single pill goes for eighty dollars."

That was a lot of money, thought Lucy. "Who buys it?"

"Addicts. It's very addicting, and once they're hooked they need three or four pills every day, or

they start feeling sick. Withdrawal symptoms."
Frankie paused. "When they can't afford the Oxy-
Contin they use heroin. It's much cheaper."

A year or two ago, thought Lucy, she would
have been shocked. But not now. The police and
court reports showed a big increase in drug-
related crimes and the town had seen several violent drug-related deaths in recent years. Doc Ryder
had expressed concern about the number of overdoses he was seeing in the emergency room. It
wasn't just Tinker's Cove, either. Even the governor's wife was trying to raise awareness of the
problem.

Still, Lucy resisted the idea that either Lily or
Eddie might be using drugs. "They're both good
kids. . . ."

"I know," agreed Frankie. "That's why I didn't
name them. I wanted to give them the benefit of
the doubt."

"That's exactly right," said Lucy. "I can't believe
either one of them would do this awful thing, steal
painkillers from a dying man."

"You're right, I'm sure you're right," said Frankie,
but her tone of voice gave her away. She wasn't
convinced and neither was Lucy.

That afternoon, Lucy ran a few errands before
picking up Sara and Renee at Fern's Famous, and
Zoe at Chanticleer Chocolate. The work permit
had come through and today was Zoe's first day,
but Lucy wasn't happy about it. She'd been in a
bad mood as she went about town, making a stop

at the town dump before picking up groceries and dry cleaning.

The rear of the Subaru wagon was full of green reusable grocery bags, dry cleaning hanging from the back of the front seat where she'd hooked the hangers around the headrest supports, and a couple of big boxes now empty of bottles she'd recycled, on the back seat.

"Gee, Mom, is there room for us?" asked Sara, when she opened the car door.

"Just stack up those boxes inside each other," said Lucy.

"They don't fit," complained Sara, struggling to jam one box inside the other. "This one's too big."

"Turn it sideways," said Lucy, wondering how a girl who got all A's in geometry couldn't figure out how to stack a couple of cartons.

"Got it," said Sara, succeeding in combining the two boxes and making room in the back seat.

The two girls jumped in and immediately began whispering and giggling.

"Can you let me in on the joke?" asked Lucy, accelerating into the road. "I had no idea chocolate was so much fun."

"It is at Fern's," said Sara, prompting a fresh round of giggling. "Especially around Valentine's Day."

"Come on, tell me," said Lucy, in a playful tone. "I've had a tough day and I could use a laugh."

"Well," began Sara. "Promise you won't tell?"

Lucy didn't get it. What was so funny and had to be kept secret, too? It didn't make sense, especially since you'd think the mood would be somewhat subdued at Fern's following Max's death. "Sure," she said. "I won't tell."

"Dora makes special chocolates that she doesn't sell in the shop. She calls them 'naughty chocolates.' "

Lucy braked hard at the stop sign. "Naughty?"

"Yeah." The girls were giggling again. "Like Hot Lips. Those are shaped like lips and are kind of spicy. They're real popular, we've been filling tons of orders from all over the country."

Lucy still didn't get it. You could buy lips wrapped in red foil at the local drugstore. They brought them out every year for Valentine's Day, along with boxer shorts printed with hearts. "That doesn't sound very naughty," she said, turning onto Route 1.

"It's not just lips," said Renee. "She has other, um, parts."

"Like boobs!" exclaimed Sara. "And, and, you know. . . ."

Lucy thought maybe she did. "Who'd 'a thunk it?" she exclaimed, chuckling to herself as she proceeded along Main Street toward Chanticleer Chocolate, where she had to pick up Zoe.

"You're not mad?" asked Sara. "Dora said you might not approve."

"I used to have standards, but motherhood has taught me to compromise." Lucy joked with the girls, but she fully intended to drop in at Fern's Famous first thing next morning to check out the naughty chocolates.

Pulling into a vacant spot in front of Chanticleer Chocolate, Lucy tooted the horn. Zoe was supposed to work until five, and it was now ten after, but there was no sign of her.

"Sara, just go inside and see what's holding her up," said Lucy.

A minute later Sara reported that Zoe would only be a few more minutes. "Tamzin's got her cleaning the display case and she's not done yet."

Lucy thought of the ice cream that was probably melting in the back of her car, not to mention other perishables like expensive winter lettuce and fresh fish. "How long do you think she's going to be?"

"A while," said Sara. "There were trays of chocolates everywhere and they've all got to be put back in the case."

Lucy wanted to go in and demand Tamzin let Zoe go for the evening, but she knew that wasn't a good idea. She'd already raised a fuss about the working papers and she didn't want to make things any harder for Zoe. But this was still darned inconvenient.

Finally, at thirty-five minutes past five, the door opened and Zoe appeared, zipping her parka.

"Sorry, Mom," she said, climbing in the back beside Sara and Renee. "Tamzin said I couldn't go until I finished."

"No problem," said Lucy, flicking on her signal and turning onto the street.

"I was afraid you'd be mad," said Zoe.

"Well, I'm pretty sure the ice cream has melted and twelve dollars' worth of fish is ruined, but it's not your fault," said Lucy. "It's Tamzin's."

"She was upset. I think that's why she made me do all that work," said Zoe.

"What do you mean?" asked Lucy, turning back onto Route 1.

"Everything was fine, she was all nicey-nice, showing me how to wrap the chocolates and tie bows and all this stuff. Not like a boss at all, like we were friends. But then Trey came in with Ms. Clarke and she was all smiley with them, but as soon as they left she turned into this really mean person. All of a sudden she was making me do icky stuff like cleaning the bathroom and mopping the floor." Zoe sighed. "I didn't think working would be so hard."

"Maybe tomorrow will be better," said Lucy, who was revising her thinking about Tamzin and Trey. Just because they weren't a couple didn't mean that Tamzin wasn't hoping to become one. Trey was awfully attractive, and wealthy, besides. Tamzin couldn't be making much more than minimum wage in the candy shop; it was probably barely enough to keep her in push-up bras and stiletto heels. Mentally slapping herself for being so catty, Lucy turned her attention to Zoe, who needed a bit of encouragement. "Was the shop busy?"

"Really busy. Valentine's Day is Sunday."

"With anybody you know? Did any of your friends come by?"

Zoe shook her head. "Tamzin took care of the customers."

I bet she did, thought Lucy, turning onto Red Top Road.

* * *

Thursday morning, Lucy met the girls at Jake's for breakfast. She couldn't resist telling them about Dora's naughty chocolates.

"There's a shop in Boston that has those sexy chocolates," Sue had told her, while Norine filled their mugs with Jake's high-test brew. "Some of them are pretty raunchy."

"I'm no prude," Pam had declared with a prim expression, "but I don't think it's appropriate to expect young girls to handle that kind of special order."

"Adolescents are very vulnerable," added Rachel, offering the insight she'd gained as a psychology major in college. "Their sexuality is just developing and is very fragile."

"Yeah," cracked Pam, "you don't want them thinking men taste like chocolate."

That sent them all into gales of laughter, including Lucy. But even as she laughed along with the others, she couldn't help feeling she didn't want her daughter exposed to such risqué products. She remembered how shocked she'd been as an impressionable girl when a catalog picturing trashy underwear had tumbled out of a pile of newspapers she was carrying out to the trash bins. She'd puzzled over the crotchless red underpants for years and, to tell the truth, the images still bothered her. As she matured and became more sophisticated, she came to believe that donning such garments turned you into a sex object, something she had no intention of becoming and which she certainly didn't want her daughters to become.

But when she stepped inside Fern's Famous, with its antiseptic white tile walls and the delicious scent of chocolate, her resolution wavered. She took in the smiling cow on the sign behind the counter and the scuffed wood floor, the ornate swirls on the antique bronze cash register and the collection of old milk cans that served as decoration, and wondered if the girls had been teasing her. All this old-timey wholesomeness seemed at odds with the production of sexy chocolates.

"Hi, Lucy," said Dora, pushing aside the red-and-white-striped curtain that separated the work area from the shop. "You should be real proud of Sara, she's a wonderful girl and a real good worker."

"Oh, thanks," said Lucy, feeling Dora already had her at a disadvantage. "That's what I wanted to talk to you about."

Dora blushed. "She told you about the naughty chocolates."

"Yeah." Lucy nodded. "I'm just not comfortable with that sort of thing."

"Come on back," said Dora. "I'll let you have a look."

Lucy followed her and was surprised to encounter Fern herself, mixing up a big batch of penuche in a huge copper kettle with a gas flame underneath it. The tiny old woman was standing on a stool, wielding a huge wooden paddle.

"Goodness, that looks like quite a job," said Lucy, greeting her.

Fern brushed back a stray lock of gray hair that had escaped from the little bun on the top of her head and paused for a second. "I'm the only one does it right," she declared, resuming her stirring. "These young'uns are too impatient."

Dora smiled. "We let her think that, it keeps her out of trouble," said Dora, leading Lucy into the packing room and grabbing several boxes from the neat stacks arranged on industrial-style metal shelves. The boxes she chose were all shiny red, unlike the usual striped ones associated with Fern's Famous.

"This is kind of a sideline of mine," said Dora, opening one of the boxes and revealing half a dozen chocolates molded in the shape of lips. "I call these Hot Lips because the chocolate is quite spicy. Max got the recipe in Mexico. Want to try one?"

Lucy thought briefly of her diet, then nodded. Taking a bite of the creamy chocolate, she was amazed at the combination of flavors. the fiery hot pepper released flavor notes from the chocolate that she had never tasted before. "Wow," she said, "That is amazing."

Dora smiled and bit into one herself. "Of all the candy we make, this is the only one I don't get tired of," she said. "Every time, it's a new experience. An explosion of flavor, that's how I describe it on the website." She lowered her voice. "Fern doesn't approve, so I market them separately on the Web. I call them 'Sexsational Chocolates.' "

"Cute," said Lucy, determined to stick to her guns. "I assume some of the chocolates are racier than these?"

"Oh, yeah," said Dora. "I've got Bodacious Bods and Big Boobs." She opened two more boxes, revealing solid blocks of chocolate. One was shaped like a muscular man's torso, complete with six-pack abs, and the other was shaped like a breast with a dried cherry for a nipple.

In spite of herself, Lucy found she was laughing.

"I know," said Dora, with a shrug. "It's not the cleverest name but, believe me, I sell a lot of Big Boobs." She paused. "The truth of the matter is, if it wasn't for my naughty chocolates, we would have gone out of business years ago. Fern thinks everybody comes for that penuche of hers, but I actually throw most of it out. And she won't raise prices on the fudge, even though the price of sugar has gone through the roof. She won't admit it, but these shiny red boxes are the real money-makers." Dora gave her a look. "And now that Chanticleer's in town, and getting so much atten-tion, well, I'd be lying if I said they weren't cutting into our profits."

Lucy felt a stab of guilt. "Ted made me write that article about them."

"Sara said her sister's working over there." Dora tilted her head in the direction of Chanticleer Chocolate. "I'm surprised you let her. That Tam-zin's a real floozy."

"I'm not happy about it." Lucy thought she'd better change the subject. "Somehow I was expect-ing something a lot racier," she said, finishing off her Hot Lips.

"That's Flora," said Dora, with a sigh. "She ab-solutely refuses to let me make anything, um, below the waist." She scowled. "I could make a lot of money with Size Matters lollipops but she won't let me go there."

"That's probably just as well," said Lucy, thinking back to the days when you only had to worry about warning kids not to run with lollipops in their mouths.

"So it's okay if Sara keeps working here?" asked Dora. "I really need the help. This is our busiest time of year."

"Oh, sure." Lucy's thoughts turned to Lily. "I suppose you'll be shorthanded when Lily goes back to school."

"Who told you that?" asked Dora, replacing the red boxes on the shelves.

"I just assumed. . . ."

Dora turned and shook her head. "I loved Max, I did, and I'll miss him. But I learned early on not to count on him. He'd promise the world, but there was never enough money to pay the rent. That's what I told Lily when he said he had money coming and she'd be able to go back to school. 'Don't worry,' he said. 'It's under control.' Now he's gone and there isn't any money, there isn't even any life insurance. All he left behind is an old truck and a snowmobile that doesn't run. It's gonna cost more to fix it than it's worth—and that's the story of Max's life." She sighed. "And now that she's been seeing a lot of Eddie Culpepper, she's not so eager to go back to school. He's just back from Afghanistan, you know, and he's pretty eager to settle down. I wouldn't be at all surprised if they got married."

"But Lily's so young," said Lucy.

"I know," said Dora. "I'd like her to wait but, well, I remember what it's like when you're young." She smiled and for a moment the years dropped away and she looked like the girl who'd fallen in love with Max.

"Have you heard anything more about Max's death from the police?" Lucy asked.

Dora shook her head. "Case closed. Accidental drowning."

"Do you believe that?"

"I didn't at first, but now I guess it must be true. Who would kill Max? Sure he had his faults, but everybody loved him, he'd give you the shirt off his back if he thought you needed it. You saw the turnout at the memorial service. He was a real popular guy."

"Yeah," agreed Lucy. "He helped me that night—the night he died—when I got stuck in the snow."

Dora smiled. "That was Max all over. I really miss him."

"You're not alone," said Lucy.

But as she left the shop and made her way to the *Pennysaver* office, Lucy's thoughts turned to Eddie and Lily. She knew Barney was worried about Eddie, saying he was having trouble adjusting to civilian life. Barney hadn't elaborated, so she didn't know if he was suffering from a full-blown case of post-traumatic stress syndrome, or just the normal sense of dislocation that accompanies major life changes like moves and new jobs. Either way it was worrying, especially in light of Frankie's suspicions. Lily had been through a lot, including her parents' divorce and her father's tragic death, and Lucy hoped this relationship with Eddie wouldn't bring her more grief.

Chapter Ten

Phyllis had raised the old-fashioned wooden venetian blinds and was taping big red paper hearts on the plate glass windows when Lucy got to the *Pennysaver* office. She paused, tape in hand, and cocked her head.

"What do you think?"

"It's very festive," said Lucy, studying the scattered arrangement. "Maybe a few more up in the left there? And what about the door?"

"One big one? A cluster of small ones?"

Lucy took off her jacket and hung it on the sturdy oak coat stand next to the door, tossed her bag on the floor next to her desk, and turned, one hand on her hip. Lifting the blinds had made the whole office brighter, she realized, and the red hearts were a cheerful counterpoint to the snowy street. "I think a scattering of small ones on the door. And maybe we should keep the blinds up." Her eyes were wandering around the office, noticing cobwebs in the corners and the shadowy shapes of insect corpses in the glass globes of the light fixtures. "This place could do with a cleaning," she said.

"That's why the blinds are coming back down," said Phyllis, yanking a cord and bringing the slats down with a clatter.

Lucy laughed, flicking on her desk lamp and booting up her computer. When the humming and whirring stopped and her desktop icons appeared, she paused. "Where's Ted?" she asked.

"Dunno. He called and said he'd be in after lunch."

Hearing this, Lucy went straight to the Internet and Googled "low calorie dessert recipes."

"We have a lot of listings this week," said Phyllis, slapping a thick pile of press releases down on the reception counter. "I guess Corney's been busy twisting arms for this *Love Is Best on the Coast* promotion."

"I promised Sue I'd enter her dessert contest," grumbled Lucy, scrolling down the list of recipes that had magically appeared. "It's not fair. I'm trying not to think about food."

"Have the girls do it." Phyllis was filing the press releases by date in an accordion file that was rather the worse for wear.

"They're busy with their jobs." Lucy's eye was caught by a recipe for low-fat cheesecake when the phone rang; it was Sue. "Funny you should call. I was just surfing the Web looking for a dessert recipe."

"Quiet day at the paper?" asked Sue.

"You could say that," said Lucy. "Phyllis put up some Valentine's decorations."

"Well, I have some news but it's not for publication," said Sue, in a low voice.

"Do tell," said Lucy, perking up.

"You're not gonna believe this," began Sue. "Remember how you saw Brad Cashman messing around with that woman in the chocolate shop?"

Lucy's eyes widened. "Tamzin?"

"Yeah. That's her. Chris said the phone was ringing all night. It was this Tamzin calling Brad."

"That's kind of pushy," said Lucy.

"According to Chris, it got so bad that Brad wouldn't take the calls. He actually turned off the phone."

"How did he explain it to Chris?" asked Lucy.

"He told her he'd flirted with Tamzin at the shop but that was all there was to it. He didn't understand why she was acting like this and he certainly didn't want anything to do with her."

"I think it was a bit more than flirting," said Lucy.

"I think you're right," said Sue, "because when she couldn't get through on the phone, Tamzin actually went to their house and made a terrific scene."

Lucy's jaw literally dropped. "What did she do?"

"Oh, she was screaming and crying and running around trying to grab Brad and kiss him, literally throwing herself at him while Chris and the girls watched."

"No!"

"Yes. She wouldn't stop. They couldn't get her to leave. They had to threaten to call the police."

"Did that work?"

"That—and a Xanax."

"So how is Chris taking it? Are they talking divorce or anything?"

"She's pretty upset. She doesn't know what to think. Brad's being a model husband—he made waffles for them all for breakfast and sent a big bouquet of flowers to her here at the school this morning—she says it's kind of making her crazy. She'd like it better if he wasn't quite so apologetic."

"I can see that," said Lucy. "I guess time will tell."

"Maybe they should talk to somebody, like a marriage counselor." In the background, Lucy heard a child crying.

"And get a restraining order," said Lucy, but Sue was already gone.

"What was that about?" asked Phyllis, raising one of the penciled lines that were her eyebrows.

Lucy considered. She didn't want to spread gossip, but Phyllis had heard most of the conversation and it seemed rude not to tell her the rest. And besides, nothing stayed secret very long in Tinker's Cove. "Tamzin from the chocolate shop has a thing for Brad Cashman and she went to his house last night and made a big scene in front of his wife and kids."

Phyllis clucked her tongue. "That woman's trouble. Do you know she gives Wilf a truffle every day when he delivers the mail?"

"Just as long as it's only a truffle," said Lucy, with a wry smile.

Phyllis scowled at a press release. "She better not mess with me, that's all I have to say."

"Me, too," said Lucy, closing out Google and opening the file for events listings. "Give me some of those press releases," she said, with a sigh. "I might as well get started."

Lucy tried to concentrate on the task at hand, but she found her mind insisted on wandering. For 'one thing, she'd written up these same announcements about children's story hours at the Broadbrooks Free Library and ham and bean suppers at Our Lady of the Harbor Church and free Friday night movies at the community center so many times that she could type them from memory. Of course, there was always the remote possibility that the movie time would change from 7 P.M. to 7:30 P.M. or that the price for the ham and bean dinners would rise from five dollars to six, which was why she really needed to pay attention.

But the harder she tried to concentrate, the more unruly her thoughts became, following their own path. And that path led straight to Tamzin Graves. What a nerve that woman had, flaunting herself at every man she met. She was practically a public menace; somebody ought to petition the selectmen to write a preservation of marriage act banning her from town. And it wasn't just husbands she was after—she went after your children, too, she realized, thinking of Zoe. They needed a family preservation act.

Lucy was chuckling at this idea when she noticed that the Newcomer's Club was canceling a planned talk by Dora Fraser until further notice.

No wonder, thought Lucy, Dora probably didn't feel up to speaking before a crowd so soon after her ex-husband's death. Max's death was especially sad, thought Lucy, since he and Dora had seemed to be reconciling. At least that's what Bill had told her and she didn't doubt it. She'd known other couples who had gotten back together after divorce. Maybe it was like slipping on a pair of worn sandals you'd put away for the winter; when you strapped them on, you found they'd been molded to your feet and fit perfectly.

In the past, Dora never hesitated to criticize Max, but now that he was gone she seemed to have found good points that outweighed his faults. Or maybe she'd simply come to accept him, warts and all, realizing that she still loved him in spite of everything. Most of their trouble seemed to involve money, that was the factor that broke up most marriages, at least according to the surveys in women's magazines. But now that the recession had arrived, everybody was having money trouble. All of a sudden people were reevaluating their priorities and discovering that relationships and family mattered more than their adjusted gross income. Maybe, she thought, that's what happened with Max and Dora. Or maybe once you loved someone, you always did—a sort of vestigial emotion.

But what about Tamzin? Lucy was sure she'd heard that Tamzin and Max were an item, even though Tamzin insisted they were only friends. Of course that's what she would say if Max had left her to return to his wife. A femme fatale like Tamzin would hardly broadcast the fact that she'd been rejected in favor of a heavier, plainer woman. She had an image to maintain.

Here Lucy had to admit she was letting her emotions get the better of her. She didn't like Tamzin, in fact, she was beginning to hate her. The woman was a predator, she stole people's husbands. She was self-centered, she thought the world revolved around her. She was blithely unaware of other people's concerns. She even thought she was above the law, if the incident with Zoe's working papers was anything to go by.

That's when Lucy decided she had to put the brakes on. Okay, so Tamzin hadn't bothered about the child labor regulations, she was hardly the first employer to ignore them. Like dog licenses and leash laws, the requirements for work permits were frequently ignored. And failing to apply for a work permit for an underage employee was a far cry from murdering someone, even someone who had jilted you.

Still, thought Lucy, the fact remained that Tamzin did have a black belt and could have overpowered Max, especially if he was drunk.

Was Tamzin a murderer? Lucy didn't know. The one thing she did know for sure was that she didn't want her daughter anywhere near the woman, who was clearly unstable. Zoe was at an impressionable age and Tamzin was a terrible role model. Lucy had high hopes for her daughters: Elizabeth had graduated from college and was successfully embarked on a career with the Cavendish Hotel chain; Sara had scored well on her SATs and was waiting to hear from the colleges she'd applied to; and

Zoe was in the top of her class. All three were serious, responsible high achievers and Lucy wanted them to stay that way. She didn't want Zoe to become a sexpot like Tamzin.

Lucy came to a decision: Zoe had to quit working at Chanticleer Chocolate. Since she was at school, there was no way Lucy could discuss the matter with her and convince her to quit. The best she could do was to send a text saying something had come up and she should call in sick this afternoon.

Moments later she got a reply: R U CRZ? T WL KL ME!

Lucy stared at the glowing letters, wondering if Zoe was on to something. Of course not, all she meant was that Tamzin was an abusive boss. She decided it was time to appeal to a higher authority and picked up the phone, dialing Trey's office at the converted sardine factory in Rockland.

"Bit of a problem," she began. "The job's not working out for Zoe. Tamzin kept her late yesterday and, well, frankly, she was really mean to her."

"Tamzin? Mean?" Trey couldn't believe it. "She's such a sweetie."

"Zoe was really upset when I picked her up."

"I'm sure she overreacted. She's very young, this is her first job, right?"

"I'm her mom and I don't like the way Tamzin treated her. That's the bottom line."

Trey immediately backtracked. "That's your prerogative, of course. But I pride myself on the company's employee relations. We value all our workers, they're our most important resource."

Lucy felt as if she were listening to a public relations spiel. Like the layoff notice Pam had received from Winchester College notifying her she'd been chosen for a special program and would be able to collect unemployment insurance. Lucky Pam!

"How about this?" Trey was continuing. "Give me a chance to talk to Tamzin. In the meantime, we'll put Zoe on leave. No pay, of course. . . ."

"Of course," said Lucy.

"But we'll keep the job open for her in case she changes her mind."

"I wouldn't hold my breath," said Lucy.

The next step, she realized with a sinking feeling, was to let Zoe know. She sent another text and braced for fireworks, a cell phone screenfull of stars and other symbols. Instead she got a phone call.

"I'm in the girls' room, I'm not supposed to phone at school."

"I know."

"Mom, I just want you to know I'm really glad. Thanks."

Lucy thought she'd misunderstood. "You're glad you're not working today?"

"I don't want to ever go back."

"You don't have to."

"Good. I think I'll stick to babysitting."

"Good choice," she said. "Take the bus home. I'll see you later."

Relieved, Lucy let out a big sigh just as Ted walked in the door. "Glad to see you're working hard," he said.

Lucy glanced at Phyllis, who ran her fingers across her lips in a zipping motion. "That's us," Lucy said. "Busy little bees."

Chapter Eleven

Ted tossed his jacket, hat, and gloves in the direction of the coat tree and made a beeline for the bathroom, causing Lucy and Phyllis to exchange amused glances. Unable to resist tidying up, Lucy picked up Ted's things, stuffed the hat and gloves in the jacket pocket, and hung it up.

"You know, Lucy, I couldn't help overhearing," said Phyllis. "I think you did the right thing, getting Zoe away from Tamzin."

Lucy turned and leaned her elbow on the battered Formica reception counter. Phyllis wasn't getting any younger, she thought, noticing the way her neck had developed crepey folds. And anxiety only served to emphasize the lines around her mouth.

"She's trouble," said Lucy, with a sympathetic nod. "One of those two-faced women who's nice to men. . . ."

"Wilf can't stop talking about her, he loves those truffles."

"As long as it's only a truffle, you don't have to worry."

"I do, though. She's prettier and sexier than I am," said Phyllis. "He doesn't see through her like a woman would, he doesn't understand why I don't like her."

"Don't be silly," said Lucy. "Wilf waited until he was practically fifty to get married and that's because he wanted to find the right woman, and that woman is you."

"I can't help worrying." Phyllis was chewing on the end of a ballpoint pen. "She's got him doing special favors, bringing her coffee from the shop next door. And not just regular coffee, skim milk lattes or some such thing. That Tamzin's got Wilf wrapped around her little finger."

Ted had emerged from the tiny toilet tucked behind the morgue looking much relieved, until he noticed Lucy standing by Phyllis's desk. Then he furrowed his brow and scowled. "Haven't you got anything better to do than gossip?"

"Actually, Ted, I was hanging up your coat," said Lucy, scowling right back at him.

"Uh, oh, sorry." Ted was momentarily shame-faced until he thought of a fresh avenue of attack. "I wish you wouldn't bad-mouth our advertisers. Chanticleer took out a six-month contract, so no more grumbling about them, okay?"

"We weren't grumbling about Chanticleer, we were talking about Tamzin," said Lucy.

"And you should be ashamed of yourselves," said Ted, self-righteously. "You should welcome her. The poor little thing is new in town and wants to make friends."

Lucy and Phyllis both laughed. "Only men friends," said Phyllis.

"That's right, Ted. You're not qualified to talk on this particular subject. Tamzin's got you under her spell, like all the other men in town."

"Right," agreed Phyllis. "We women have a special sense that warns us about husband stealers like Tamzin. It's like when chickens know a storm is coming, or the wildebeests stampede because a lion's on the prowl."

"Heaven help us if the women in this town stampede," muttered Ted. "Considering their average weight is two hundred pounds, there'd be nothing left. The place would be flattened."

"Not funny, Ted," said Lucy. "Besides, the fact that Tamzin's a man-eater isn't all that I object to. She hired Zoe without getting a work permit and then she treated her badly and made her work extra time. It's Zoe's first job—and she's a rotten boss."

Ted shook his head. "You know what kids are like. . . ."

"So don't hire a kid," snapped Lucy. "She hired Zoe because she thought she could exploit her."

"That's a reach, Lucy. Put yourself in Tamzin's shoes. . . ."

"Ha! I'd break my neck in those stilettos!"

"See! That's what I mean. What's really bothering you is pure female jealousy of someone who's more attractive. . . ."

"Watch it, Ted," warned Phyllis.

Lucy decided she'd better not say what she was thinking and instead marched over to the coat tree and pointedly lifted Ted's jacket off the hook and dropped it on the floor, in the exact spot it had been before she'd picked it up for him. Then she stomped over to her desk, plopped herself into her chair, and clicked on the solitaire game.

"I'm sorry, Lucy," said Ted, stooping to retrieve his clothing.

Lucy was staring at the screen, clicking her mouse and moving cards.

"I'm really, really sorry. I don't know what I was thinking."

"Hmph," said Lucy, starting a fresh game.

Ted seated himself in the spare chair next to Lucy's desk. "The thing is, Lucy, I need you to do something for me. I need you to take some photos at Chanticleer Chocolate for the ads."

Lucy was moving cards, pretty sure she was going to win this game. "Why can't you do it?" she asked.

"Uh, this is embarrassing."

"I knew it!" crowed Lucy. "Pam won't let you!"

Ted was staring at the scuffed floor. "That's right."

The little cards were dancing around on the computer screen, celebrating Lucy's win. She smiled at Ted. "Can't do it today. I left my camera home."

"You should always bring it," said Ted, unable to resist putting Lucy in the wrong. Lucy cocked an eyebrow in his direction and he backtracked. "Tomorrow will be fine."

"Good," said Lucy, reaching for the phone. Darn it, she'd called the place so often in the past few days that she'd memorized the number, which was taking up way too much precious brain space.

She winced, hearing Tamzin answer with "Chanticleer Chocolate" in a phony French accent.

"Hi, Tamzin, Lucy Stone here at the *Pennysaver*," she began, in a tone that was all business. She certainly didn't want to get into a discussion about Zoe's need for a leave of absence after only one day on the job; she'd leave that to Trey. "Ted wants me to take some photos for the ad campaign."

"Great!" From her enthusiastic tone, Lucy guessed Tamzin was also eager to avoid the subject of Zoe. "When do you want to come?"

Lucy considered her schedule. She sure didn't want to go out of her way for the woman. "Maybe tomorrow morning, on my way to the office. Eight-thirty?"

"We don't open until nine." Tamzin made it clear she was doing Lucy a favor. "I'm happy to come in early for you, though."

"Well, thanks, Tamzin," said Lucy, happily. She was on a winning streak today. "See you then."

Friday was the sort of day that would send any sensible person diving back under the covers. It was well after sunrise when Lucy drove down Main Street, but the streetlights were still lit, which meant the sun was not providing enough light to trip the sensors that turned them off. In other words, it was dark as night at eight-thirty in the morning.

The gloom wasn't the worst of it, though. Sleet, frozen rain, whatever you wanted to call it, was coming down hard, plopping on the windshield of

Lucy's car faster than the wipers could get rid of it. The road was filling with the slushy stuff, too, and every now and then the rear wheels would start to fishtail. The car's automatic all-wheel drive caught it every time, but it was still unnerving and Lucy's stomach lurched when she felt the car start to slip.

Maybe, she thought, swallowing down the coffee and bile taste that filled her mouth once again, maybe she should have had something more than black coffee for breakfast. Of course, she reminded herself, she hadn't had time to eat anything because she'd put off getting out of bed to the very last minute. Behavior like that wouldn't win her the mother-of-the-year award, or the wife-of-the-year award, either. She usually got up and made breakfast for Bill and the girls, but this morning she simply hadn't had the energy. Even now she had to resist the urge to turn the car around and go back home and back to bed, just like the snoring old man in the nursery rhyme *who went to bed and bumped his head and couldn't get up in the morning.*

Really, there was something to be said for opting out, especially on a day like this when she had to photograph Terrible Tamzin. Talk about adding insult to injury. If there were ever a day she'd like to skip, a day she'd like to pretend never happened, it was this Friday, actually the twelfth, but felt like an unlucky Friday the thirteenth. There was nothing to look forward to even after the photo session. When she finished at Chanticleer she had to go back to the office to write up the water commission's meeting, the highlight of which was the superintendent's assurance that the town had plenty of water.

Sure they did, thought Lucy, remembering last summer's floods and casting her eyes at the dark clouds filling the sky. Water in all its forms—ice, snow, rain, sleet, salty ocean, freshwater ponds, and streams—was one thing they had plenty of and, frankly, she could do with less of it.

She remembered a commercial for Aruba she'd seen on TV last night and pictured the sunshine, the sandy beach and turquoise Caribbean water. Boy, what she wouldn't give to be there. Now, that would be a great way to celebrate Valentine's Day: in a swimsuit, pale white skin slathered with sunscreen, sipping a piña colada, while Bill nibbled on her toes.

Not that Bill would ever do such a thing, she thought resentfully. Some men had foot fetishes, but Bill could truly be said to have a foot phobia. He didn't even like to see her barefoot. And instead of her being the focus of his adoring attention on Valentine's Day, this most personal of holidays had turned into a marathon. She had a to-do list that was a mile long. She had to make a dessert for the contest, pick up Bill's suit, jolly him into wearing it, and somehow find a way to stuff herself into her tight black skirt. Maybe skipping breakfast hadn't been such a bad idea after all, she decided, patting her now almost-flat tummy.

There was no problem finding a parking spot today. Main Street was practically deserted and Lucy thought of her old friend Miss Tilley's assertion that there was so little traffic when she was a girl that she and her friends used to play tennis in the road right in front of Slack's Hardware. Lucy parked in front of Chanticleer Chocolate and sat for a minute, lost in thought.

She was thinking of how things had changed even in her lifetime. When she and Bill first came to Tinker's Cove, the town had been more self-sufficient—you could get everything you needed right in town. There was a grocery store, drugstore, post office, liquor store, hardware store, a five and dime, and even a small department store with household linens and clothes to fit everyone in the family from newborn babies to grandmas. Through the years many of those old, established businesses had vanished, one by one, replaced by national chains. Now, if you wanted a new set of sheets or some pot holders, good luck to you. You had to travel to one of the big box stores that had sprung up out by the interstate or else you had to take your chances and order from the Internet.

Holidays were simpler, too. They were primarily family events, nobody thought of capitalizing on a holiday to bring tourists to town. Lucy remembered the kids making valentines for friends and family out of lace doilies and red construction paper. She'd make cupcakes for dessert, with pink icing and conversation hearts on top. Bill would bring home a box of Whitman's chocolates for her, which she shared with the kids after she'd plucked out her favorite caramels (easily identified from the chart on the inside of the box top), and that was that.

Sighing, she decided she'd put it off long enough, it was time to face the music. Or rather, Tamzin, with her fake boobs and false eyelashes, the glistening lips and the jeans that were so tight you wondered how she ever got them on, not to mention tucked inside those thigh-high boots.

Lucy pulled the fur-lined hood of her parka over her head and climbed out of the car. Ducking her head to avoid the sleet that pelted her face, she ran around the car and onto the sidewalk, seeking the shelter of the yellow Chanticleer awning. She was reaching for the door handle when the door flew open and Roger Faircloth barreled into her.

The man was obviously upset. He grabbed her by the shoulders with shaking hands and Lucy grabbed his sides, afraid he would fall. Noticing his pale face, shiny with sweat, and his panicked expression, Lucy thought he was having a heart attack.

"Roger, what's wrong? Shall I call the rescue squad?"

He couldn't manage to speak but nodded. Lucy needed to be able to reach inside her purse for her cell phone but she was still supporting Roger, she couldn't let go of him for fear he would fall. She decided the best thing would be to go inside the shop, where they would be out of the weather, Roger could sit on one of those oh-so-cute café chairs, and Tamzin could make the call.

But when she suggested going inside the shop to Roger he became frantic, shaking his head and saying no over and over. Lucy didn't know what to do, all that came to mind were those old black-and-white westerns where the cowboy hero was always slapping some hysterical woman. She couldn't slap Roger, she had to get help for him.

"Come on, Roger," she said, "we can't stay out here in the weather."

The man was sobbing and shaking, but he finally allowed her to guide him toward the door. Pulling it open, she heard the musical chimes ring once again and her nostrils were filled with the heavy scent of chocolate. Chocolate and something else. But what?

"Tamzin, I need help," she yelled. "Call nine-one-one."

There was no answering cry from Tamzin, which Lucy figured was typical. The woman was so self-absorbed, she was probably putting on fresh lip gloss or something and was too busy to make the call. She looked around the shop, past the tables stacked with blue-and-yellow boxes of chocolates and behind the counter, searching for the phone. It was then Lucy suddenly understood why Roger was so upset. At first, she thought it was just some sort of promotion, a giant chocolate displayed on the marble table behind the counter. A giant chocolate in the shape of a naked woman, a "Sex-sational Chocolate" bigger and fancier than anything Dora ever dreamed of. But when she took a closer look, she realized it was Tamzin; her naked body had been stretched out on the table and coated with chocolate.

Lucy's stomach heaved and, dragging Roger with her, she ran out of the store and stood on the sidewalk, gasping for fresh air. Tamzin was dead, somebody had killed her. Somebody with a wicked sense of humor.

Chapter Twelve

Lucy's car was parked right outside the shop so she helped Roger across the slippery sidewalk and opened the door for him. He made no attempt to seat himself, but stood, obviously in shock, leaning heavily on her arm and unaware of the globs of icy sleet that were falling on their heads and sliding down their faces. Lucy wasn't feeling too good herself. She was shaking and nauseous and realized a dark shadow was falling across her vision. She knew she had to sit down and lower her head or she'd faint and then she'd be no good to anyone.

"Come on, Roger," she said, coaxing him. "You've got to get in the car. We'll sit here and I'll call nine-one-one."

A glimmer of understanding flitted across his blank, staring eyes. Lucy turned him 'round and, imitating the maneuver she'd seen Rachel use with Miss Tilley, she guided him into the seat and lifted his legs one by one until he was properly seated. Bending down to seat him cleared her head, but she still felt dizzy and queasy when she took the driver's seat and started rooting in her big purse for her cell phone.

Finding it, she rested her head on the steering wheel and pressed the numbered keys. The dispatcher answered right away and Lucy told her she'd found Tamzin Graves's body at Chanticleer Chocolate.

"Is the victim conscious?" asked the dispatcher.

"No."

"Is the victim breathing?"

"No."

"Can you perform CPR?"

"Yes, I can," answered Lucy, who'd taken a course soon after her grandson Patrick's birth. "But there's no point. She's been dead for a while."

"Are you sure?"

Lucy was losing patience. "She's covered with chocolate!"

"Like she fell into it?"

"I don't know, but I've got an elderly man here who discovered her and he's in shock and we need some help."

"That's the thing—because of the sleet we've had a bunch of accidents and I don't have any units available. And if she's already dead, there's really no hurry."

Lucy couldn't believe what she was hearing. She glanced at Roger, who was breathing heavily, his face pale and waxy. "I've got an elderly man here in shock, he needs help."

"Maybe you could drive him to the ER?"

Give me a break, thought Lucy. "That would mean leaving a crime scene and I don't think I should do that."

"Are you sure it's a crime? Maybe it was an accident."

Lucy pictured Tamzin's body in her mind, neatly arranged on the marble table with her hands crossed over her stomach and completely covered with shiny dark chocolate. Her killer must have spent most of the night creating the macabre scene. This was no hit-and-run killing. The murderer wasn't content to simply eliminate Tamzin; he, or maybe she—Lucy conceded the killer could have been a woman—went to a lot of effort to humiliate her. It was on a par with Max's murder, she realized with a start. The two had most likely been killed by the same person. But why? And why did the killer feel the need to arrange the bodies so dramatically? First it was Max, found trussed in fishline with a lure hooked to his lips, and now it was Tamzin, turned into a giant chocolate bar.

"Hello? Are you still there?" It was the dispatcher breaking into her thoughts.

"Yeah."

"You're in luck. I've got an available unit and I'm sending it right over."

"Good," said Lucy, noting with alarm that Roger was reaching for the door handle.

"No, Roger. You have to stay here and talk to the police."

"I'll buy chocolate for Helen another day," he said, sounding like he'd just happened to find the store closed and needed to adjust his schedule. If he remembered finding Tamzin's body, it seemed he was determined to forget it. "I want to see Helen."

"You'll see Helen soon," said Lucy. "But first you have to talk to the police and tell them everything you saw."

Roger was quiet for a few minutes, staring straight ahead at the icy drops plopping onto the windshield, following their descent down the glass. "I was only there a minute or two before you arrived," he said. "I could go and you could tell them what you saw."

"I could do that," she said, "but they'd want to talk to you eventually."

"You wouldn't have to mention me at all. They don't need to know I was here," said Roger.

"No, Roger. You need to stay here. I think you might need medical attention."

"I'm fit as a fiddle," declared Roger, reaching once again for the door handle just as a police cruiser pulled up and parked at an angle, neatly blocking the Subaru.

"We're not going anywhere, Roger," said Lucy, watching as Officer Todd Kirwan stepped out of the cruiser and approached them; when he was beside the car she lowered the window. Inside the cruiser she could see Barney calling in to headquarters on the radio. At least that's what she thought he was doing.

"What's the problem?" asked Todd, leaning on the door. He was a tall, good-looking kid with a crew cut, one of Dot Kirwan's brood.

"We found a body in the shop," said Lucy, pointing at Chanticleer Chocolate. "And I'm a little worried about Roger here, it was a terrible shock for him."

At that point Roger seemed to pass out, his head dropped forward and his whole body slumped against the car door. Todd quickly called for an ambulance on his walkie-talkie, then reached across Lucy and felt Roger's neck to check his pulse. "Strong and steady," he said, with a shrug. He'd barely finished extracting himself from the car when they heard a siren. Lucy saw Barney get out of the cruiser and make his way to the shop. He went inside at the same moment the ambulance arrived. Her attention turned back to Roger and she was sure she saw his eyelids flicker when the ambulance crew approached the car; for a brief second she wondered if he was faking unconsciousness to avoid being questioned. Then the door opened and the emergency medical technicians began the process of extracting him. Seeing nobody was paying attention to her, Lucy joined Barney in the shop.

He was a big man, bulky in official cold-weather blue from head to foot, and was standing with his legs planted far apart and his hands on his hips, studying the situation. Lucy could tell he was thinking hard because he'd drawn his eyebrows together and had lifted one hand to his face to scratch his chin.

"Somebody's got a mean sense of humor," she said.

Barney scowled at her. "You shouldn't be here. This is a crime scene."

"I know," said Lucy. She heard the doors of the ambulance slam and the wail of the siren as Roger was carried off to the emergency room. The musical chimes on the little door rang and she turned to see Todd Kirwan enter.

Spotting Tamzin's body, he stopped in his tracks and gave a low whistle. "That's one hell of a chocolate tart," he said.

Barney started to reprove him when the chimes sounded once more and the police chief, Todd's brother, Jim Kirwan, arrived, accompanied by State Police Detective Lieutenant Horowitz.

Horowitz's glance raked the shop, taking in the body and landing on Lucy. "Did you find the body?" he snapped.

"No. Roger Faircloth found her. . . ."

"He went into shock," said Todd. "The ambulance just left with him."

"I got here a minute or two after Roger," said Lucy.

Horowitz cocked a pale eyebrow. "You're losing your touch," he said.

Lucy had worked with the lieutenant for years but she still never knew if he was joking or serious, whether he liked or disliked her. He never seemed to change; he'd looked gray and tired the day she first met him and that's how he looked today, with his long upper lip, grayish eyes, and sardonic smirk.

"I was supposed to photograph her for an ad," said Lucy. "I set it up yesterday; we agreed to meet at eight-thirty this morning, before the shop opened."

"So what was that other guy, Faircloth, doing here?"

"I think he wanted to buy some chocolate for his wife. He said something like that before he passed out."

Horowitz was writing it all down. The chief, meanwhile, had ordered the other officers to set up crime scene tape across the sidewalk where a small knot of curious townsfolk had gathered.

"So you came here with your camera . . . ," prompted Horowitz.

"Yeah, I'd just got to the door when Roger ran out, all upset. I thought he was having a heart attack so I brought him inside and yelled for Tamzin to call nine-one-one and that's when I saw her body. I took Roger outside to my car and called from there on my cell."

"Did you know the victim?"

It was the question she'd been dreading. "It's a small town and I work for the newspaper. I know everybody."

Horowitz sensed he was on to something. He lifted his pen, waiting for her to continue.

"My daughter Zoe, the youngest, had an after-school job here for one day." Lucy shrugged. "It didn't work out."

Horowitz wasn't about to let it go. "How come?"

"She's just a kid, she just turned fourteen. She wasn't ready for a job."

Horowitz looked skeptical. "I think there's something you're not telling me."

"I didn't want Zoe working here but Tamzin went behind my back and hired her but didn't bother to get the work permit. . . ."

"And why didn't you want Zoe working here?"

Lucy didn't want to be the one to tell Horowitz about Tamzin's reputation, it was bad enough the woman was dead. "Like I said, I thought she was too young. She should concentrate on her school-work."

"Oh, right, and the moon is made of green cheese," said Horowitz.

"Okay, okay. I saw Tamzin in a compromising situation with a neighbor of mine, a man who happens to be married."

Horowitz didn't actually exclaim ah-ha; it was there but unspoken. "Name?"

Lucy sighed. She didn't want to involve Brad and Chris but she knew Horowitz wouldn't give up. "Brad Cashman," she said. "But he wouldn't have anything to do with something like this."

"That's for me to decide," said Horowitz. "Anything else you don't want to tell me?"

"No, but I have some questions I'd like to ask you," said Lucy, as the crime scene workers began arriving, shouldering her aside.

"No comment," snapped Horowitz. "I may need to talk to you some more, so don't leave town."

"Darn," said Lucy. "You mean I'll have to cancel my Caribbean vacation?"

Horowitz grinned. "If I don't go, you don't go."

Released from questioning, Lucy left the store and headed for her car, only to discover strips of yellow crime-scene tape were fastened to the antenna.

"Uh, what's going on?" she asked the nearest officer, who happened to be Todd Kirwan. "Why can't I drive my car? It's not connected to the crime."

Kirwan looked down at her from his lofty six-feet-plus. "It's just temporary," he said. "There wasn't anything else to attach the tape to."

The sleet was still coming down and Lucy was half soaked and cold. She wanted to get into her car, crank the heat up as high as it would go, and drive home where she would hop into a steaming hot bath. Instead she sighed and reached for her camera, snapping a few photos of the crime-scene techs going into the store. Then she walked on down the street to the *Pennysaver* office.

Phyllis looked up when she entered. "What's going on down the street?" she asked.

Lucy noticed immediately that Ted's desk was empty. "Where's Ted?" she asked.

"He's at some conference or other in Portland, he told me but I don't remember." Phyllis bit her lip, coated in Tangerine Tango. "Might be the freedom of information act, or maybe wind power. He's gonna be gone all day."

"Figures," muttered Lucy. "He's here when you don't want him and he's gone when you need him."

"Why do you need him?" Phyllis and Lucy had long ago come to the conclusion that Ted was mostly a nuisance, except for signing their pitifully small paychecks. "Whatever's going on down there," she tilted her head in the direction of Chanticleer Chocolate, "you can handle it. What is it? A gas leak?"

Lucy plopped herself into her desk chair and swiveled it around to face Phyllis. "Somebody killed Tamzin Graves."

Phyllis's orange mouth got very small and her turquoise-shadowed eyes got very large. "No!"

Lucy nodded and pulled off her hat and gloves. "Yes. I saw the body."

"I can't say I'm sorry," admitted Phyllis. "For one thing, I didn't really know her and for the second thing, well, now I don't have to worry about her stealing Wilf." She tapped her lip with a finger tipped in matching Tangerine Tango nail polish; her diamond wedding set glittered, catching light from the antique gooseneck lamp on her desk. "Come to think of it, I bet a lot of wives and girlfriends had a motive for killing her. Do you think a woman did it?"

Lucy had unzipped her jacket and pulled off her boots; she shoved her feet into the battered boat shoes she kept underneath her desk and shuffled over to the coat tree, where she hung up her parka. The hat and gloves she arranged on top of the cast-iron radiator.

"Maybe," said Lucy, going back for the boots. "She was coated in chocolate." Lucy bent down to set the boots in front of the radiator and shove the toes beneath it.

Behind her she heard a crash. The sudden noise made her heart jump and she whirled around, adrenaline pumping. "What was that?"

"Nothing. I dropped my Rolodex." Phyllis was on her knees, picking up scattered index cards. "What do you mean, coated in chocolate?"

Lucy heard her but her mind was busy adding up this and that and coming to a conclusion she didn't like. "She was naked and coated with chocolate," she said, thinking that was clue number one.

"It made me think of Max, the way he was found. The killer was making a statement." That was the second thing she didn't like, because she could only think of one person who had a motive for killing both Tamzin and Max.

"I wonder," mused Phyllis, who was now seated at her desk and putting the cards back on the Rolodex. "How would you even go about coating somebody in chocolate? I mean, I can barely get the stuff to stick to strawberries. Coating an entire body would be a huge project." She paused, whirling the Rolodex. "And messy, too."

"There was no mess," recalled Lucy, thinking that there was only one person in town who knew enough about chocolate to manage such a trick. And that person, the same person who had a motive for killing both Tamzin and Max, was known for her wicked sense of humor.

Chapter Thirteen

Lucy went back to her desk, sat down, and opened a new file. She typed, slowly, recording her recollections of the crime scene. She made no attempt to write sentences, she simply wrote down her recollections as they occurred to her: the cloying scent of chocolate, her frustration with the dispatcher, the detached professionalism of the crime-scene technicians. She felt it was important to make a record while it was all still fresh in her mind and she could remember everything exactly the way it happened. She typed almost automatically, finding herself emotionally detached. It was as if she were seeing it all through a thick glass. It didn't seem like something that had really happened, it was more like a lurid scene from a TV show or a movie.

Oddly enough, she discovered, it was Roger she found most puzzling. Not his original reaction; the unexpected discovery of a body would unsettle anyone. It was later, when he attempted to leave the scene. Why didn't he want to talk to the police? And did he really lose consciousness due to shock, or was it feigned? Why did she think there was something dodgy about Roger?

She was sitting there, hands poised above the keyboard, when the door opened and Corney breezed in, clutching an armful of red and white Valentine's banners. "What's going on at Chanticleer Chocolate?" she demanded.

"Tamzin's been murdered," said Lucy.

"Coated in chocolate," added Phyllis, with a prim nod.

Suddenly, the banners clattered to the floor and rolled every which way, followed by a fluttering cascade of brochures. "Oh . . . my . . . oh!" exclaimed Corney, at a loss for words.

"Yeah," said Lucy, stepping carefully over the scattered banners and coming to her side. "Are you okay?" she asked, reaching for a chair and sliding it toward Corney. "Maybe you better sit down."

"Thanks." Corney lowered herself onto the chair and watched while Lucy gathered up the flags, with their big red cupids against a wavy pink and white background, and propped them against the reception desk. "I don't know what came over me." She clutched her purse to her chest and turned to Phyllis. "Did you say she was coated in chocolate?"

"That's right," Phyllis couldn't wait to tell the rest. "Naked, too."

Corney's jaw dropped. "How?"

"I have no idea. The crime techs are there, I suppose they'll figure it out," said Lucy, who was on her knees, gathering up the brochures.

"Maybe it was some sort of weird sex thing that went wrong," said Corney. "Like dabbing whipped cream here and there."

"Weird is right," sniffed Phyllis.

"I don't think so," said Lucy, wondering if Corney had a rather interesting sex life. She stood up and set the stack of brochures on the reception counter. "I think the chocolate must have been applied after she was dead. It was all very neat and tidy."

Corney gave her a curious look. "Really," she said.

"Can I get you something? A cup of tea?" asked Lucy. She was in caregiver mode, going through the motions.

"No." Corney shook her head. "I should get going. I have all these *Love Is Best on the Coast* banners and calendars to distribute." She gasped, suddenly grasping the implications of Tamzin's murder. "The weekend! Valentine's Day weekend! All our work and planning! Now it's ruined!"

"Yeah." Phyllis gave a sympathetic nod. "I know I'll never think of chocolate the same way again."

"Don't say that!" protested Corney.

"Why not?" Phyllis shrugged. "Better face facts. Chocolate's not sexy anymore. It's over."

"I'm not so sure," said Lucy, slowly. She still had that odd feeling of distance, as though she were watching herself from a far-off point. "It's certainly sensational. This is going to be all over the news— think of the free publicity. Tamzin's murder is going to attract a lot of interest."

Hearing this, Corney seemed to revive a bit. "Media will come, for sure," she said, brightening.

"And thrill-seekers," said Lucy. "People are ghouls. Trust me, they'll want to see the place where it happened."

"You're right, Lucy." Corney was on her feet, gathering up her flags and brochures. "I've got no time to waste. I better get these delivered right away!" She paused at the door. "Poor Trey! He'll be devastated." She reached for the knob. "I'll give him a call," she said, "but not just yet. Better give him a little time to let it sink in, get over the shock." Then Corney was gone. They could see her through the plate glass window, chatting away on her cell phone as she marched purposefully down the street.

Lucy sat back down at her computer, intending to continue working on her memories of the crime scene, but found the well had gone dry. She couldn't concentrate, she discovered, as her thoughts darted all over the place: Had she remembered to take the chicken she intended to cook for dinner out of the freezer? Thank heavens Zoe hadn't been the one to discover Tamzin's body. Good thing she nipped that problem in the bud. What about Sara? The news was going to be all over town. Would the girls be frightened? Maybe they should all be frightened—was there really a serial killer loose in town? Or did the killings have something to do with Tamzin and Max's relationship? How many lovers had Tamzin really had? Would they be upset? Would it be obvious? Would the male population of Tinker's Cove be wandering aimlessly around town, sniffling and dabbing their tears with handkerchiefs? Was that why Roger was so upset? Was he really in the shop to buy Valentine's chocolates for Helen? And what about dinner? What could she cook, instead, if she hadn't remembered to thaw that chicken?

She was suddenly startled out of her thoughts by Ted's booming voice. "Why didn't you call me?" he bellowed, slamming the door behind him. "A woman is killed and covered in chocolate and you don't think it's news?"

"I thought you were at a conference," said Phyllis. "I wasn't sure I could reach you."

"I have a cell phone," said Ted, glaring at her.

"I didn't want to disturb you," said Phyllis.

"This is news! This is what I do! Disturb me!" Ted was jumping around like Rumpelstiltskin, stamping his feet on the scuffed plank floor and rattling the wooden venetian blinds hanging over the plate glass windows.

"Calm down," said Lucy, in the tone she used for her children. "It's under control. I was on the scene minutes after Roger Faircloth found her body. I'm the one who called nine-one-one."

"Oh," said Ted, momentarily losing steam, then rallying to defend himself. "I didn't hear that part."

"How did you hear about it?" asked Lucy.

"It was all over the conference. People were asking me about it, since they know I'm from Tinker's Cove." Once again his temper flared. "I felt like an idiot, I was the last to know what was happening in my own town."

"Somebody must've called somebody," mused Lucy. "Darn cell phones. Thanks to Twitter, everybody knows everything the minute it happens." She paused, considering the ramifications of instant news. "We're obsolete, aren't we?"

"Not while I've got breath in my body," declared Ted. "We're going to find an angle, something nobody else has. And we've got five days before deadline to do it."

"Well, I was there," said Lucy. "I actually saw the body. Here, I'll send you the file."

"That's a start," said Ted, pulling out his chair and sitting down at his desk, still wearing his coat and boots. Slowly, he began unwinding his scarf, which he tossed on the chair he kept for visitors, and unbuttoned his coat, shrugging out of it. Little puddles formed around the boots, which remained on his feet. He switched on his computer and opened Lucy's file, leaning forward to read it. When he finished, he leaned back in his chair, shaking his head. "I hope you girls are sorry about all the mean things you said about that poor woman."

Lucy and Phyllis exchanged puzzled glances. Was this a typical male reaction? Was Tamzin now a blameless victim?

"Well," said Phyllis, in a judgmental tone, "it does seem to me that her behavior might have had something to do with her death."

"Blame the victim," said Ted, angrily. "She didn't kill herself, you know."

"I know that," said Phyllis. "But maybe she contributed to it."

"I think you're on the wrong track here," said

Lucy, thoughtfully. "Don't forget Max Fraser's murder. What I think we've got here is a single killer who likes to make a statement."

Phyllis took in a sharp breath. "A serial killer."

Ted was rocking in his chair. "A real sicko." His expression brightened. "This is going to be a hell of a story." He drummed his fingers on his desk. "If only I can get somebody official to confirm your theory. . . ."

The wooden blinds rattled again and Lucy looked up to see a big white satellite truck rumbling down the street. "NECN is here," she said. "You're going to have plenty of competition."

"Yeah," said Ted, rising to the challenge. "But we've got a big advantage. We know the lay of the land." He reached for his phone. "Have you called Trey Meacham for a comment yet?" Receiving a no from Lucy, he proceeded to make the call.

Phyllis and Lucy were all ears, listening as he probed for a comment.

"Really sorry to hear the sad news," Ted began. "When did you hear? Oh, so the police have already contacted you? They just left? What did they tell you? Well, I understand. Once again, just want to say how sorry I am."

Scowling, Ted put the phone down rather harder than necessary.

"The police told him not to talk to the media?" ventured Lucy.

"How'd you guess?"

"Par for the course. Did he say anything you can use?"

"He's terribly shocked and Tamzin was a stellar employee who will be greatly missed."

The blinds rattled again; this time it was the WCVB truck from Boston.

Watching it drive by, Ted came to a decision. He was on his feet and putting his jacket back on. "I guess I'll head on over to the police station and see what's going on."

"Sounds like a plan," said Lucy, wondering what her next step should be.

"No sense you hanging around here," said Ted, who kept close tabs on her hours and didn't want to pay her for doing nothing. "Phyllis can handle the listings. I've got your stories on the finance committee and selectmen's meetings. I can call you at home if I have any questions."

Lucy wasn't pleased, she didn't want to miss out on a big story, and it showed in her expression.

"But, Lucy, thanks for everything you did," he added, wrapping the scarf around his neck. "That was good work."

Watching as he hurried out the door, Lucy had the urge to grab the ends of that scarf and strangle him. "You know," she said to Phyllis, as she logged off her computer, "sometimes I understand what drives people to kill."

Phyllis adjusted the harlequin reading glasses that had slipped down her nose. "We might want to, but we don't. It's a big difference."

Driving home and thinking about lunch, Lucy realized she'd only worked four hours, which didn't amount to much money at all. Certainly not enough to compensate her for what she'd been through. She'd found a body, she'd been physically sickened and emotionally ravaged, and how much would she actually clear after taxes? It was enough to make you think about signing on to work nights at the big box megastore that had recently opened out by the interstate—if they'd have her.

Pulling into the driveway, she climbed out of the car and sloshed through the slush, noticing that the paint on the porch trim was peeling, revealing gray patches. Now that she was really looking she noticed the entire house could use a coat of paint. Oh, well, she told herself, as she climbed the steps, if the economy didn't pick up by spring, Bill would have plenty of time to paint. There was a bright side to everything.

Libby certainly thought so, greeting her with ecstatic wiggles and tail wags. Lucy gave her a handful of dog treats and considered her lunch options while she took off her coat and boots. It was definitely a day for comfort food, she decided, scuttling her diet and reaching for the peanut butter and jelly.

After polishing off a huge sandwich and a big glass of milk, she decided she'd better get cracking on the dessert she had promised to make for Sue's contest. Chocolate was obviously out of the question. Just the smell would make her sick, not to mention the look of the stuff. Shiny and brown and fragrant, no, she wasn't going there.

Opening the fridge and standing there, just like the kids did when they were looking for a snack, she noticed a tub of cottage cheese and a couple of bars of cream cheese. Cheesecake! Why not? She had an easy, delicious recipe. And, suddenly inspired, she remembered the blueberries she'd frozen last summer. What if she topped the cheesecake with blueberries, cooked with a little maple syrup for sweetener? Soon she was busy, happily mixing and stirring and remembering sunny summer days when she and the girls had picked the tiny blueberries that grew at the far end of the yard, where the woods began.

Looking out the window now, she saw a dismal view. The yard was filled with gray slush, the sky was gray, the trees were bare of leaves. Even the pointed balsams were black in the dim winter light. But here in her kitchen, the dog was snoozing on her plaid cushion, yipping every now and then as she chased rabbits in her dreams. The refrigerator door was covered with colorful photos of friends and family; many were of little Patrick, her grandson. The curtains were blue-and-white check, her beloved regulator clock was ticking, and the gas hissed as the oven heated. She was warm and busy and all around her was evidence she was loved and appreciated: a colorful pottery pitcher Elizabeth had sent from Florida "just because I knew you'd love it," the wooden bread box Bill had made for her, the KEEP CALM AND CARRY ON tea towel Sue had given her after their trip to England last year.

Suddenly she seemed very fortunate and she thought of Tamzin, killed and laid out in a gruesome display, objectified and ridiculed. Lucy hadn't liked her, but she didn't deserve that. Nobody did, she thought, stirring an egg into the cheese mixture, not realizing she was crying until a hot tear fell on her hand. And then another and another, as her body was wracked with tears of rage and regret. First Max and now Tamzin, both killed so horribly. It was more than she could stand.

Chapter Fourteen

Saturdays sure weren't what they used to be, thought Lucy, as she loaded the dishwasher with last night's snack dishes and this morning's breakfast crockery. She remembered lazy mornings when she and Bill slept late, then made plans for the rest of the day over a leisurely breakfast. Later, when the kids were little, they used to let them watch Saturday morning cartoons while they lingered in bed until the kids got bored and came in for a midmorning romp. That all ended, however, when the kids became teenagers. Now she and Bill were at the mercy of sports schedules and coaches, AP exam coaching sessions, and part-time jobs. This morning she not only had to make sure Sara got up and was fed and dressed, but she had to drive her and Renee to work because Frankie usually had open houses on Saturdays. Revising her original thought, she added Realtors. Like all the parents of teenagers, they had to adjust their schedules to accommodate the demands of others.

Now that Sara had her driver's license, she could drive herself except for the fact that Lucy needed the car later to take Zoe to her volunteer job at the Friends of Animals shelter. And there was always the possibility that Ted would call with a last-minute assignment, which often happened when a big story like Tamzin's murder was unfolding. It would be nice if they could afford a third car for Sara, she thought, straightening up and stretching her back, but that wasn't possible these days. Simply adding Sara as a driver had pushed their insurance premium so high that it was straining the family budget.

Glancing at the clock, Lucy realized they were running late. "Sara!" she yelled up the steep back stairway that led from the kitchen to the upstairs bedrooms. "I'm going out to start the car!"

Sara yelled back. "I'm almost ready!"

Lucy checked the thermometer that hung on the porch post and learned it was ten degrees outside. A mite nippy, she thought, but at least the sun was shining. Yesterday's slush had frozen solid overnight, so she put on her boots, reminding herself to watch her step and to expect icy patches on the road. She'd have to drive slowly and leave plenty of time for braking.

"Sara!" she yelled once more, pulling her knit beret over her ears and pulling on her gloves. "We've got to go!"

There was a huge clatter as Sara crashed down the stairs and landed in the kitchen, where she paused to pull her hair back into a ponytail. "No sense fussing with my hair since I have to wear those ugly shower cap things."

"Dress warm, it's freezing," Lucy advised, picking up the carefully wrapped cheesecake she intended to drop off at the contest and going out to warm up the car. Moments later, Sara popped out of the house, coat and scarf flapping.

"Brrrrr," she said, hopping into the car beside Lucy. "You weren't kidding."

"The sun's out, I think it will warm up," said Lucy, switching on the radio. "Might even get up to twenty."

"I think Elizabeth had the right idea," said Sara. "While we're freezing up here, she's working on her tan in Florida."

Lucy was backing out, humming along to a Beatles tune. "I don't think she gets too much time to lie around the pool—she's not a guest, she's the hired help."

"She gets plenty of time off," said Sara, in a sour tone. "And she doesn't have to wear a shower cap when she's on the job!"

Lucy chuckled, picturing her oldest daughter in the tailored Cavendish uniform with an embroidered "C" on the blazer pocket, as she made the turn into Prudence Path and pulled up at the La Chance house. She gave the horn a little toot and looked over at her son Toby's house, hoping to catch a glimpse of Patrick. "I thought Toby and Patrick might be playing outside but I guess it's too cold," she said, disappointed.

"I bet they're watching cartoons," said Sara. "I used to love Saturday mornings."

Lucy smiled, remembering how she and Bill

took advantage of the kids' passion for cartoons to indulge in a little passionate activity of their own.

The song had changed and the Rolling Stones were singing "Gimme Shelter" when Renee ran out of her house and hopped into the back seat.

"Wow, it's cold," she complained, fastening the seat belt.

"I don't know why you girls refuse to zip your jackets," said Lucy. "They put zips and buttons on them for a reason."

Sara rolled her eyes. "We don't want to look like dorks."

"So you look like popsicles instead," retorted Lucy, as the song ended and commercials began to play. Lucy was driving slowly, wondering who could possibly be interested in an adjustable mortgage after the recent financial crisis and how exactly did Dr. Myron Bush reverse baldness, at the same time keeping an eye out for that tricky black ice. She'd made it to the end of Red Top Road when the news came on.

Police have made an arrest in the Chanticleer Chocolate murder case. Dora Fraser, 38, of Tinker's Cove, was arrested late yesterday, according to state police. Fraser, who works at a rival chocolate shop, is accused of strangling Tamzin Graves and then coating her nude body with chocolate in what police have termed "a bizarre ritual slaying." In other news. . . .

The newscaster continued his report but nobody in the car was listening. They were sitting, silent and stunned, trying to absorb what they'd heard.

"Do we go to work?" asked Sara.

"I can't believe it," said Renee.

"I was afraid of this," said Lucy.

Sara's head snapped around. "You were?"

"Do you think she did it?" asked Renee, leaning through the gap between the two front seats.

"No. Of course not. I wouldn't let you work for a murderer, now would I?" said Lucy, cautiously making the turn onto Main Street. "It's because of her wicked sense of humor, the way she's always joking."

"The police must have more than that," said Sara. "You can't be arrested for making jokes."

"You're right," said Lucy, wondering what evidence the cops had found that incriminated Dora. She also wondered how long it would be before they charged her with murdering Max, too.

"Mom, do you really think the store will be open?" asked Sara.

"Only one way to find out," said Lucy, hoping she'd learn more about Dora's arrest at the shop.

When they pulled up in front of the familiar storefront, with its red-and-white-striped awning and curtained windows, the OPEN sign was prominently displayed on the door. Lucy led the way, marching right in, followed by the girls, who hung back reluctantly.

"Come on in! I won't bite!" said Flora, in her usual bossy tone. She looked the same as always, with her short salt-and-pepper hair and pink poly pantsuit. Her eyes didn't have their usual sparkle, however, and she looked pale and drawn.

"We heard the news about Dora," said Lucy. "The girls weren't sure. . . ."

"It's business as usual," said Flora. "I'm manning the counter and you girls can go on back and start filling the mail orders."

When they stood in place, she made a little shooing motion with her hands. "Go on. I'm not paying you to stand around gaping."

The girls shuffled off through the curtained doorway and Lucy approached the counter, adopting a sympathetic expression. "I can't believe the police suspect Dora," she began.

"It's nonsense," said Flora.

"I know Dora likes a good joke but she'd never kill anybody," prompted Lucy.

"Of course not."

Flora was known for being close-mouthed, but Lucy was hoping distress would make her a bit more talkative. So far this was tough going. "Did they say what sort of evidence they've got against her?"

"Nope."

"They just came and arrested her?"

"Yup."

"When was that?"

"Last night, around eight o'clock. They came to the house." Flora paused. "Good thing she hadn't put on her pajamas like she usually does to watch TV."

Lucy could just imagine the scene. Police rushing into the cozy old Victorian, guns drawn, upsetting potted plants and knocking over tables. "That must have been terrible."

"They were very polite, I'll say that for them."

Lucy realized she'd let her imagination run

away with her. "Even so, it must have been very upsetting. How are Lily and Fern?"

"They're not crying into their milk, that's for sure. They're checking out lawyers; we want to get the best for our Dora."

"Of course," said Lucy, struck with the woman's brisk efficiency and determination. The police probably hadn't gotten Dora into the cruiser before Flora was organizing the family and assigning jobs. "Let me know if I can do anything."

Flora gave her a look. "Lucy Stone, I've known you forever and I like you fine, but I know you work for the paper so don't be thinking I'm going to tell you anything I don't want to see in print."

Lucy felt as if she'd been slapped across the face, but she had to admit the woman had a point. "I understand," she said, turning to go. At the door, she paused and turned. "The offer to help still stands, and I won't print anything you tell me is off the record."

Flora narrowed her eyes and crossed her arms across her chest. "Hmph," she said.

Typical Mainer, thought Lucy, leaving the shop.

The dessert contest was taking place at the Community Church so that's where Lucy went next. The parking lot was a slick sheet of glass so she walked slowly, keeping her weight forward and praying she wouldn't slip and drop the cake. Sue was inside the basement fellowship hall, instructing her husband, Sid, where to set up tables.

"After the judging we'll be selling portions of the desserts, as well as coffee and tea," she was saying, when she spotted Lucy. "Hi, Lucy. You're the first." Sue waved a hand at the large, empty room with a stage at one end and a kitchen at the other, separated by a serving counter. "We're not ready yet. You can put your entry on the kitchen counter. What did you make? Can I have a peek?" she asked, crossing the room.

Sid, a dark-haired man with a mustache, was lifting one of the big folding tables off the wheeled rack where they were stored. "Hi, Lucy," he called. "How's the family?"

"Everybody's fine," she replied, setting the cake on the counter. "It's cheesecake," she told Sue. "With blueberries."

Sue frowned, picking at the foil with one finger. "Cheesecake?"

"Yeah. What's wrong with cheesecake?" Lucy asked, defensively.

"Somehow blueberry cheesecake doesn't say Valentine's Day to me. It says summer, maybe at a clambake."

"Too bad," snapped Lucy. "Cheesecake's what I felt like making. . . ."

"Yeah, I can see how you didn't want to mess with chocolate, after finding Tamzin's body," admitted Sue. "I'm just telling you because I don't think the judges are going to love cheesecake."

"I like cheesecake just fine," said Sid, flipping one of the tables over and unfolding its legs. His tight T-shirt revealed his muscular build; he worked as a closet installer and stayed fit, carrying heavy prebuilt components upstairs and down and wrestling them into place.

"Did you hear the news?" asked Lucy. "Dora's been arrested for Tamzin's murder."

Sue put the cheesecake down. "Are you sure?"

"Yeah. It was just on the news."

Sue was silent for a moment, absorbing this news. "Well, if you ask me, she did us all a favor. That woman was nothing but trouble."

"Meow," said Sid, grabbing another table.

"If it wasn't for the heavy lifting—and his spider-killing ability—I wouldn't keep him around," said Sue. "What about Max? Do they think she killed him, too?"

"The radio didn't say, but I wouldn't be surprised." Lucy leaned her back against the counter and pulled off her gloves. "The killings were similar, bizarre, and Dora does have an odd sense of humor."

"I can't say I miss Max, myself, and I bet I'm not the only one," volunteered Sid. "He'd beg you to help with a job and then if he paid you at all, he paid late."

"I dunno," said Lucy, thoughtfully. "From what I've heard, he was pretty popular, in spite of his money problems. And if there's one person in town I'd expect to really miss Max, it would be Dora. There was something going on between them, even if they were divorced."

"And Lily," added Sue. "He loved his daughter, and she loved him. You've got to give him that." She gave Lucy a look. "Why don't you take your coat off and help us out here?"

Lucy looked at the vast empty room and the waiting racks of tables and chairs; just looking made her back ache. "Uh, thanks for the irresistible invitation but I've got a bunch of errands to do."

"Be like that," muttered Sue.

Lucy ignored her. "How's Chris? Are she and Brad okay?" Lucy was feeling guilty about mentioning Brad to the police.

"I think they'll be just fine, now that Tamzin's out of the picture."

"I wonder," mused Lucy. "Did the cops question Chris? She had a motive, after all."

"They did," said Sue. "But she had an alibi. We were together Thursday night, working late, writing up student reports."

"How late did you work? She could've gone to the shop afterwards and knocked off Tamzin."

"No way. Brad took the SUV that day because of the weather, so she didn't have a car. He dropped her off in the morning and I drove her home that night." She paused, clearly remembering something. "In fact," she said slowly, "the lights were on at Chanticleer when we drove by and I remember thinking it was awfully late for anybody to be in the store, especially since they don't actually make the chocolates there. I even looked at the clock in the car. It was a little past nine." She shuddered. "Do you think that's when the murder took place? Isn't that creepy?"

"Yeah," said Lucy, wondering if the police had established a time of death for Tamzin's murder.

Sue's eyes widened. "Oh my gosh, I saw. . . ." She immediately turned toward Sid. "Don't forget the mike, okay?"

He nodded and continued arranging chairs.

"What did you see?" asked Lucy. "Or should I say, who?"

Sue was looking down at the floor. "Dora. I saw

Dora," she whispered. "She was right in front of Chanticleer."

"Are you sure? What was she doing?"

"Nothing, really." Sue was hugging herself. "For all I know, she was just walking down the street. But I did say something to Chris about it. Like, how come she wasn't walking on the other side of the street, some stupid crack like that."

"And Chris probably told the cops."

Sue nodded. "I feel sick about it."

"It's not your fault." Lucy squeezed her lips together. "I'm sure the police have other evidence."

"I don't think Dora is a murderer," said Sue, "but we did see her near the scene of the crime."

"Poor Dora. This explains a lot—it seems she had means, motive, and opportunity," said Lucy, realizing a little seed of doubt was sprouting in her mind. "Well, I gotta run. See you later, Sid," she called, heading for the door.

Outside, in the car, she thought about what Sue had said. It certainly didn't look good for Dora. She was probably the only person who had the skill to paint a body with chocolate, and witnesses had seen her at the shop the night of the murder. But as Sue had said, they didn't actually make the chocolates at the Tinker's Cove shop. The copper bowl and the marble-topped table and the other candy-making equipment were just for show. If Dora was the killer, she would have had to bring the chocolate that was used to paint Tamzin's body. How did she do it? And why did she bother? And what happened to Tamzin's clothes? When you thought about it, there were a lot of unanswered questions about the murder.

When she parked in front of the dry cleaners she noticed Trey's Range Rover was also parked on the street; maybe she'd get a chance to ask some of those questions. She hurried inside, hoping to catch him before he left, but there was no need. He was waiting patiently at the counter for the clerk to find his clothes.

"Hi," said Lucy, standing next to him and digging in her purse for the little green receipt. "I'm awfully sorry about Tamzin."

"Thanks, Lucy," he said, in a solemn voice.

"Three-three-oh-four-five, here it is," proclaimed the clerk, a gray-haired woman in her fifties, coming around the wall of hanging, plastic-bagged clothes. "Misplaced," she said by way of explanation, setting Trey's boxed shirts on the counter. "I didn't realize you wanted them boxed." She made it sound like an unreasonable request. "That'll be eight dollars and forty cents."

Trey handed over a ten dollar bill and turned to Lucy. "I'm still in shock, if you want to know the truth. Poor Tamzin. She didn't deserve this."

"Shocking," said the clerk, counting out his change. "I told my boss, there's no way I'm staying here after dark. I'm closing the shop at three-thirty. Folks'll just have to come early."

"It's hardly the sort of thing you'd expect in a little town like this," said Trey.

"It's outrageous! We've had two murders, right here in town." The woman's chin shook with indignation as she shut the cash drawer. "You can't be too careful these days."

"That's for sure," said Lucy, handing her the green slip of paper and turning to Trey. "I know they arrested Dora Fraser—did the police tell you why they suspect her?"

"Pretty obvious, don't you think?" replied Trey. "Tamzin was dating her ex, and then there's the fact her business was suffering due to Chanticleer's success. . . ."

"Those don't seem very compelling to me," said Lucy, as the clerk hung Bill's suit on the rack. "You're not really in competition with Fern's Famous. You attract an entirely different clientele." She paused, remembering how he'd touted the truffles as an affordable luxury, a status symbol. "I mean, you're selling a lot more than chocolate."

Hearing this, Trey's expression hardened, but Lucy didn't give it much thought. She was digging in her purse for her wallet.

"If you ask me, anybody who kills somebody else must have a screw loose," the clerk was saying. "I won't rest easy until she's locked up for good. That'll be eight seventy-five."

Lucy was thoughtful, handing over a twenty. "I suppose the police think she killed Max, too."

"I wouldn't be surprised," sniffed the clerk.

"Dora's sure made a lot of trouble for me. I don't know when the cops are going to let me reopen," said Trey. "And I have to find a new store manager."

Lucy couldn't believe it. Was the man out of his mind? A woman was dead and he was complaining about losing business. "What about Tamzin's family? Have you been in touch? What are the funeral plans?"

For a moment, Trey seemed at a loss. "I haven't really . . . I mean, I don't actually know. I'll have to check with HR." He pulled out his iPhone and began texting. "It's early days yet, of course, but the company will help any way we can."

Lucy didn't know what she expected. Sure, there had been rumors about Trey and Tamzin having a relationship, but that didn't mean it was true. Maybe he really was nothing more than her employer. She took Bill's suit off the rack where it was hanging and turned to go, discovering that Trey was holding the door for her.

"Hey!" called the clerk. "Don't forget your change!"

"Oh, right," said Lucy, embarrassed at her mistake. She went back to the counter and Trey continued on his way; she heard him slam the door of the Range Rover before speeding down the street.

The clerk handed Lucy her money. "You know, I thought he and that woman were real close. He was at the shop a lot, and sometimes they left together, when she closed."

"Really?" Lucy was tucking the cash into her wallet.

"Yeah. I have a clear view from here," said the clerk, nodding toward the plate glass window.

Lucy turned and discovered it was true. The WCVB truck was parked directly opposite, blocking her view of the drugstore, and a reporter was being filmed standing on the sidewalk in front of Chanticleer Chocolate.

"They seemed awfully affectionate," continued the clerk. "She'd be holding his arm and he'd open the car door for her, like a real gentleman. I even saw them kiss a couple of times."

"Not to speak ill of the dead, but I heard Tamzin was a very affectionate girl," said Lucy.

"That sort always gets in trouble," said the clerk, clucking her tongue.

Leaving the store with Bill's suit, Lucy wondered about Trey and Tamzin's relationship. They had seemed quite friendly when she'd interviewed them, but she hadn't really thought anything serious was going on between them. Now it seemed she may have underestimated their relationship. Or maybe the clerk had overestimated it. Two good-looking people, single, working together. It wasn't like they were kids or anything, they were a man and a woman and these things happened. It didn't necessarily mean they were truly intimate and involved in each other's lives.

And Tamzin wasn't shy about making her availability known. She might even have been using her sexuality to advance professionally. She certainly wouldn't be the first woman who'd slept her way to the top. And, to his credit, Trey had seemed shaken by her death.

Maybe he was still in shock, she thought, carefully hanging Bill's clean suit inside the car. A sudden loss could make your mind play tricks, make you forget details. She remembered how she'd struggled to remember appointments and keep the family on track after her mother died. Come to think of it, she was still struggling, but now it was just due to an overpacked schedule.

Lucy slid behind the wheel and consulted her list. Next stop: the post office. She had a box of books and clothing that Elizabeth had asked her to send to her in Florida.

Lucy was thoughtful, wondering if some small choice might have changed the direction of Tamzin's life and saved her from her terrible fate. If her mother, perhaps, had insisted she dress more modestly, or if her father had encouraged her to study harder and become a professional. What if she'd become a doctor instead of a chocolate shop manager? What if she'd taken another path and become a famous actress? Could she have changed her destiny? It was impossible to know; she didn't really know anything about Tamzin's background. She didn't know if she'd slipped down the social ladder, or if working at Chanticleer Chocolate was a step up; she had no idea what obstacles Tamzin had faced.

Lucy was wondering what information Tamzin's obituary might provide when she rounded the corner by the Quik-Stop and saw an ambulance with its lights flashing parked by the air machine. Slowing for a better look, she saw her friend Barney sitting on the raised concrete slab that protected the gas pumps, with his head in his hands. What was going on? She pulled off the road and parked, then hurried to his side. As she approached she saw he was crying; tears were rolling down his crumpled bulldog face.

"Barney! What's the matter?"

He looked up, blinked, and brushed at his eyes with his gloved hands.

"It's Eddie," he said.

Lucy looked around and spotted Marge's car, which Eddie had been borrowing, parked by the Dumpster, apparently undamaged. A sudden wail of the siren indicated the ambulance was leaving;

she watched as it departed, lights flashing. A police cruiser remained, and Officer Todd Kirwan approached with a sympathetic expression.

"They're taking him to the hospital," he said, leaning down and touching Barney's shoulder. "They think he's going to make it."

Barney nodded, but made no effort to move.

"What happened?" asked Lucy.

Todd turned to her, speaking softly. "It's his kid. Just back from Afghanistan. He OD'd."

"Eddie? On drugs?"

Todd nodded. "Heroin. He was shooting up, we found the needle."

Lucy's eyes widened. Now Frankie's suspicions about Eddie and Lily didn't seem so ridiculous. But what a terrible waste. She knew drugs were a problem everywhere, Tinker's Cove included. She'd seen the number of arrests rising, she'd written a number of obituaries for young people who didn't seem to have much going on in their lives but had loved animals, had lots of friends, and died unexpectedly of unexplained causes. She'd had her suspicions but somehow she'd managed to insulate herself. She'd been in denial, thinking drugs were something that happened to other people. She had never been personally affected, until now.

"It's everywhere," said Todd.

"Come on, Barney," she said, taking his huge hands in hers. "I'll give you a ride to the hospital."

He looked up at her. "I've got to get Marge." He shook his head. "How am I gonna tell her?"

"We'll go together," she said. "Where is she? Home?"

Barney seemed to be struggling to remember, trying to see through his fogged emotions. "She was taking a cake to that dessert contest."

Good heavens, thought Lucy, thinking of the now-crowded church hall, filled with happy, busy volunteers getting ready for the contest. Poor Marge! She'd just gotten her son back, safe and sound, from the war and now she might lose him. It was too cruel.

"Come on," she said, tugging at Barney's hands. Slowly he rose to his feet.

"You go back to the station, file the report," he told Todd.

The young officer nodded. "I hope, uh, I hope Eddie's okay."

"Yeah," said Barney, straightening his shoulders. He turned to Lucy. "Let's go."

It was only a short drive to the Community Church, where Marge was just coming out of the door, an empty pie basket slung over her arm. She was wearing a flattering knit hat and scarf that matched her green eyes and smiled as they pulled up, recognizing Lucy's car. When she noticed Barney in the passenger seat, her brow furrowed in concern.

Lucy braked and Barney got out, slowly, and lumbered clumsily across the sidewalk to his wife's side. He lowered his head, speaking to her, and Lucy saw Marge's face crumple. Then, taking Barney's arm, she hurried to get in the car.

"Let's go, Lucy," she said, taking charge. "As fast as you can."

In a matter of minutes Lucy reached the small "cottage" hospital that served the town's basic medical needs; the ambulance was parked outside the ER entrance. Lucy dropped Marge and Barney off at the door and parked the car. When she joined them in the waiting room, they were talking to Doc Ryder.

"He was lucky," the doctor was saying. "A few minutes later and, well, this story would have a different ending."

"He's going to be okay?" asked Lucy.

"Well, let's just say his chances are good at the moment," said the doctor. He took Lucy's elbow and guided her to a corner of the waiting room, apart from Marge and Barney. "We've got a real problem on our hands," he said, shaking his head. "This is the third overdose this week."

Lucy's jaw dropped. "Third?" She knew that Tinker's Cove was a small town, with a population of less than five thousand. Three overdoses in one week constituted an epidemic.

"It's out of control," said Doc Ryder. "We've always had a problem with drugs here in town but I've never seen it this bad. The stuff is pouring in from somewhere."

Lucy knew that illegal drugs had long been available to those who wanted them, but it wasn't terribly obvious. There were plenty of secluded areas in town where deals could be conducted; plenty of places where a user could get a fix unobserved. Police occasionally made a bust and sometimes the illicit traffic erupted in violence, as it had last year when Rick Juergens and Slash Milley were murdered. But most people in town had little or no contact with drugs except those they bought with a prescription.

"People need to know what's going on," said Doc Ryder, peering at her over his half-moon glasses.

"I'll see what I can do," said Lucy. "I'll check with Ted and give you a call next week."

"You know how to reach me," said the doctor, giving her a nod before going back to Marge and Barney. They made a tight little circle and Lucy felt it was time for her to go; she wasn't needed here. She suddenly felt an overwhelming need to make sure the girls were okay, to reassure herself that they were safe and sound and straight.

Chapter Fifteen

Lucy was leaving the hospital when she saw Max's big old silver pickup truck speed into the icy parking lot, taking the turn too fast. She held her breath, watching as the driver zoomed into a vacant spot and braked hard. The door opened and Lily jumped out, still wearing her red-and-white-striped apron with the FERN'S FAMOUS FUDGE logo.

Lucy waited inside the doorway and grabbed the girl's arm as she hurried in.

"Eddie's going to be okay," she said. "You can slow down."

Lily whirled around. "Let me go," she said, pulling her arm away. The girl was a nervous wreck, twitching and shivering.

"Take it easy," said Lucy, in mother mode. "Everything's going to be okay."

Even as she spoke she realized how ridiculous her words were. Things weren't okay for Lily, far from it. Her father had been murdered, her mother was in jail, and her boyfriend had just overdosed.

"Where's Eddie?"

"In the ER," said Lucy, pointing down the hall.

Lily started to run off and Lucy called after her. "His mom and dad are already there."

Lily stopped in her tracks and suddenly hunched over, as if in pain. "They are?"

Concerned, Lucy approached her. "Are you okay?"

"Yeah, yeah, I'm fine." Lily was nodding like a bobblehead doll. "What are they doing here?"

"They're his parents, they love him." Lily was clearly in some distress, trembling from head to toe. "Do you want me to take you to them?"

"No!" she shouted. "No, no, no!"

"Okay," said Lucy, who was completely confused. "Let me buy you a cup of tea," she suggested. "It will warm you up and help you relax."

"Tea." Lily said the word slowly, as if she'd never heard of it.

"Yes. Tea. We'll have a cup of tea in the cafeteria and you can pull yourself together and then you can see Eddie." Lucy had to admit her motives were mixed. She wanted to help Lily, who was obviously in trouble, but she also hoped to ask her a few questions about her mother.

Lily was staring at her warily, as if she sensed a trap. "Who are you, anyway?" she demanded.

"I'm Sara's mom. You know, Sara works at the shop with you."

"Right." Lily bit her lip. "Mom's gonna be mad. I better get back to the shop."

Lucy's jaw dropped. Dora was in jail, awaiting arraignment for murder, and had bigger things to worry about. But before she could say a word, Lily disappeared back through the door. Lucy started after her, but by the time she got outside, Lily was in the truck and speeding out of the parking lot.

Shaking her head, Lucy headed for her own car, pulling the list of errands out of her pocket. Post office. Right. She checked her watch and discovered she just had time to make it before it closed at noon. But as she drove along the familiar roads, she struggled to figure out what was going on with Lily. The poor girl was clearly an emotional mess, but who could blame her? Considering everything that had happened to her, it was no wonder she was struggling. Thank goodness she had her grandmother and great-grandmother, Flora and Fern, to take care of her.

Leaving the post office, Lucy noticed the lights were on in the *Pennysaver* office and decided on impulse to stop in. As she suspected, Ted was there, hunched over his desk.

"Hi," she said. "What are you doing here on a Saturday? You should be getting ready for the ball tonight."

Ted laughed. "I won't need much time, but Pam is making a day of it. She's getting the works at the Salt Aire Spa."

"Lucky her." Lucy felt a twinge of jealousy but resolutely ignored it. "Did you hear about Dora?" she asked.

"That's why I'm here. The cops had a press conference this morning. Horowitz was unusually chatty."

"Really?" Lucy had taken off her hat and gloves and was loosening her scarf. "What did he say?"

Ted stopped typing and looked at her, twisting his mouth into a scowl. "I don't know. Maybe I'm hallucinating or something, but I got the feeling something was going on. It's all circumstantial, there were no witnesses. . . ."

"You'd hardly expect a witness."

"It's more than that. They didn't have a weapon, no concrete evidence. Just a theory."

"That she was a woman spurned?" Lucy's voice was dramatic.

Ted nodded. "Yeah. She killed Tamzin out of jealousy, and they're reopening the investigation into Max's death, figuring to charge her with that, too."

Lucy sat down, mashing her hat, gloves, and scarf together in her lap. "I expected as much." She sighed. "What about Tamzin? Any family?" She paused. "How old was she, anyway?"

Ted laughed. "You women are all alike—that's what Pam wanted to know, too."

"And?" prompted Lucy.

"Forty-six."

"I knew it!" crowed Lucy. "I knew she was no spring chicken!"

"She was well preserved, you've got to give her that," said Ted. "And there's a husband. . . ."

"A husband?"

"Well, an ex. Career army, in Afghanistan. They

stayed in touch, there were letters and photos in her apartment."

"I had no idea." Lucy suddenly felt ashamed of her uncharitable opinions of Tamzin.

Ted shrugged. "Nobody did."

When Lucy returned to the church basement later that afternoon for the judging, she found the air was heavy with the scent of sugar and chocolate. The tables Sid had arranged under Sue's instructions were now covered with white cloths and packed with desserts of all kinds, arranged by category. There was a table with nothing but pies and fruit tarts, another with cookies and cupcakes, and several others devoted to all sorts of chocolate treats. Smaller tables with red balloon centerpieces and chairs were scattered around the room, ready for the customers who would buy the treats after the judging, and then consume them along with tea and coffee. Just looking at all the goodies was enough to cause a diabetic coma, but nobody was interested in checking them out. Instead, everybody was talking about Dora's arrest. That was fine with Lucy, who was relieved that news of Eddie Culpepper's overdose hadn't reached the grapevine yet.

"She was always a prankster," recalled Franny Small, her face unnaturally smooth and tight thanks to a recent face-lift. Franny owned a wildly successful jewelry company and could afford anything she wanted; her Lexus was parked outside. "I remember she got in trouble when she was in high school—something about an effigy of the principal."

"It wasn't an effigy," offered Luanne Roth, who had recently contacted Lucy about publicizing the twentieth reunion of her class at Tinker's Cove High School. "We were in the same class, you know, and there was quite a fuss. It was a sign. A bed sheet they hung from the roof that said something bad about Mr. Wilkerson; he was the principal then. I can't remember exactly what it said but it was insulting."

"They let her graduate but they kicked her out of the National Honor Society," said Lydia Volpe. Now retired, Lydia had taught kindergarten to all four of Lucy's kids. "It was quite a scandal at the time. The police prosecuted and she was on probation and had to perform community service and couldn't go to college right away. They postponed her admission until her probation was completed." She paused, her huge brown eyes momentarily unfocused as she dredged her memory. "I don't know if she ever did go, now that I think about it."

"I think she went right to work in the shop," said Luanne.

"She got pregnant," said Franny, with a little sniff.

"That's right," agreed Lydia. "We had quite a little flurry of teen pregnancies around then."

"Well, I know Dora has a unique sense of humor, but getting in trouble for a high school stunt is one thing and murder is another," said Lucy.

"A double murder," offered Dot Kirwan, joining the knot of gossipers. They all looked at her expectantly, knowing she was the police chief's mother and most likely had the latest information. "They're most likely charging her with Max's murder, too."

"Now that I don't believe," said Luanne. "They've been on and off ever since junior high school. I mean, even though they're divorced, I still think of them as a couple. I think everybody who was in school with them does. They were always fighting and making up. The girls would side with Dora and the boys with Max; it was high drama in the cafeteria. A real soap opera, a new installment every day."

"Well, if it was a soap opera, this was the final episode," said Dot. "They've got witnesses who saw Dora on the ice, arguing with Max, the evening before he was killed."

If that was true it was bad news for Dora, thought Lucy, who remembered Barney telling her that Dora said the last time she saw Max was at the house, when he came to help her with her car. Did she lie, or were the witnesses mistaken? Was it Dora, or someone else?

"Max had been seeing a lot of Tamzin," said Luanne, who worked at the Irish pub by the harbor. "They came in for drinks quite a few times."

"A classic love triangle with a tragic ending," said Lydia, welling up with tears. "I remember Max and Dora, they were in some of my first classes. I had such high hopes for them—especially Dora. She was such a bright little thing."

Lucy gave her a hug. "Well, she's innocent until proven guilty."

"That's right," said Dot, with a smart nod. "If you ask me, I don't think Dora would hurt a fly."

"You know she makes those dirty chocolates," said Franny, pursing her lips with disapproval. "She sells them on the Internet."

"I've seen the chocolates—they're not offensive," said Lucy. "My own daughter works there, packing them, and I certainly wouldn't let her handle anything I didn't approve of."

"Dora's always marched to her own drummer," said Dot, "but that doesn't make her a murderer."

"Is the case against her strong?" asked Lucy. "They must have evidence. . . ."

"Circumstantial," said Dot. "And she's a smart girl. Last I heard, she's refusing to talk to investigators—you know most perpetrators are only too happy to incriminate themselves. My Jim says if it wasn't for the fact that the bad guys aren't too smart and love to talk, they'd hardly convict anybody."

"I saw Flora this morning," said Lucy. "She said they're looking for a lawyer."

"Smart," said Dot, with an approving nod. "That's the other thing in Dora's favor. She's got a lot of support from her family."

"That's for sure," agreed Lydia. "Flora was always there for every conference, every school event. And Fern, too. And then when Lily came along, all three of them would show up."

Sue was tapping on a glass with a spoon, so conversation ceased as everyone focused on the panel of judges gathered beside her. Sue then made the introductions, but Lucy wasn't listening because she recognized them all: Roger Wilcox, chairman of the board of selectmen; Hildy Schultz, who owned a bakery; and Fred Farnsworth, executive chef at the Queen Victoria Inn. They were nodding and smiling and saying nice things about all the entries, but Lucy's mind was miles away, thinking of Dora, sitting in the county jail. As a reporter Lucy had been there numerous times, covering various stories. It was one of her least favorite assignments; she hated the moment the door clanged shut behind her, even though she knew she could leave whenever she wanted. Nevertheless, she always sympathized with the inmates, who couldn't.

Of course, Dora was tough. She was probably better able to withstand the indignities of imprisonment than most. And, as Dot had mentioned, she had plenty of support from her family. If anybody could successfully conceal a saw in a cake and smuggle it in to the jail, it would be Flora, she thought, as a little smile flitted across her lips.

Thinking about that tight family of women, who all lived and worked together, she wondered if perhaps Dora was protecting somebody else. Not Fern, she was too old to manage such elaborate murders. She could probably bash somebody on the head or shoot them, but staging the bodies the way the murderer had was a big job and Lucy doubted she had the strength. Flora, however, was a big woman with a lot of determination. And she'd been handling heavy sacks of sugar and other ingredients her entire life. Flora was also judgmental, and used to getting her way, according to Miss Tilley, and had forced Max to marry Dora when she got pregnant. Perhaps Flora didn't approve of the divorce and would rather see Dora as a widow than a divorcée with an ex who kept hanging around. Lucy was wondering if Flora wasn't a likelier suspect for the murders than her daughter when Dot elbowed her in the ribs.

Lucy was recalling her strange encounter with Lily and wondering if she wasn't an even likelier suspect—after all, Flora had bragged about Lily's skill at hunting and dressing deer—when Lydia poked her in the ribs.

"Lucy! They called your name!"

Lucy blinked. "What?"

"Once again," Sue was saying into the microphone, "our first-prize winner is Lucy Stone for her Maple-Blueberry Cheesecake!"

Stunned, Lucy made her way through the crowd toward the judges. When she was in place behind the table, Sue continued, reading from a card.

"The judges all agreed that this cheesecake showed an imaginative and original use of local ingredients. It was refreshing and light and surprisingly low in calories, the perfect end to a coastal dinner."

"And I might add, absolutely delicious," said Fred Farnsworth, leaning in to the microphone.

Everybody laughed and applauded, except for Sue, who looked rather annoyed as she handed Lucy an envelope. "The grand prize is a dinner for two at Chantarelle. Congratulations and bon appétit, Lucy."

"Thank you," said Lucy, still not quite comprehending her triumph. "This is a real surprise."

"I'll say," muttered Sue, under her breath, as there was another round of applause. She held up her hand for silence. "And now, I encourage everyone to sample the delicious entries—the five dollar per plate cost goes to support the Hat and Mitten Fund, which provides winter clothing for local children. Tea and coffee are also available."

Putting the mike down, Sue thanked the judges while Lucy tucked the envelope into her handbag. Then she asked Sue if she could help with the serving as people started to mob the tables where the desserts were displayed.

"It looks like they could use some help with the pies," said Sue, scanning the crowd, which was thickest around the table displaying that category of entries. Cupcakes were also popular, as were the cookies, but Lucy noticed that few people had gathered at the table with brownies and chocolate cakes.

"Chocolate's gotten some bad press lately," said Lucy.

"Absolutely," declared Sue. "If that poor woman hadn't been coated with chocolate, I'm sure my Better-Than-Sex Brownies would have won. The entries were blind, you know, so they could have picked mine. But right now it's hard to think about chocolate without picturing Tamzin's body and it takes your appetite away."

"I'm sure that's it," said Lucy, before heading over to the pie table.

"People are sick of chocolate," added Sue, in a parting shot.

When Lucy picked up Zoe at the Friends of Animals shelter, she discovered the news about Eddie was finally out.

"Mom! Did you hear? Eddie Culpepper over-dosed at the Quik-Stop. He's in the hospital."

"I know." Lucy scowled, waiting for Zoe to fasten her seat belt. "How did you hear about it?"

"I got a text from Sara."

Hearing the click, Lucy shifted into drive. "How did she know?"

Zoe gave her a patronizing look. "From Lily, of course. At the shop. She and Eddie have been dating."

Lucy braked at the road. "You know about that?"

"Yeah." Zoe's tone implied that everybody knew this, everybody except her stupid mother.

"Does Lily use drugs?" Lucy kept her tone off-hand, as she turned onto Oak Street.

"No way. She's anti-drug, anti-alcohol."

Lucy was beginning to think this was a bit of protective camouflage. Now that she thought about it, it seemed that drugs might explain Lily's odd behavior at the hospital. "How do you know all this stuff?"

Zoe shrugged. "I dunno. I hear stuff. Sara and her friends talk." She paused. "I guess they think I'm deaf or something." She laughed. "I'm the little sister. It's like I don't exist."

Lucy thought she had a point. "What else have you heard?"

Zoe's tone was serious. "Plenty, but you'll have to pay."

In spite of everything that had happened, in spite of Dora's arrest and Eddie's overdose, Lucy found herself chuckling as she turned into the driveway. But her emotions were ragged and she was on the verge of tears when she entered the warm and homey kitchen. Determined to distract herself, she got busy making supper for the girls.

Lucy saved the news of her prize until they were dressing, hoping to present it to Bill as a sweetener before she dragged him off to the Hearts on Fire Ball. She knew he was less than enthusiastic about wearing a tie, much less an entire suit, and he hadn't danced in years. Probably not since their own wedding reception, come to think of it.

"Guess what?" she said, leaning into the mirror and brushing mascara onto the back of her upper lashes, the way she'd read about in a magazine at the dentist's office. It seemed impossibly difficult and required a great deal of concentration, but whoever wrote the beauty column insisted it was important to first coat the lashes, then to use the tiny brush to lift them.

"What?' growled Bill, straining to button the collar on his starched shirt.

"I won the dessert contest and the prize is dinner for two at Chantarelle."

Bill wasn't impressed. "What's Chantarelle?"

"It's fabulous, everybody raves about it."

"It's not here in town," he said, warily. "Is it in Portland?"

"Actually, it's in Portsmouth."

The collar was flipped up and Bill was looping a tie around his neck. "New Hampshire?" he demanded, his tone verging on outrage.

Lucy sensed her plan was not working. "That's where Portsmouth is, last time I checked," she said.

"No need to get all sarcastic," he said, scowling at his reflection in the full-length mirror behind the bedroom door and undoing the knot.

"Let me do that," said Lucy, screwing the cap on the mascara and setting it on her dresser.

"That's a heck of a drive for dinner," he said, surrendering the tie to her.

"The food is supposed to be well worth the trip," said Lucy, sliding the knot up to his chin. "There. You look very nice."

She was only wearing her bra and a half-slip and Bill slipped his hands around her waist. "You should go like this," he said, pulling her close.

"Whoa, boy," she cautioned, stepping away from him. "We're running late."

He sighed and reached for the hanger with his pants. "The portions in those fancy places are always so small," he said.

"That's so you can savor the flavors," said Lucy, applying lipstick. "After a few bites you don't really notice the taste anymore." She pressed her lips together and examined the effect, then added a slick coat of gloss. "At least that's the theory."

Bill was fastening his belt. "And you can't relax, there's always some waiter fussing around, trying to grab your plate."

"Well, for your information, Sue was very put out when I won the prize. I think she wanted it." Lucy was fastening the waistband of her good black skirt, pleased to discover it fit easily. The diet was working.

"Maybe you should give the certificate to her, then," said Bill, adjusting his jacket on his shoulders.

Lucy was pulling her lace blouse over her head, so Bill didn't hear her reaction, which was just as well. When she emerged, her hair was tousled and her eyes were blazing.

"You look amazing," said Bill. His expression was a combination of surprise and awe, as if he were seeing her anew and liked what he saw.

Lucy was about to ask if she didn't look too fat but bit her tongue. Moments like this didn't happen very often, especially when you'd been married for more than twenty-five years and had four kids. "So do you," she said, smiling and smoothing his lapels.

She wasn't just saying it, she realized, he really did look great. He still had plenty of hair, mostly still brown but gray at the temples, and he wore it a bit long, so a lock fell over his brow. His beard also had a touch of gray, but it made him look distinguished. He was slim and stood tall and straight in the suit, which still fit even though he'd had it for years.

"Thanks for doing this," she said. "I know you're not really keen on dress-up occasions."

"It's good to break out of a rut, once in a while," he said, offering her his arm. "Shall we go?"

Chapter Sixteen

The VFW was decorated to the hilt for the ball, but it was still, unmistakably, the VFW. All the red crepe paper streamers and heart-shaped balloons in the world couldn't disguise the scuffed wood floors and the walls that needed a fresh coat of paint, scarred as they were by all the notices that had been taped up and removed through the years. There was also that VFW smell, a combination of stale cigarette smoke, booze, and pine-scented cleaning fluid.

The organizers had done the best they could—the round tables were covered with floor-length white cloths, topped with smaller red ones, and a single red rose in a chunky milk glass vase served as a centerpiece on each table. The colored cloths set off the VFW's basic white china to advantage, and a red cloth napkin was tucked in each industrial-strength wine goblet.

When Lucy and Bill entered, the DJ was playing classic Beatles tunes and a disco ball was throwing spots of light around in the darkened room. Lucy had the déjà vu that she'd been in the same place before and realized she was thinking of her high school prom.

Smiling at the recollection of her awkward self, dressed in four-inch heels and the ridiculous slinky black dress she'd insisted on wearing despite her mother's objections, she was pleased when Bill took her hand and led her to the table where their friends were sitting.

There was a flurry of greetings as air kisses and handshakes were exchanged, and soon Lucy was seated at the table while Bill went to get drinks from the bar. It was odd to see everyone dressed to the nines, since dress in Tinker's Cove tended to be extremely casual, especially in winter when everyone clomped around in duck boots and bulky down coats and jackets.

Sue was especially gorgeous, dressed in the lace camisole she'd bought last spring in London and a pair of skin-tight black satin pants. Her bare arms were golden, evidence she'd spent some time at the tanning salon. Lucy was tempted to warn her about the dangers of tanning, but bit her tongue. Sue would just laugh at her. It was definitely annoying that Sue managed to look fabulous, always had tons of energy, and was never sick despite a diet that consisted of little but black coffee and alcohol, with the occasional indulgent gourmet dinner.

"You look great," said Lucy, remembering the day they'd gone shopping together in London. "That camisole was a terrific buy."

"I barely had time to get dressed," said Sue.

"The dessert contest didn't wrap up until almost six and the clean-up committee didn't show. Poor Sid got pressed into duty when he came to pick me up."

Sid ran his finger around his neck, trying to loosen his collar. It was too small and his ruddy cheeks made him look as if he were about to burst and pop a button. "It was a big success, though," he said, beaming proudly at Sue. "Tell them how much it made for the Hat and Mitten Fund."

Sue leaned forward. "Believe it or not, over a thousand dollars."

"That's a lot of cookies," said Pam, who'd recently given up Nice 'n Easy and her ponytail for a neat, silvery cut that hugged her head. Her day at the spa had refreshed and rejuvenated her; her complexion was glowing, and she looked gorgeous in an electric blue sari she'd probably picked up in a vintage clothing shop. It was the sort of thing I would feel ridiculous wearing, thought Lucy, but it looked great on Pam.

"It's a lot of hats and mittens," said her husband, Lucy's boss, Ted. He was seated beside Pam, nervously stroking his tie, as if he needed to check that it was still in place and hadn't slithered off somewhere.

"That fund does so much good—you should be really proud of yourself, Sue," said Rachel. "You made the contest a big success."

Rachel had gone to the beauty salon where they'd clipped and curled her long black hair, which she usually wore pinned up in a loose knot. Sensible as always, she was wearing a burgundy cashmere sweater dotted with sparkly beads that

was warm as well as flattering, and a long black
skirt.

Her husband, Bob, was the only one of the men
who seemed comfortable in his suit. He was a
lawyer and often wore a jacket and tie. "I've got a
scoop for the *Pennysaver*," he said, with a nod to
Ted. "I've been hired to defend Dora Fraser."

"I knew they were looking for a lawyer. Flora
said she wanted the best and I guess she got it,"
said Lucy. "What do you think her chances are?"

"I really haven't had time to look at the case,"
he said, as Bill returned with a beer for himself
and a glass of white wine for Lucy. "They called me
this morning. I'll know more next week, after I
talk to her."

Ted fingered his napkin and Lucy figured he
was adding up column inches in his head, working
out whether the story was worth the expense of
adding a page. "Lucy, you can follow up on that,
right?"

"Sure." Lucy didn't want to think about work or
murder or Eddie's drug overdose; she wanted to
enjoy herself. She took a sip of her wine and reached
for Bill's hand.

"I went to the hospital today to visit Joyce Ren-
nie—her husband is in the play and they just had a
baby girl—and I ran into Barney and Marge," said
Rachel. "They said Eddie was in the ER, but then
they hurried off. I hope it's nothing serious."

Darn it, thought Lucy. Here we go. "It was
drugs," she said. "He OD'd. . . ."

Everyone fell silent for a moment.

"Poor Marge and Barney," said Rachel.

"Is he going to be okay?" asked Pam.

"Doc Ryder said he'd make it, but he almost died," said Lucy.

"PTSD, post-traumatic stress disorder," murmured Rachel. "It's not unusual after what these kids go through over there."

"That's true, as far as it goes," said Lucy. "But Doc Ryder told me there's been a recent epidemic of overdoses. He wants us to do a story about it."

"We already ran that interview with the governor's wife," said Ted, in a defensive tone. "I'd like to give it a rest, maybe revisit the issue in a month or so."

Lucy struggled to hold her temper. "Sooner would be better than later," she argued. "We could save lives." She felt a nudge on her ankle and realized Bill was signaling her that she'd said enough on this particular topic.

"Drugs are a fact of life these days," said Ted. "They're everywhere. It's hardly news."

"Sadly, that's true," offered Rachel, with a sad smile.

Recognizing defeat, Lucy glanced around the room. Chris and Brad Cashman were seated at a nearby table, along with Frankie and the Faircloths, as well as some people she didn't recognize. It seemed a lively group, however, and there were frequent bursts of laughter. She looked around for Corney but didn't see her; maybe she was busy with some last-minute details.

Lucy had only had a sip or two of wine before the high school–student waiters began serving the fruit cup appetizers that preceded the VFW's famous rib roast dinner.

"Canned fruit!" exclaimed Sue, picking out the

tiny bit of maraschino cherry and popping it in her mouth. "I haven't had fruit salad since I was a kid." She cautiously speared a bit of pear and tasted it. "Now I know why I haven't had it—it's gruesome."

"I kinda like it," said Sid.

"Me, too," said Lucy, digging in as the DJ started playing a Four Tops tune. "It takes me back—in fact, this whole thing is like a trip down memory lane."

"I wonder if that's what Corney had in mind," said Rachel. "Somehow I think she was going for something more glamorous."

Lucy glanced around the room, but once again didn't see any sign of Corney. "There was a committee, wasn't there?"

"The activities committee is pretty square," admitted Pam, who was an active Chamber member and served on the publicity committee.

"Old guard," agreed Ted, cocking his head at a table of older men and their tightly permed wives. "Insurance, insurance, real estate, and banking."

They were laughing at his joke when the waiters took away the chunky glass compotes that had held the fruit salad and brought plates loaded with huge slabs of beef, mountains of mashed potatoes topped with craters of gravy, and haystacks of grayish French-cut green beans amandine.

Sue's eyes widened in horror as her plate was set in front of her. "This explains a lot," she said, pushing it away and reaching for her wine.

"What do you mean?" asked Pam, who was busy cutting her meat.

"The fat epidemic!" explained Sue. "Huge portions, tons of salt, it's no wonder Americans look the way they do if this is how they eat."

"Oh, you're right," said Rachel. "You know I prefer organic food and Bob and I mostly eat grains and veggies, but once in a while," she said, taking a bite of beef and savoring it, "I just love a big piece of juicy red meat."

"Amen," said Bob.

By the time the dessert plates—cherry pie à la mode—and coffee cups were removed, Lucy was feeling guilty about slipping off her diet and was uncomfortably aware of her control-top panty hose. The DJ was playing a slow dance so she begged Bill to take a turn on the dance floor. "I've absolutely got to move or I'll burst," she said, grabbing his hand.

He got up reluctantly, earning sympathetic looks from the other guys, and followed Lucy onto the dance floor where a handful of couples were moving to the music, mostly swaying back and forth. Lucy had endured cotillion dance classes when she was in seventh grade, letting repulsive pimply boys in button-down shirts and sports jackets that smelled of cleaning fluid put their arms around her so they could learn the waltz and fox-trot, and she found it frustrating that nobody, including Bill, seemed to know how to dance anymore.

Still, it was nice to slip her right hand into his and feel his other arm around her waist, and Bobby Darrin sure knew how to melt a girl's heart. She tried to keep her toes out of his way as they moved around the patch of parquet that served as a dance floor, trusting him to keep her from colliding with the other dancers.

The Faircloths, she noticed, danced beautifully together and made a lovely picture as they glided smoothly, perfectly in step with each other. Frankie and her partner, fellow real estate agent Bud Olsen, were having a good time, laughing as they struggled to keep time to the music and each other. When the inevitable happened, and they crashed into Lucy and Bill, there were giggles and apologies all round. Frankie just had time to tell Lucy the Faircloths had finally made an offer on a Shore Road house before Bud swept her away in a dramatic twirl.

"Did you hear?" she asked Bill. "Frankie sold a house to the Faircloths."

Bill was interested; real estate had been at a virtual standstill for months. "Where?" he asked.

"I think she said Shore Road."

"The only place for sale out there is the old McIntyre mansion," said Bill. "It's listed for a million and a quarter."

"I wonder what they offered," said Lucy.

"Check with Frankie," urged Bill, as the song ended. "Maybe they'll be looking for a contractor."

Lucy noticed that Frankie was making her way across the room in the direction of the ladies' room, so she followed and eventually joined her in front of the mirrored counter, and began to refresh her lipstick.

"So the Faircloths finally found a house they liked," said Lucy.

"Finally is the word," said Frankie, with a huge

sigh. "I must have showed them fifty or more houses. I swear we covered the coast from Kittery to Camden several times over. Then they decided to make an offer on the very first place I showed them."

"The McIntyre mansion?"

Frankie nodded, leaning forward and running her finger along her eyebrow. "It needs work, but they said they're excited about remodeling."

"How much did they offer?" asked Lucy.

"Just under a million," said Frankie, screwing up her lips. "It's a low offer, but the place definitely needs updating. The wiring and plumbing are last century, the kitchen is a nightmare. I don't know if the McIntyre kids—well, they're all in their forties, not really kids—it's a question of how much they want the cash. If they don't need the money, they could decide to wait for the market to improve."

"It must be hard for them to let it go," said Lucy. "They've spent every summer there since they were kids."

"They told me they don't get to use it much, now that their folks are gone. One is in Turkey, works for some bank; a couple of others are out on the West Coast. It's a big responsibility and they can't keep it up. It needs a roof; just keeping the lawn mowed is a big expense."

Lucy nodded. It was a familiar story. "Well, I hope the sale goes through. It would be a nice commission for you—and maybe a job for Bill."

"And I could use it," said Frankie, dropping her lipstick into her purse and clicking it shut.

Lucy was following her out the door when her

cell phone rang, so she sat on the droopy, slipcovered sofa to take the call, afraid it was one of the kids. That whole awful episode with Eddie was stuck in her mind. No matter how well you thought you knew your kids, how much you trusted them, there were always surprises and experience had taught her that trouble always came when you were least expecting it. Wasn't that always the way? When she and Bill finally got a rare night out together, some emergency invariably seemed to come up. But when she glanced at the phone, she saw it was Corney who was calling.

"Hi!" she said, wondering what had kept Corney from the ball. "Where are you? I thought you'd be dancing the night away."

"I wish," whispered Corney. "I think I'm being held against my will."

"What do you mean?"

"Trey suggested we have a little, you know, before going to the ball and I foolishly agreed. I read in a magazine that sex gives you a terrific glow, much better than makeup."

"I read that, too," said Lucy.

"It didn't exactly work out."

"What do you mean?"

Corney's voice got even lower. "He suggested handcuffs, said they'd be fun."

Lucy resisted the temptation to laugh. "And?"

"Well, here I am, stark naked and handcuffed to my bed. Thank heavens the cell phone was on the night stand. I could just manage to reach it, kind of shoved it along with my nose until I could grab it."

"Where's Trey?"

"That's why I'm calling. He left me here. I need you to come and free me."

"He left?"

"Yes."

Lucy didn't understand. "He handcuffed you and then left? Left the house?"

"Yes! I begged him to unlock them but he just laughed and walked out."

"What a bastard!"

"Yeah." There was a pause. "So will you come?"

"What he did is against the law," said Lucy, primly "This is a matter for the police."

"Are you crazy? I'm naked. This is Tinker's Cove! Do you think I want the Kirwan kids and Barney Culpepper seeing me like this?"

"You have a point," said Lucy. "But what can I do? I don't have the keys."

"They're right here. They're on the dresser. I can't reach them."

"Okay," said Lucy, finally accepting the fact that she was going to have to leave the party to help Corney. "I'll be there in ten minutes."

"I'll be here," said Corney. "I'm sure not going anywhere."

Chapter Seventeen

When Lucy returned to the ball she found Bill standing with a group of friends near the bar. They were all holding glasses of beer and were engaged in a loud, play-by-play discussion of the Superbowl. Lucy didn't want to interrupt them, they were all in high spirits with plenty of laughing and backslapping and she didn't want to be a ball-and-chain sort of wife. Instead she caught Bill's eye and held up her car keys, then tapped her watch. She hoped he'd take her sign language to mean she was leaving the party for a few minutes.

He didn't. Looking puzzled, he left the group and crossed the room. "What's going on?"

"I have to leave for a few minutes . . . ," she began.

"Why? Is one of the kids in trouble?"

"No, no," she hurried to assure him. "It's Corney." She paused, trying to come up with a reason why Corney needed her. "It's her car. It won't start and she needs a ride."

"Want me to come? I've got jumper cables, maybe I can get it started."

What was it with men? she wondered. She'd been after Bill for weeks to replace the toilet seat in the powder room. She'd even bought a new seat and tried to do the job herself but wasn't strong enough to loosen the bolts that held the broken one in place. Somehow he wasn't interested in a little job that would take him two minutes, but now when she didn't want his help he was suddenly Dudley Do-Right.

"Don't be silly," she said. "You're having a good time with your buddies and I'll be back in no time."

"Are you sure?" he asked. "I don't mind going. It's cold and you're not really dressed for it."

Lucy realized he had a point. Unused to walking in heels, she'd had to hang on to his arm just to cross the icy driveway. She hadn't wanted to mess up her hair by wearing a hat and her good black coat wasn't nearly as warm as her parka.

Lucy was about to give up and confess the truth when Sid, who had loosened his collar and stuffed his tie into his jacket pocket with one end dangling out, joined them and punched Bill in the arm. "Whassup, buddy?" he asked.

"Lucy needs me. . . ."

"No, I don't," said Lucy, interrupting him with a smile. "I can handle this."

"Well, that's good because the Bruins game is on the TV in the bar and Montreal's got two players in the penalty box."

Bill was clearly torn. "Go on," she said. "I'll be back before those Canadiens are back on the ice."

"Okay," he said, as Sid clapped an arm around his shoulder and dragged him off to join the crowd of men gathered in front of the TV.

Buttoning her coat as she stepped outside, Lucy had second thoughts about her mission. The temperature had dropped while they were inside, and a stiff breeze had blown up. The cold air hit her like a slap in the face and she hurried to pull on her gloves. Her ears were already burning from the cold and she covered them with her hands as she slipped and slid across the icy parking lot. She almost fell when she reached out to open the car door but saved herself by grabbing the roof.

Finally in place behind the steering wheel, she realized the car wasn't any warmer than the parking lot. At least she was out of the wind, she told herself, as she started the engine and cranked the heat up as high as it would go.

The roads were deserted as she drove along under the star-filled sky. There was no moon but the stars were very bright. Orion was hanging so low she felt as if she could reach out and touch the archer's belt; the Big Dipper pointed to the North Star, just as it had in the days when escaping Southern slaves followed it to freedom in the North. In fact, a number of houses in town were said to have been stops on the Underground Railroad that led to Canada.

Corney had recently moved into a brand-new house on Shore Road and Lucy remembered how she'd proudly showed off all the modern advances— gas fireplaces that turned on with the touch of a remote, jacks in every room for phones, TVs and

computers, a dream kitchen with granite counter-
tops and energy-saving stainless steel appliances,
even a heated toilet seat.

Lucy wasn't jealous; she loved her antique
home with all its quirks. But at this moment, driving through the dark and silent streets, she wouldn't
mind a heated car seat. She was shivering in her
short silky skirt and lace blouse—even under her
coat they felt cold against her skin. Why hadn't she
dressed like Rachel, in a long skirt and sweater?
She suspected Rachel had worn warm boots under
that long skirt, too. Which reminded her, she kept
an old pair of boots in the car for emergencies,
along with a blanket.

Warm air was finally beginning to blow from
the vents when she turned onto Shore Road and
approached Corney's house, which sat on a double lot overlooking the ocean. It was a gorgeous
spot in summer, when you could sit on the porch
and watch the sailboats tacking back and forth,
but winter was a different story. Tonight, the ocean
was angry and she could hear the waves rhythmi-
cally pounding the rocks below. Lucy was wondering if Corney regretted her choice of location
when she noticed that Trey's Range Rover was
parked in the driveway.

What did this mean? she wondered, as she
braked and came to a stop in front of the house.
All the windows were dark but Lucy knew Corney
had expensive, custom-built window coverings that
blocked the light. Inside, every light could be on
and you'd never know it from the outside if the
shades were drawn.

Lucy sat there a minute, wondering what to do.

Corney had said Trey was gone, but if he had left, he was back. Or maybe he'd just left the bedroom and was lurking inside. Perhaps he'd even gone back to the bedroom and picked up wherever he'd left off with Corney. Lucy was tempted to leave; she certainly didn't want to interrupt the pair in a romantic moment.

Maybe romantic wasn't exactly the word, she thought, considering the handcuffs, and maybe Trey was a kinky guy who got off by abusing women. Sometimes that sort of thing went too far. Corney had called for help, she couldn't drive away without making sure everything was okay.

She couldn't just walk up and ring the bell—what should she do? Time was passing, pretty soon Bill would start to worry. She had to do something and do it fast, she decided, turning into the driveway opposite Corney's. Nobody was there this time of year; the Whittleseys were summer people.

Bracing for the shock of cold air, she opened the door and went around to the back of the car, where she opened the hatch and found her emergency stash. She draped the blanket over her head and wrapped it around her shoulders and shoved her feet into the boots; then she clomped across the street feeling like a Muslim woman in a chador. Except that she doubted any devout Muslim woman would be out alone at night trying to peep into her neighbor's windows.

Reaching Corney's porch, Lucy looked for a gap in the blinds or curtains, without success. That meant she'd have to walk around the house, on the lawn, where the snow wasn't shoveled. She stepped off the porch, expecting to sink into deep snow, but found instead that a crust had formed that supported her, though it occasionally broke through. Even so, her feet went down only a few inches when that happened, so she soon reached the rear porch, where a patch of light on the snow revealed an uncovered window. She hurried across and peered inside, discovering the kitchen.

It was empty, and so was the adjoining dining area and family room. Lucy stood there, noticing that nothing was out of place. The counters were bare, the farmhouse sink was empty, only one pot, a large cast-iron frying pan, was sitting on the stove. There was no sign of a struggle, no evidence that anything was wrong.

There was also no sign that anything was right. If only she could catch a glimpse of Corney, alive and well. Opening a bottle of wine, perhaps, or settling down on the couch to watch TV. Snuggling up beside Trey, even.

The silence was beginning to worry her. She decided she had to find out what was going on inside the house, even if it meant discovering Corney and Trey in an embarrassing situation. Corney had called her for help and hadn't canceled the request, she reminded herself, reaching for the doorknob. She had a responsibility to make sure her friend was safe.

To her surprise, the door opened, and she stepped inside. She'd been there many times and knew the layout. A formal dining room was just beyond the kitchen and a central hallway led to the living room and study, which were separated by another hall that led to the guest bath and the master suite beyond. There was no sign that anyone was in the house besides her; it was absolutely quiet. The windows were shut tight against the cold; you couldn't even hear the roar of the ocean waves.

The warm air inside the house was making her nose run so she reached for a paper towel from the roll on a decorative black wirework holder. She was just blowing her nose, as quietly as possible, when she heard a piercing scream.

She stopped, frozen in place as adrenaline surged through her body, ready to fight or flee. Fleeing definitely seemed the best option but she couldn't leave Corney. She remained in place, trying to decide if the scream was one of pain or pleasure, fear or delight. Unsure what to do, she considered calling for help. But Corney had specifically said she didn't want the police. Too embarrassing, she had said.

You couldn't die of embarrassment, thought Lucy, only too aware that a double murderer was still on the loose. Before she could change her mind, she dialed 9-1-1 and told the dispatcher there was an intruder at Corney Clarke's on Shore Road.

No sooner had the dispatcher said she'd send a unit right over than Lucy regretted making the call. She decided the best thing would be to go outside and explain the situation. It would be awkward, but she knew all the officers on the force and they knew her. They'd probably just think it was a big joke and everyone would have a good laugh. If they insisted on checking out the house, well, the flashing lights and radio noise would give Corney and Trey time to make themselves decent.

And if Corney was angry with her, well, darn it, she shouldn't have called her in the first place. She was supposed to be dancing the night away, not standing in somebody else's kitchen, listening to the hum of the refrigerator and waiting for the cops.

She was about to go outside when another scream ripped through the nighttime silence.

This time Lucy was sure. That was a scream of pure terror. She looked around for a weapon, anything, but Corney's counters were bare. She yanked a drawer open, but all she found were rolls of wrap. Another drawer held silverware. Where were the knives? Her eyes fell on the stove where that hefty black cast-iron frying pan was sitting on a burner. Better than a knife, she decided, grabbing it. She could use it as a shield, too.

Holding the pan in front of her with two hands, she started down the darkened hall, toward the bedroom. As she proceeded she heard muffled sounds, moans and whines that could have come from a cat. She reached the door and paused, listening, trying to figure out what was happening on the other side. She reached for the knob, then decided it was too risky to go into a situation blind, and withdrew. What if it was a home invasion like the recent one in nearby Gilead, and Trey was a captive, too? Those guys, two strung-out drug addicts, had been armed with a gun and a machete. She was simply not prepared to face something like that. She'd be better off going back outside, where she could try to peek through a bedroom window.

Hurrying back down the hall to the kitchen,

she stepped outside onto the porch. The cold hit her like a hammer and she drew the blanket more tightly around herself. Clutching the frying pan to her chest, she stepped off the porch into knee-deep snow. Scrambling awkwardly, as quickly as she could in the snow that clung to her boots, she headed for the one window where she saw a crack of light. Her teeth were chattering and she was shivering as she peered inside the bedroom, all aglow from the pink light bulbs Corney insisted were most flattering to her skin.

The gap in the curtains was small and Lucy didn't see much skin, only Corney's bare pink legs, only one leg really. Trey Meacham was kneeling, fully dressed, between her legs and it looked as if she was trying to kick him.

Just then, Lucy was caught in a bright light and a male voice ordered, "Police! Drop it and raise your hands over your head."

Lucy whirled around, squinting against the powerful beam of light and trying to decide who was holding the flashlight. "He's—he's killing her!" she yelled, pointing at the window.

"I'm armed. Drop the frying pan and raise your arms over your head."

"Okay, okay," said Lucy, complying. "I made the call. I'm not the intruder. Corney called me. She's in trouble."

"Walk slowly." The flashlight beam indicated the direction he wanted her to take, around the side of the house to the front yard. "Keep your hands above your head."

"For Pete's sake!" declared Lucy, frustrated beyond belief. "I'm Lucy Stone. I'm not a peeping

Tom. There's a murder going on inside . . . at least I think it's a murder."

"What's going on here?" Lucy recognized Todd Kirwan's voice, coming from behind whoever was holding the flashlight.

"What's going on is this guy thinks I'm a peeping Tom and meanwhile Trey Meacham is attacking Corney inside the house."

"Uh, sorry, Lucy. This is Will Martin, he's new to the force, he's filling in while Barney's on leave," said Todd, striding past him and stepping onto the porch, where he banged loudly on the door with his flashlight. "POLICE! OPEN UP!"

Noticing that young Officer Martin had joined Todd on the porch, Lucy decided discretion was definitely the best part of valor. She sure didn't want to face Trey and Corney if she'd misunderstood the nature of their encounter. Picking up the frying pan, she placed it on the porch and then slipped away, as quietly as she could.

She'd reached the corner of the house when the door opened and she heard Trey asking, "What's the trouble, Officer?" His voice was calm and cool, polite.

She ran, as fast as she could, to her car.

Chapter Eighteen

The car had cooled down while Lucy had tried to figure out how to help Corney, but she didn't notice. She was burning with embarrassment and exertion—fleeing the scene through the snow had taken a lot of energy. Now she was trying to catch her breath as she fumbled with the keys and started the car. It took a great deal of restraint not to floor the gas pedal, but she knew it would be foolish to speed on the icy roads, and she sure didn't want to attract attention by peeling off down the street at high speed.

As she drove along the dark, empty roads she tried to figure out what to do next. The clock in the car said it was already nearly ten. The ball was probably in full swing and she knew she ought to go back, although she was hardly in the mood. How was she going to join her friends in the festivities when her mind was across town, worrying about Corney? They would be joking and laughing and probably drinking a bit too much and she'd be wondering what was happening on Shore Road.

She replayed the scene she'd glimpsed through the curtains, trying to figure out what was going on. If it was sex, it wasn't like any sort of sex she'd ever been involved in, though she was pretty sure her experience in this department was rather limited. But if it wasn't sex, but an attempted murder, why would Trey want to harm Corney? He might be a bit kinky but he hardly seemed like some psycho who got off by killing women. Could he have killed Tamzin? That murder had some sexual overtones, the way the killer stripped the victim and covered her with chocolate. But what about Max? His death didn't fit that mold at all. He was a guy, for one thing, and emphatically heterosexual. The police thought Dora was the killer, and maybe they were right, which meant that if Trey was a killer, then there were two murderers operating in Tinker's Cove. Considering the town's small population, that seemed a statistical impossibility. Although Lucy knew that lightning sometimes did strike twice, she couldn't believe that was the case here.

She believed Dora was innocent, so maybe Trey was the real killer, but that also seemed a stretch. He was successful and admired—what would he possibly have to gain by killing Max? And if he was the murderer, why would he have risked discovery by attempting to kill Corney? She admitted to herself that she might not like Trey very much, but that didn't mean he was a murderer.

Reaching the VFW, where the lights were all

ablaze and the thumping beat of rock music could be heard even in the parking lot, Lucy resolutely put thoughts of murder in the back of her mind. A handful of smokers were shivering on the porch as Lucy entered; inside she sniffed a heady mix of perspiration, perfume, and booze. The DJ was playing "Y.M.C.A." at top volume and a few serious party animals on the dance floor, including Pam and Sue, who were dancing together, were waving their arms in the shapes of the letters.

Bill was sitting at the table with Rachel and Bob, swirling his half-full glass of beer and staring at the dwindling foamy head. She slipped into the empty seat next to him and he snapped to attention. "Where were you?" he asked, his voice thick.

"I told you. Corney had car trouble."

"Right." He looked around. "Where is she?"

"In the end she didn't feel well and decided to stay home."

"That's a shame," said Rachel. "She worked so hard to organize this shindig and now she can't enjoy her success."

Bob, clearly a bit tipsy, raised his glass. "To Corney!"

Rachel shook her head. "I can see I'm going to be driving the car home tonight."

Bill nodded and leaned toward Lucy, putting his hand on her knee. "Speaking of which, I'm ready to go anytime you are."

Lucy found she was disappointed. The DJ was playing a new song, "Heard It Through the Grapevine," and Lucy was itching to dance. "Oh, come on, let's just dance a couple of songs."

"You know I feel like an idiot on the dance floor," said Bill, draining his glass. "Another round, Bob?"

"Sure," said Bob, getting a look from Rachel.

"All these guys want to do is drink," she said. "I'll dance with you, Lucy."

Lucy grinned and hopped up. "When we first got here I was reminded of my high school prom, but now that the girls are all dancing together it's more like middle school."

"Yeah," agreed Rachel, as they joined the twisting and writhing dancers. "Except in middle school the guys were interested enough to stand on the sidelines and watch the girls dance."

"Now they don't even watch," said Lucy, staking out some dance floor territory next to Pam and Sue.

"They watch . . . sports," said Sue, cocking her head toward the bar where a crowd of men had gathered to stare at the basketball game on the TV.

"They're missing out on a lot of fun," declared Pam, as the song ended. "Let's do the Macarena," she yelled to the DJ. "And the Chicken Dance!"

Rachel caught Lucy's eye. "You know, I think I better get Bob home or he'll have a heck of a hangover tomorrow. And he's got that case. . . ."

"Right," said Lucy, her thoughts turning back to Corney's predicament. "I should get home, too."

Pam and Sue were already crossing their arms and slapping their hips, keeping time to the music, so Lucy wiggled her fingers in a little wave and followed Rachel back to their table. When she got there, she realized her phone was ringing. She picked up her purse and drew it out, heading for the quiet of the ladies' room. It was Corney, again.

"Are you all right?" asked Lucy.

"I'm scared." She paused. "And confused."

"What happened?"

"I'm not sure. That's why I'm scared. What if he comes back?"

"You've got an alarm system, don't you?"

"Yeah," said Corney. "He could disable it, couldn't he? I've seen it on TV. A snip of the wire, they open the window. . . ."

"Lock all the windows, and the doors, too. Any way, he's not going to come back. Not after the cops came."

"I told you not to call the cops," hissed Corney. "Talk about embarrassing—and they weren't any good at all. Trey wrapped them around his little finger. He got all chummy with Todd Kirwan, told him it was just sex play and Todd, sweet lad that he is, just wanted to get away as fast as he could. That young one, on the other hand, was sure fascinated with my predicament. Couldn't take his eyes off me while Trey was unlocking the handcuffs. He did that first—then gave me a sheet so I could cover myself, the bastard."

"I'm sorry," said Lucy. "But I couldn't see through the door and I was worried it was a home invasion. That's why I called the cops. I was scared, too," admitted Lucy. She dropped her voice as a couple of women entered the ladies' room. "Do you think he really wanted to hurt you?"

"I honestly don't know. I'm so confused. He had his hands on my neck, but I think that's supposed to make everything more intense or something. A lot of men like it rough, remember what those girls said about Tiger?"

Lucy did. It had been quite a revelation. "Trey's got a big ego," ventured Lucy. "Maybe that's something these Type A guys need."

"Well, I'm done with him, that's for sure. I don't care how successful he is, I don't need to be treated like that."

"Absolutely," agreed Lucy. "How did it start? I mean, weren't you all dressed up for the ball?"

"Yeah. I was dressed to the nines. I spent the entire day getting ready. Manicure, pedicure, hair, facial, the works. I had a new dress, Valentine red, fabulous shoes. And he was in a tux when he arrived, gave me a box of truffles. The big one. The *grande*. I offered him a drink, I had a bottle of champagne on ice. We were sitting in the living room, in front of the fire. It was lovely. We chatted, light stuff, you know. I was in a great mood, I felt flirty, you know?" She paused. "Maybe I went too far."

"I don't think you should blame yourself. I don't think you had control of the situation," said Lucy.

"I did in the beginning," said Corney. "I invited him in, I had the champagne ready."

"When did it change? Did he drink a lot of the champagne?"

"No. He hardly had any."

Another dead end, thought Lucy. "What were you talking about?"

"I think I said I was going to Mexico in a week

or two. I asked if he was going to get away some-place sunny this winter."

"That sounds innocent enough."

"I know. It's not like it was personal or anything. Just small talk, cocktail party chatter."

"Maybe he couldn't get away himself this year," said Lucy. "The economy is still pretty bad, a lot of people are cutting corners."

Corney's tone was thoughtful. "I don't think that was it. It was more about me, something I said. I just had this feeling the atmosphere had changed."

"What did you say?"

"I think I said I was looking forward to drinking *sangria* and using my high school Spanish!"

"And what happened then?"

"He put down his glass and stood in front of me and put his hand under my chin and sort of pulled me up and kissed me and said there was no hurry about getting to the party."

Lucy shook her head. "Speaking Spanish is a turn on for a lot of men. Bill loves to see those Almodovar movies just to hear Penelope Cruz do that lispy thing."

"I do have a Castilian accent," said Corney. "Maybe I said *thangria* instead of *sangria*."

"That's probably it," said Lucy, realizing she'd been talking too long and Bill was still at the bar. "I've gotta go. Take a sleeping pill and I'll see you in the morning."

"Thanks, Lucy. You've been a pal."

Chapter Nineteen

Lucy took the wheel for the drive home, and Bill immediately fell asleep, snoring loudly as she followed the familiar route home. She was left to her own devices, and her thoughts followed their own meandering track. So Corncy was going to Mexico, and she spoke Spanish. A lot of people went there. James Taylor had a song about it. Mexico. What was it with Mexico?

Chocolate was discovered in Mexico, at least she thought it was. The Aztecs drank it in their religious rituals, but it was a bitter, unsweetened drink. One of the explorers—Cortez, Magellan, Columbus—she wasn't sure who, but she did know one of them brought it back to Europe, where it created a sensation when some genius came up with the idea of adding sugar. The rest was history. And now the health experts were saying that dark chocolate was good for you, so she didn't even have to feel guilty about that secret stash of chocolate bars she kept in her night stand.

But the popularity of dark chocolate was a relatively recent phenomenon. Lucy remembered how the kids would refuse to eat it and the little miniature bars would linger in the bowl of Halloween candy until she finally finished them off. Until then, in fact, she'd always chosen milk chocolate but after eating those few, spurned bits of dark chocolate, she came to prefer it.

Now, of course, dark chocolate was just the beginning of a chocolate revolution. Trey had been proud of his unusual flavors and she knew he was part of a larger trend. Even Dora was mixing up hot-pepper-flavored chocolates for her Hot Lips, which, come to think of it, she'd learned from Max. Hadn't Dora said something about Max picking up the recipe in Mexico?

Okay, so maybe both Max and Trey had gone to Mexico, and Corney was planning to go there, too. A lot of people went to Mexico. Even Bill's parents, in fact, had a time-share in Cancun. They loved it and spent a few weeks there every winter. They didn't speak Spanish, they said they didn't need it. They had little contact with actual Mexicans, except for the time-share employees, but spent their time with other Americans. Lucy figured that was probably the case with most English speakers in Mexico, who lived in a sort of parallel universe to the natives, encountering them only when they bought something in a shop or ate in a restaurant. Bill's parents, however, stuck to the time-share's own restaurant, fearing the native food would make them sick. And they never drank the water without boiling it first.

Lucy chuckled to herself, remembering Bill's mom Edna's hilarious account of how the first thing she did upon arrival every year was to fill every pot with water, bring it to a boil for ten minutes, and then load all the pots into the refrigerator. Lucy doubted it was really necessary but you couldn't convince Edna, who wouldn't even make coffee with unboiled water.

"What's so funny?" asked Bill, waking up when she turned into the driveway.

"I was thinking about your mother," said Lucy, braking.

"My mom is funny?"

"Sometimes," said Lucy. "It's been a while since you spoke with her. Why don't you give her a call tomorrow?"

"I will," said Bill, stumbling on the porch steps.

"Take it easy," said Lucy, taking his arm and guiding him inside. She doubted he'd remember much about the evening tomorrow morning, least of all his promise to call his folks.

Bill wasn't the only one with a thick head on Sunday morning—Corney complained of a hangover when Lucy called to check on her.

"I couldn't sleep, so I had some brandy," confessed Corney. "I finished the bottle."

"It wasn't full, was it?" asked a horrified Lucy.

"I don't remember," admitted Corney. "All I know is that it's empty now. It's sitting on the kitchen counter, mocking me."

"My father used to swear by something called a

prairie oyster," said Lucy. "I think it's a raw egg with Worcestershire sauce and something else. Maybe tomato juice."

"That sounds disgusting," said Corney.

"The hair of the dog, that's the thing," said Bill, pulling a beer out of the refrigerator.

"Try a beer," advised Lucy. "That's what Bill is doing."

"I think I'll just throw up and go back to bed," said Corney.

"No sign of Trey?" asked Lucy.

"No." Corney paused. "You know, I think I probably overreacted. It's just been so long since I was with a man I think I forgot how they are."

Lucy didn't think using handcuffs and trying to strangle your partner were typical male behaviors, but she didn't say anything for fear of upsetting Corney. She'd been through a traumatic experience and it would take time for her to process it. In the meantime she would need sympathy and support. "I'll stop by later," promised Lucy. "Just to make sure everything's all right."

"Thanks, Lucy," said Corney, her voice a bit shaky.

Hanging up, Lucy dialed Fern's Famous, where Flora answered the phone.

"How's Dora?" she asked.

"About how you'd expect, if you were innocent and accused of killing two people and sitting in a stinky jail cell," said Flora, in her matter-of-fact tone.

"I heard you hired Bob Goodman," said Lucy. "He's the best."

"He's charging enough," said Flora, adding a little *humph*.

Lucy knew Bob's rates were extremely fair, but doubted Flora knew that many lawyers charged hundreds of dollars per hour. "Maybe they'll catch the real murderer before it goes to trial," said Lucy. "I'm following up on something that might help. Do you know when Max was in Mexico?"

"Well, it was when Dora got pregnant with Lily. He got her pregnant and hightailed off. I had to go down and bring him back and make him do the right thing."

"So that was about twenty years ago, something like that?"

"That'd be about right."

"There's another thing," said Lucy. "Do you know anything about the tuition money Max promised for Lily?"

"Promises, promises," snorted Flora. "Max was always making promises."

"Do you have any idea where he was going to get it?"

"I do not," said Flora. "As far as I know, he was broke, he was always broke." She paused. "Maybe his rich old uncle died and left him a bundle. Maybe he was blackmailing somebody. Maybe he won the lottery. I really don't know. What I do know is that if he got a dollar, he spent it."

Lucy was thoughtful. Flora had meant it as a joke, sort of, but blackmail could be a motive for murder. "Do you really think Max was blackmailing somebody? Where'd you get that idea?"

"Same place I got the idea about the rich uncle

and the lottery ticket. Where do people get money if they don't work for it? Trust me, Max wasn't much of a worker. Maybe he was going to sell something, maybe he had a buyer for that snowmobile of his. Like I said, I really don't know where Max thought he was going to get twenty thousand dollars for Lily. All I know is that he never did."

"Right. Well, thanks Flora. Say hi to Dora for me. Let her know I'm thinking of her and doing everything I can to catch the real killer."

Flora didn't reply immediately and Lucy suspected she probably didn't think much of her investigative abilities, so she was surprised when Flora finally spoke. "You be careful, Lucy."

"I will," promised Lucy, touched by Flora's concern. "I surely will."

Turning to her morning chores, Lucy loaded the breakfast dishes into the dishwasher, wiped the counters, and swept the floor. She was just finishing running the vacuum around the family room when the girls appeared, looking for rides.

"Can I take the car?" asked Sara.

"What for? I thought your job ended with Valentine's Day."

"I've got a study group meeting at Jenny's house. It's a group project on women's suffrage."

"And I'm going to Friends of Animals," added Zoe. "I'm filling in for Laurie—she went on that ski trip."

Lucy thought for a minute. Bill was under the weather now, but he'd probably want his truck later. Besides, he didn't like anyone to drive it except himself. She could let Sara take the Subaru, but that would leave her without transportation and she had promised to stop in at Corney's. "No. I'm going to need the car," she said.

Sara wasn't happy with her decision. "What about the truck?"

"Don't push it," said Lucy, laughing. "Your father's not in a mood to share this morning." She wrapped up the vacuum cleaner cord. "I'll take you."

Lucy made the familiar trip, first dropping Zoe at Friends of Animals and then letting Sara off at Jenny's house. She went on to the Quik-Stop for gas, feeling guilty about adding to the nation's thirst for foreign oil and resentful that she didn't really have a choice, and picked up a sports drink for Bill's hangover. When she was leaving the store, a man with a buzz cut and a decided military bearing held the door for her. She thanked him and hurried to her car, but when she started the engine a little hunch popped into her head. She waited until the man left the store and watched as he strode off down Main Street, observing that he appeared to be in his early fifties and extremely fit. She was certain she'd never seen him in town before.

Acting on the hunch, she drove slowly until the car was alongside him, then rolled down the window. "You're new in town, aren't you?" she asked. "Can I help you with anything?"

He turned, an amused expression on his face. "I know this is a small town but. . . ."

Lucy interrupted him. "I'm Lucy Stone. I'm a reporter with the local paper. I really do know everybody in town," she said, handing him her card. "And I'm thinking you might be Tamzin Graves's ex-husband."

"You must be a really good reporter," he said, raising an eyebrow. "I'm Larry Graves and I was married to Tamzin for a couple of years."

"I'm very sorry for your loss," said Lucy, in a serious tone.

Graves's expression hardened. "She didn't deserve this."

"I know." Lucy paused, thinking that survivors often wanted to talk about their lost loved one. "You know, I'm going to have to write an obituary for her and I don't know much about her. Maybe you could help me?"

Graves hesitated a moment, then nodded.

"How about a cup of coffee?"

"Sure," he said, reaching for the car door.

When he was seated, Lucy continued driving down Main Street, toward Jake's. Graves sat beside her, large and silent, and she remembered hearing he was in Afghanistan.

"You must have some case of jet lag," she said. "How long is the flight from Afghanistan?"

"Actually, it was only a short hop, from Cape Cod. There's a training facility at Camp Edwards—a little village and a lot of sand—it's to give the troops a feeling for what they'll encounter in the Middle East. I'm one of the instructors."

"Oh." Lucy pulled into a parking spot in front of Jake's and braked. "But you were in Afghanistan?"

"Yeah." He fell silent, climbing out of the car. "I've been back stateside for six months or so," he said, as they climbed the steps and went inside the coffee shop.

The morning crowd had gone and Norine, the waitress, was busy clearing tables and tidying up. "Sit anywhere you want," she said.

Lucy chose a booth at the back. "This is on me," she said, as Norine set two menus down in front of them. "Have whatever you want."

"Just coffee, regular," he said, pulling off his hat and shrugging out of his jacket. His buzz cut was sprinkled with gray, Lucy noticed, and the skin was stretched tightly over his cheekbones. His eyes were very blue.

Lucy ordered a black decaf for herself, then pulled out her notebook. "I hope you don't mind if I take notes?"

Graves shrugged.

"First of all, I need your full name and rank. . . ."

He raised an eyebrow and slid a business card across the table. "Not my service number?"

She smiled back, taking the card. "That won't be necessary."

"It's major. Major Lawrence Graves, United States Army, currently stationed at Camp Edwards in Massachusetts." Norine set the coffees in front of them and he busied himself adding cream and sugar. .

"And you were married to Tamzin?"

"Yeah." He nodded, stirring his coffee. "For three years, back in the nineties. She was in her early thirties. Beautiful. I never knew such a beautiful woman."

Lucy nodded, wondering how to broach her next question. "She made quite an impression here in town. . . ."

Graves laughed. "I bet she did—especially with the male half of the population."

"Well, yes," said Lucy. "Was she always so . . . ?"

"Promiscuous?" Graves took a long drink of coffee. "She was."

"Is that why you divorced?"

"Yeah."

"But you stayed in touch?"

"Sure. It was a lot easier being her friend than being her husband."

"So what was she really like?"

"She grew up in Troy, it's one of those towns in New York State that have fallen on hard times. She couldn't wait to get out and joined the army; that's where we met. She's the only person I ever heard say she loved boot camp, but she thrived on physical challenges, she just loved the workouts, the obstacle courses, the runs. And she really liked being with all those guys."

"How come she left?"

He shrugged. "She was stuck in Texas and didn't like it much, so when she got twenty years— enough for a pension—she didn't reenlist. She always loved New England so she came up here to Maine. She loved this town, she said she'd never been happier."

Lucy felt the pull of a great sense of guilt. "I'm so sorry. . . ."

"It's not your fault," said Graves. "You didn't kill her, did you?"

"I could have been nicer to her."

"It's okay. She never had a lot of girlfriends," he said, signaling Norine for a refill. When she'd filled his cup and he'd gone through the rigmarole of tearing open the little paper pouches of sugar and poured in the cream, he made eye contact with Lucy. "So what do you know about this guy she was working for? This Trey Meacham?"

Lucy shifted in her seat, uncomfortably aware that the situation had changed and she was now the interviewee instead of the interviewer. "I don't know him very well," she said, feeling that the incident with Corney was something she shouldn't talk about. Corney deserved to have her privacy protected.

"But you told me you know everybody in town," he said, challenging her.

"I may have exaggerated," she said, attempting a chuckle.

Major Lawrence Graves was not amused and Lucy had the feeling she was up against a skilled questioner, someone who was able to get information from toughened Taliban fighters. "How big is this chocolate operation of his?"

"Oh." Lucy was relieved. This was something she could talk about. "There are four stores: Kittery, Camden, Bar Harbor, and here. The chocolates are made in Rockland, in a converted sardine factory, and there's a shop there, too. I haven't seen the corporate balance sheet, but Trey himself seems quite prosperous—he drives a Range Rover—and the chocolates have won prizes."

"Is he a local guy?"

"You mean, did he grow up here?"

"Yeah."

"No. He left a high-powered career in public relations, I think, and started Chanticleer Chocolate about a year ago."

"Did he and Tamzin have a relationship?"

"That's open to debate," said Lucy. "They certainly seemed friendly."

"What about this woman they say killed her? Dora Fraser?"

"She's a local woman, her family owns a fudge shop so she was a competitor with Chanticleer. Also, Tamzin had a relationship with Dora's ex-husband and she may have been jealous."

"I don't buy it," said Graves. "I don't think a woman could take Tamzin. She was into martial arts, she taught hand-to-hand combat."

Lucy brightened. "That's what I think, too. I don't see Dora as a double murderer."

Graves's eyebrows shot up. "Double?"

"Dora's ex-husband was killed last month when he was ice fishing. Knocked on the head and tangled up in fishline and shoved through the ice. They're charging Dora with that, too. Or trying to. I'm not sure of the status of the investigation."

"Wow, this is some nice town you've got here."

Lucy decided not to respond. "Are there any funeral arrangements yet for Tamzin?" she asked.

He drained his cup and set it down. "Her family is still back in Troy. They'll have a service and she'll be buried there."

"Thanks for your help," said Lucy. "I guess you'll be heading off to Troy?"

Graves caught her in his gaze. "Oh, no. I'm staying right here until I find the bastard who killed her."

The cool, calculated way he said it took her breath away. "Oh," she said, her voice a whisper. "Good luck."

"Luck will have nothing to do with it," he said, reaching for his jacket and pulling his watch cap over his head. "I have a mission and I intend to complete it. Thanks for the coffee."

Lucy watched as he left the coffee shop, feeling a bit like a bystander in a superhero movie. Graves, it seemed, was no ordinary mortal, he was battle ready and itching for a fight. She was convinced he had the skills and the mental preparedness to fight his enemies and even kill them.

Reaching for her purse, she picked up the check and went over to the cash register. "Who was that guy?" asked Norine. "He looks like one tough customer."

"That was Tamzin's ex-husband," said Lucy, handing her a five-dollar bill. "He's a soldier."

"Well, I'm glad he's on our side," said Norine, giving Lucy her change.

But as Lucy left the coffee shop and hurried to her car, she wondered if Graves was really the avenger he said he was. As a reporter she'd covered a number of murders and the sad fact was that most of the victims were women who'd been killed by their husbands or lovers. Graves said he wanted to find Tamzin's killer but was that nothing more than a smoke screen to hide his own guilt?

She climbed into the car and started it, thinking that the more she knew about Tamzin, the less she knew. Here she'd thought she was nothing but a trashy sexpot and now she had learned she was a soldier for twenty years and even taught hand-to-hand combat. It seemed crazy. Yet in spite of all that, somebody had overpowered her and killed her. Who could have done it? And why? This was one story she couldn't wait to write; it was going to upset a lot of people's preconceptions about Tamzin, that was for sure. And it was going to blow a very big hole in the case against Dora.

Lucy was already composing sentences as she headed for home, detouring along Shore Road to stop by Corney's place.

When Corney opened the door, Lucy saw that Corney had definitely had a tough night. Her eyes were puffy, her face was blotchy, and there were faint bruises on her neck and wrists. Her short blond hair hadn't been brushed and was sticking out all over her head. "Oh my goodness," Lucy exclaimed, wrapping her friend in her arms and giving her a hug.

"I feel awful," said Corney, "and I look worse."

"You had a bad time," said Lucy. "Trey's bad news."

"You can say that again." Corney sat on one of the stools at the breakfast bar. "A lot of it's my own fault. I never should've drank all that brandy. I always try to sleep on my back, but when I woke up this morning my face was squished into the pillow."

"Don't blame yourself," said Lucy. "You're the victim here. Those are terrible bruises on your neck You're lucky to be alive."

"No, Lucy, you've got it wrong. He's just a big guy. He doesn't know his own strength—and I bruise easily." She got up and went over to a mirror that hung on the wall, examining her face and running her fingers beneath her eyes, smoothing out the bags. "Do you happen to have any Preparation H?"

This was the last thing Lucy expected to hear. "Not on me," she said.

"It's the best thing for bags under your eyes." Corney flipped up the collar of her blue fleece robe, holding it beneath her chin with two hands and hiding the bruises. "You know, I think he really likes me."

Lucy had done a couple of stories on the rape crisis center in Gilead and knew that Corney's re-action wasn't unusual. The counselors there said one of the most difficult obstacles to getting rape convictions was the victims' tendency to blame themselves for causing the incident in the first place, believing it was something they did that made their partner become violent. She knew she had to use a gentle approach if she was going to convince Corney that she hadn't deserved to be assaulted.

"I'm sure he does like you," said Lucy, seating herself on one of the rustic stools that were lined up at the island. She was recalling Larry Graves's interest in Trey and wondering if he suspected Trey had killed Tamzin. Now that she knew about his assault on Corney, it seemed possible, but what about Max? Was there some link between Trey and Max?

"Last night, you said something about how Trey's mood changed when you mentioned you were going to Mexico."

"Yeah." Corney took a big gulp of coffee. "I said I was going to this little town on the Baja coast. A lot of surfers go there and I know he likes to surf, at least he did when he was younger. He was always talking about surfing."

Somewhere in Lucy's brain a connection formed and she felt a mounting excitement. "Max surfed, too. In Mexico. What's the name of the town?"

"Playa del Diablo."

"Devil's Beach?"

"I didn't know you knew Spanish," said Corney.

"I don't," said Lucy, slipping off the stool. "Mind if I use your computer?"

"Not at all. It's down the hall, next to the guest bath."

Lucy followed Corney's directions and found a small, very messy office. The desk was covered with stacks of papers, the bookcase was crammed with cookbooks and design books, and a bunch of Valentine's flags were propped in a corner. A box of promotional brochures was sitting on the desk chair, and Lucy couldn't find anyplace to put it except on the couch, where stacks of newspapers and magazines were already taking up most of the space. She sat down and booted up the computer; she was waiting for the Internet connection when Corney joined her, plunking herself down on the couch amid all the piles of print media.

"You've found my secret," said Corney, crossing her legs and revealing a fuzzy blue slipper that matched her robe. "I can organize other people's stuff but I can't get a handle on my own."

"Like the shoemaker's barefoot children," said Lucy, typing PLAYA DEL DIABLO in the search box. A few moments later she was rewarded with colorful pictures of a pristine beach and muscular, tanned surfers with very white teeth. "Looks like you're going to have a fantastic time in Playa del Diablo."

"Oh, that's just PR. I bet they're all eighty years old and toothless. And the beach is probably covered with globs of tar and oil." Corney propped her feet on a storage box marked TAX RETURNS. "That's the trouble with being in public relations—you never believe anything."

Lucy chuckled and began a search for Mexican newspapers. Playa del Diablo didn't have its own paper, but nearby Cabo San Lucas did and its archives were available for a small fee. "Corney, I need your help here."

Corney groaned as she got up and shuffled over, kicking a pair of high-heeled shoes out of her way. She leaned over Lucy's shoulder to read the screen, then opened a desk drawer and pulled out a credit card. "It's my shopping card," she said. "I keep it handy, in case I want to order something."

Lucy vacated the chair and Corney plopped down and began typing in the numbers. It took a couple of tries but she finally got it right and was inside the archives. "It goes by year. What year do you want?"

Lucy told her and she entered the date. "What now?"

"Just keep scrolling through. I'm looking for anything about Max or Trey."

"Talk about a needle in a haystack," complained Corney. "How do you think we're going to find . . . uh, whoa! Here we go!"

"What is it?" asked Lucy, spotting a photo of several surfers and recognizing youthful versions of both Max and Trey. "What does it say?"

"*American killed in surfing accident,*" translated Corney, reading the accompanying story. "*Wes Teasdale drowned yesterday when hit by a loose board . . . his companion Trey Meacham was tragically unable to save him.*" Corney leaned back in the chair. "Poor Trey. That must have been terrible. Imagine seeing your friend drown in a horrible accident."

Lucy had a different take. "Maybe it wasn't an accident," she said. "And maybe Max knew it."

Chapter Twenty

Excited about finding a connection between Max and Trey, Lucy dialed the state police barracks and asked for Lieutenant Horowitz, half expecting her call to be transferred to voice mail. He was there, however, and took her call.

"You're working on a Sunday?" she said, in a surprised voice.

"And so, apparently, are you," he replied.

"I guess I am," said Lucy. "I'm actually with Corney Clarke. She was involved in a very unpleasant situation with Trey Meacham last night."

"Umm," said Horowitz, sounding bored.

"Well, I've found some evidence that casts doubt on Dora Fraser's guilt. It points instead to Trey Meacham."

Horowitz sighed. "Go on."

"It's a connection between Trey and Max that goes way back, about twenty years ago, when they were both in Mexico. A friend of theirs, Wes Teasdale, was killed in a surfing accident, but I don't think it was an accident at all. I think Trey actually murdered Wes. And when Trey showed up here in Tinker's Cove, I think Max may have attempted to blackmail him."

"Whoa," said Horowitz. "This was twenty years ago?"

"Yes. You see, I knew there was a connection between Tamzin and Trey, of course, but I couldn't figure out why he would kill Max. But Max told Dora he was going to come up with the money for Lily's college—and how else would he get twenty thousand dollars if he wasn't blackmailing Trey?"

There was a long pause before Horowitz spoke. "You've really done it now," he said. "Off the deep end. Completely crazy. My advice is to take two aspirins and call a psychiatrist."

Lucy was disappointed, she'd really expected a bit more enthusiasm. "I'm probably not explaining it well. I'm sure I'm on to something."

"It's more like you're *on* something," said Horowitz, ending the call.

"What did he say?" asked Corney, as Lucy pocketed her phone.

"He told me to seek professional help," said Lucy, chagrined.

Corney laughed. "I think you may be making a mountain out of a molehill. According to the newspaper article, the Mexican authorities were convinced Teasdale's death was an accident."

"I doubt they really conducted any sort of investigation," said Lucy. "Bill's mom and dad have a time-share in Mexico and they say the police are notoriously corrupt. They make phony traffic stops and threaten to arrest you, but if you give them fifty bucks they let you go." She chewed her thumbnail. "Don't you see? Max and Trey knew each other, there's a connection. They have a shared past in Mexico and I think they were involved in more than gathering chocolate recipes."

"That doesn't necessarily mean that Trey killed Max," said Corney, yawning. "I'm beat."

"Oh, sorry," said Lucy, hopping to her feet. "I'd better let you get some rest."

"Thanks for everything, Lucy," said Corney, giving her a hug.

"Make sure you lock the door after me," advised Lucy, reaching for her coat. She had zipped up and was digging for the car keys in her purse when she found the card Larry Graves had given her.

Should she call him? she wondered, as she left the house and made her way to the car. He had seemed very interested in Trey Meacham, she remembered. Of course, Tamzin had probably mentioned Trey to her ex-husband. The two were friends, he said. They probably communicated regularly. It was natural to talk about your job and your boss. But Graves had particularly asked about Trey, as if he had a special interest in him. Jealousy? Maybe, but he seemed to have put that behind him. It was easier to be her friend than her husband, that's what he said, and Lucy took it to mean he wouldn't be hurt when she went with other men.

In the car, Lucy waited for the engine to warm up and fingered the card. Graves was a tough guy and she wasn't sure what his reaction would be to this new information. She didn't want him to go off half-cocked and do something he would regret. On the other hand, she didn't feel she had a right to withhold information he might find valuable. He had loved Tamzin, after all, and clearly felt a need to resolve her death. Lucy didn't think he was motivated by revenge as much as the desire to achieve justice. Somebody had killed Tamzin and desecrated her body and he wanted to make sure that person paid for the crime.

And, face it, she told herself, she didn't owe Trey a thing. His behavior to Corney was inexcusable—and suspicious. Trey might seem like a nice guy but his treatment of Corney had revealed another side to his personality. There was definitely something a bit off about Trey. Coming to a decision, she dialed his cell phone but Graves didn't answer; the call went straight to voice mail.

Disappointed, she shifted into drive and headed for home. Today was Valentine's Day and she couldn't help hoping there might be something special waiting for her; Bill usually had some little surprise for her. She had a card for him—one of the big, expensive ones—and was planning a special dinner, his favorite meat loaf, with butterscotch brownies and ice cream for dessert.

Pulling into the driveway, she stopped the car by the mailbox, irrationally hoping to find some red envelopes. She smiled, finding one, hand-delivered and signed with a crayon scrawl, from Patrick.

When she went inside the kitchen, she found a vase filled with a dozen perfect red roses in the middle of the kitchen table, with a note from Bill. It was one word: ALWAYS. She pressed the card to her chest and bent down to inhale the flowers' scent, savoring the moment. He loved her, he really, really did. He'd remembered. She felt as if she were floating on air as she took off her winter jacket and danced around the kitchen, humming a little tune. "Love, love, love," she sang, gathering butter and brown sugar and walnuts to make the brownies. She was just about to grease the pan when her cell phone rang.

She half expected it to be Bill, checking to see if she'd found the flowers, but it was Larry Graves.

"I found a link between Trey Meacham and Max Fraser," she said. "They were in Mexico about twenty years ago."

"Tamzin called me, terrified, just before she was killed," said Graves. "A big package from Mexico came to the shop and when she opened it she found cocaine. She was going to take it to the police, but she never made it."

Of course, Lucy thought, drugs. The chocolate business was a perfect cover. Suddenly, an image popped into her mind. It was Trey, standing in the dry cleaner's shop. She'd said something about how he was selling a lot more than chocolate. She'd meant that the chocolates were something special, a luxury item that implied the discriminating consumer deserved only the very best. But his expression had implied something very different; he'd looked shocked and had hurried out of the shop. It was as if she'd hit a nerve, and she was pretty sure exactly what that nerve was. He was selling more than chocolate; he was selling drugs. And she was willing to bet he was making a lot more money from the illegal drug operation than he was from his overpriced chocolates.

"I called the police but they didn't believe me," said Lucy.

"I don't want to go on record with this, it's just between you and me, but I'm on my way to Rockland, to the factory," said Graves. "Could be quite a scoop for the town's best reporter."

Lucy was suddenly energized; she felt like a racehorse waiting for the gate to open. "I'll bring my camera," she said.

This was better than roses, thought Lucy, as she followed the road up hill and down dale to Rockland. She felt exhilarated, chasing down a story that wasn't some stupid puff piece assignment from Ted but one she developed herself, following her hunches and taking the initiative. And what a story it was! Everything was coming together. She was not only solving two murders, and clearing Dora in the process, but nailing Trey would cut off the supply of drugs that was pouring into the region. Not forever—she wasn't naïve enough to believe that—but long enough that a lot of users would have time to go to rehab and get themselves straightened out. She couldn't wait to see Ted's face when she presented him with the story of the year, complete with photos. And best of all, it was her story.

They'd know soon enough, of course. NECN and CNN and the Boston stations and newspapers would be all over it, but that would be later. She was breaking this story, a story that was going to be big, really big. Maybe they'd even interview her. She could just see herself chatting with Deborah

Norville. "How did you break this story?" Deborah would ask. "Well, it was nothing more than good investigative reporting and a little bit of luck, Deborah," she'd say. "I followed a hunch and learned the luxury chocolates were a front for illegal drugs from Mexico."

But when she arrived at the old waterfront sardine factory, the parking lot was empty. She wasn't sure what she'd expected, Larry Graves had been pretty vague, but she'd definitely gotten the feeling that something was going to come down. A raid maybe? She drove around the building, looking for the major, but there was no sign of life at all and she was beginning to wonder if she'd misunderstood and jumped to the wrong conclusion.

The five-story building was handsome; she had to admit Meacham had done a terrific job restoring the classic nineteenth-century factory. The brick had been cleaned and pointed, and the windows, which were lined up in symmetrical rows, had been repaired. Even the tall bell tower that once called workers to their shifts had been restored. The plowed parking lot was freshly paved and lined, dotted here and there with hardy young trees, and a handsome carved wood sign with the trademark rooster identified the former cannery as the home of Chanticleer Chocolate.

Somewhat frustrated that Graves had turned out to be a no-show, Lucy decided that rather than waste her time, she might as well snap a few photos of the factory. She found the structure surprisingly photogenic in the slanting afternoon sunshine: the ranks of windows offered an interesting visual, the tall bell tower made a dramatic image shot from its base, and the original doors, now freshly painted, featured elaborate hand-forged hinges. She was just focusing her camera when the door opened and Trey stepped out.

"What are you doing here?" he demanded. His tone wasn't exactly pleasant and Lucy felt uneasy.

"Just taking photos," she said, with a big smile. "I can't believe what you've done with this old place. It used to be such an eyesore, all covered with grime, most of the windows cracked or broken. Ted wanted a photo for the paper, for an article on repurposing older buildings."

"Oh," he said, sounding mollified. "Why don't you come in? The machinery is pretty interesting, too, especially the big copper kettles."

Considering her suspicions about Trey, Lucy didn't think that was a good idea. She made a show of glancing at her watch. "Actually," she said, stepping backwards, "I'm running late. Maybe another time."

"It will only take a few minutes," he said, wrapping an arm around her shoulders and drawing her toward the door. "Believe me, it's worth the time. You're going to get some great photos."

Every instinct told her to run, but Trey had maneuvered himself so that he was beside her and was exerting pressure on her back, pushing her through the door. She tried to pull away but his arm tightened around her shoulders when he felt her withdrawing. It was extremely awkward; Lucy wasn't sure if Trey really wanted to show her the machinery or if he was abducting her. Looking over her shoulder for some means of escape, she saw a number of police cars arriving with lights flashing and realized the raid had finally materialized. The timing couldn't have been worse; now she was in the middle of it. She made a desperate effort to escape, shoving Trey and pulling away, but he only tightened his grip on her.

"Don't move or I'll shoot," he said.

Lucy felt cold metal pressed against her temple.

The police cruisers—there were four of them— came to a stop about thirty feet away, where a row of evergreen bushes provided some cover. A door on the first one opened and Lieutenant Horowitz stepped out.

"Stop!" yelled Meacham. "I've got a gun and I'll use it."

Horowitz's arms went up. "We can work this out," he said. "There's no need to shoot."

"I've got a hostage. You make any moves and I'll shoot her."

"Nobody's moving," said Horowitz.

Caught in Trey's grip, Lucy's teeth were chattering. She noticed that he was shivering, too, and the hand holding the gun was shaking. The next thing she knew he had dragged her inside the building and the thick wooden door had closed behind them.

"Did you call the cops?" he demanded.

Lucy shook her head. "No! I only came to take pictures."

He jabbed the gun into her back. "Move. We'll go in the office."

Lucy obeyed, walking woodenly in the direction he indicated, toward a door with a frosted glass panel painted with the word OFFICE. Once they were inside the large room, which was filled with old-fashioned wooden desks and had big windows overlooking the parking lot, he pushed her into a chair and snapped a handcuff on one arm. Lucy wondered if they were the same pair he'd used on Corney.

He looped the other cuff around the arm of the chair and when he snapped it shut she realized how helpless she was and a huge shudder ran through her body. She was a hostage, entirely at the mercy of a twisted killer, and she could only hope the police outside knew what they were doing. Trey gave the wheeled chair a shove, placing her in front of one of the big windows, where she was a sitting duck. She had a clear view of the parking lot, where a steady stream of police vehicles was arriving and a group of black-clad SWAT team members were taking up positions surrounding the building.

If shooting broke out, Lucy decided, her only chance would be to try to tip the chair over and fall to the ground. That plan was flawed, however, because she'd have to survive the first volley of shots and her exposed position made that unlikely. Mind whirling, she remembered hearing somewhere that if you ever found yourself in a hostage situation you should try to develop a friendly relationship with your captor. It was worth a try, she thought. "I'm supposed to be making brownies and meat loaf," she said, trying to keep her voice steady.

"This wasn't exactly on my agenda," muttered Trey, sounding nervous.

She decided to keep up the small talk. "Do you have a date for tonight?" she asked. "It's Valentine's Day."

Trey had positioned himself behind a heavy oak filing cabinet, probably a relic from the sardine cannery, and was staring out the window.

"I was going to call my mom."

This whole situation was surreal, thought Lucy, and getting even weirder. "That's nice," she said, feeling a bit more confident. "I was going to make meat loaf for my husband, it's his favorite. With mashed potatoes and gravy. And I was going to have ice cream for dessert. We have two daughters. . . ."

"I have a bad feeling about this," said Trey, just as the phone rang. "Answer it," he said. "Put it on speakerphone."

Lucy slid the chair closer to the nearest desk and reached for the phone with her free hand, getting it on the fourth ring. "Hello," she said.

"I'm Brian Sullivan. I'm a trained negotiator." A warm, relaxed voice filled the room.

"I'm Lucy Stone," she replied, looking at Trey for permission to continue. When he nodded, she said, "I'm the hostage. I'm handcuffed to a chair."

"We're going to get you out of this, Lucy. Are you the only hostage?"

Getting a shake of the head from Trey she replied. "I don't know."

"Who is with you?"

Lucy looked once again to Trey but this time he drew his finger across his throat. "I have to go," she said, and hung up.

Develop a relationship, she reminded herself. "He sounded nice," she said.

"Nice!" barked Trey. "They want to put me in jail for life."

"Not for life," said Lucy. "You don't get life for dealing."

He looked at her. "I think we both know I did more than that."

"There were mitigating circumstances," said Lucy. "Max tried to blackmail you, didn't he? He knew what happened in Mexico, with Wes Teasdale."

"Wes? Wes drowned. He was a lousy surfer." Trey scratched his chin with the gun. "No, Max wasn't blackmailing me. He wanted in on the drugs."

"He knew about the drugs?" asked Lucy.

"Yeah. From Mexico. We did some stuff together a long time ago. He knew the chocolate business was a good front—I used the cocoa shipments to smuggle in coke, heroin, even oxy; you can get it cheap down there."

The phone rang again, but Trey shook his head, signaling she shouldn't answer it. The rings continued for a while, and Lucy could hardly stand it. She felt panic rising in her chest with every ring and tried to concentrate on breathing, just breathing. Finally the rings stopped. "That was annoying," she said.

"Yeah," agreed Trey.

"It was really clever, the way you killed Max. The cops thought it was an accident."

"Max helped, he was really drunk. It was easy."

"Did you plan it?"

"No. We'd set up a meeting on the ice, he liked to fish at night. Said he'd show me how it was done. One thing led to another. He got mad, took a swing at me. I swung back and he went down, fell on his gear, and got tangled up. That's what gave me the idea to kind of embellish his body."

"The thing I wondered about is how you got him through the ice—how'd you do that?"

"I knew there was that punky spot and I just slid him over—the trick was not to go through myself. It was a near thing, I almost did."

Lucy wished he had, she wished it more than anything she'd ever wished, but she wasn't about to let him know that. "That was lucky," she said, trying to sound as if she meant it.

"I don't think you really mean that," he said, with a crooked smile. Lucy almost liked him, she realized, wondering if this was that Stockholm syndrome she'd heard so much about.

"What about Tamzin?"

"She opened a package of cocoa beans and found a brick of coke. She said she wouldn't tell anyone but I didn't trust her, she was always talking about that ex-husband of hers and what a hero he was. I couldn't risk it."

"Why the chocolate coating?" she asked.

"I wanted to make it look like Dora did it," he said.

"Very clever," said Lucy, as the phone started ringing again.

Trey was looking out the window, where the parking lot was filling up fast with official vehicles with red and blue flashing lights. "It's like Christmas out there," he muttered. Then, in a tone of amazement, he added, "Look at that sky."

A spectacular winter sunset had tinted the overarching sky a gorgeous shade of pink and a handful of fluffy white clouds were rimmed with gold. It seemed as if God himself could reach down and touch the earth, making everything right.

"I'm not going to jail," said Trey. His voice was low and decisive. "If I'm going out, I might as well do it in a blaze of glory."

Then he was gone and Lucy was left alone with the ringing phone. She answered it. "He's left. I don't know where. . . ."

Just then a dark shape tumbled past the window, landing with a heart-stopping thud.

She sat, absorbing what had happened, and waited for the SWAT team to release her.

"He was up on the tower," one of the officers told her, as he unlocked the handcuffs. "He climbed up on a ledge and stood there, facing the sun. Then he stretched out his arms and just stepped off."

"Is he dead?" asked Lucy.

"Oh, yeah."

She stood up and stretched, then, feeling woozy, thought better of it and sat back down.

"Do you need a medic?" the officer asked.

"No, I'll be okay," she said, noticing Larry Graves standing in the doorway. "Where were you?" she asked. "You were supposed to meet me here."

He shrugged, a sheepish expression on his face. "I got lost. The GPS didn't work." He paused, studying her face. "I'm really, really sorry."

Lucy tried standing again and this time she didn't feel dizzy. She felt good, she decided. It was definitely good to be alive.

"Don't be," she said. "You were right. I got a hell of a story."

Chapter Twenty-one

The police had set up a temporary crisis management headquarters in a trailer in the parking lot outside the chocolate factory, and that's where Lucy was taken to be debriefed. Brian Sullivan, the negotiator with the warm voice, interviewed her, and she was surprised to find he was short, slight, and balding, a complete contrast to the mental picture she'd built based on his voice.

"I just want to go over the video with you," he said. "We had a very sensitive listening device, but it didn't pick up everything and I need you to fill in the blanks."

He pointed to a video monitor and when the snow cleared she saw a grainy picture of the office, shot through the windows. Meacham was a shadowy figure, never seen in full as he remained partially hidden behind the file cabinet. She, on the other hand, was front and center, handcuffed to the chair. It was an unsettling image.

An audio technician arrived and was soon able to match his recording with the video and Lucy was able to see and hear the worst hour of her life all over again. It went excruciatingly slowly, however, because the process was halted frequently so Lucy could supply missing scraps of dialogue. She tried her best to be accurate, but oftentimes the technician would determine that her memory didn't match the fragments of sound on the tape and she'd have to try all over again. She was completely exhausted when they finally said she could go.

She wasn't sure how she was going to get home and was trying to decide if she could manage to drive herself when the door opened and Bill arrived. She rushed into his arms and he held her tightly, smoothing her hair and covering her face with kisses, and that's when she burst into hysterical tears.

"It's all over, you're safe, you're safe," he said.

"I know," she blubbered, unable to stop sobbing.

"The cops said you were amazing, really cool, did everything right."

"I want to go home," she finally said, wiping her eyes with her hands.

Bill gave her one of his big white handkerchiefs and just seeing it and holding it made her start crying all over again. "I love you," she said, sputtering.

He gave her a big squeeze. "You can show me later. But for now, you owe me a meat loaf dinner."

"Okay," she said, letting him take her hand and lead her out into the night.

* * *

On Monday morning Ted was already at his desk when she arrived. "How are you?" he asked.

"Kind of shaky," she said.

The door opened and Phyllis came in, wrapped in a colorful poncho with matching hand-knitted hat and gloves. She was carrying a big bouquet of flowers. "These are for you," she said, engulfing Lucy in a multicolored hug.

It was all too much for Lucy, and the tears began flowing again.

"Oh, for Pete's sake, the story of the year and my ace reporter is too emotional to tell it," muttered Ted, as the bell on the door jangled furiously and Frankie blew in, all in a dither.

"The story of the year—that's what I've got for you!" she exclaimed, waving a sheaf of papers in her gloved hand.

"We've got it. Lucy was there when Trey committed suicide."

"Trey? Suicide?" Frankie was puzzled.

"Haven't you heard?" asked Ted.

"Renee and I spent yesterday *chez ma mère*, she lives in Portsmouth. Why? What happened?"

"It's a long story," said Lucy. "What's your news?"

Frankie couldn't wait to tell them. "It's the Faircloths. They're gone!"

"But I thought they were buying the McIntyre place," said Lucy.

"Yeah, so did I." Frankie waved the papers. "I've got a purchase and sales agreement right here, but when I went over to the Salt Aire to get them to sign it, the desk clerk told me they'd left sometime in the night without paying their bill. It's over five thousand dollars."

Lucy wasn't sure she'd heard right. "They skipped out on their bill?"

"Yeah. When housekeeping went in this morning, they were gone—and they even took the bathrobes!" Frankie paused. "But they did leave a twenty for the maid, along with a note thanking her for excellent service."

"Classy," said Ted.

"Not really," muttered Frankie. "I devoted every waking moment to those people and now I'm out a hefty commission. I was counting on that money."

"They seemed so nice," said Lucy. "I saw them dancing Saturday night at the ball and they made a lovely couple."

"*Seemed* is the operative word here," said Phyllis.

"You said it," agreed Frankie. "It turns out they're a pair of scam artists. They've been doing this for months, maybe years. They lost their house to foreclosure so they've been moving around to inns and B&Bs, living it up in the style to which they're accustomed and leaving a trail of unpaid bills. The clerk at the Salt Aire said they got an e-mail from the innkeeper's association just this morning, warning about them. They left a big bill at the Queen Vic, too."

Ted was reaching for the phone. "I'm calling the printery," he said. "I think we're going to need some extra pages this week."

Lucy was nodding. "And people say nothing happens here in the winter!"

* * *

Punxsutawney Phil had predicted six more weeks of winter on Groundhog Day and for once he seemed to be right. March roared in like a lion, but this particular lion turned out to be a pussycat, bringing bright sunshine and warm temperatures. When Elizabeth came home for a long weekend before starting her next assignment at the brand new Cavendish Hotel on Cape Cod, the snow was gone and buds were swelling on the forsythia bushes. Lucy had cut some branches a week or so earlier and they were already in bloom, a yellow explosion on the dining room sideboard.

Lucy was putting the finishing touches on her table, laying out the silver serving spoons, and the scent of cooking turkey was heavy in the air. A series of sharp barks from Libby announced the arrival of her dinner guests, Marge and Barney Culpepper and their son, Eddie.

"It's like Thanksgiving," declared Zoe, when they were all sitting at the table.

"We have a lot to be thankful for," said Lucy.

"You can say that again," said Barney, with a nod to Eddie.

He was fresh out of rehab and looked great, thought Lucy. He was letting his military brush cut grow in and the slightly longer, curly hair softened his appearance. He smiled often, paying special attention to Elizabeth. Lily, he said in answer to Lucy's pointed inquiry, was away in Switzerland, apprenticing with a master chocolatier.

Elizabeth seemed to be enjoying herself, which was a big change from her returns home during college breaks, when she complained about there being nothing to do and couldn't wait to get back to Boston. Now that she was working and fending for herself she had a new appreciation for home, where Mom took care of the cooking and cleaning and even did her laundry.

When they'd polished off the shrimp cocktail and turkey with stuffing and gravy and all the fixings—Bill's payment for fixing the door at the *Pennysaver*—Lucy suggested moving into the living room for coffee. Sara and Zoe were delegated to clear the table and load the dishwasher; Elizabeth and Eddie went off together to hear a local band and catch up with high school friends at the Irish pub down by the harbor.

"Eddie looks terrific," said Lucy, pouring a cup of decaf for Marge.

Bill lit the fire he had laid earlier. When he was satisfied that it had caught, he produced a bottle of brandy and, receiving a nod from Barney, poured two glasses. "What's his legal situation?" he asked.

Barney took the snifter and raised it to the light, admiring the golden liquid, then took a sip. "Mmmm," he said. "Well, he took my advice for once and agreed to cooperate with the DA. He got a good deal, no jail time, probation for a year with random drug and alcohol tests, and of course rehab. You never know, but it looks like he's staying clean."

"He's thinking about going to college," said Marge, holding her saucer with one hand and lifting the cup with the other. "He's looking into physical therapy. Maybe because of the guys he knew who got wounded. He says he wants to help people."

"I guess he already has," said Lucy, sitting down on the couch with her coffee. "He's named some of the dealers Meacham was supplying. The drug task force is finally making real progress." She paused. "I didn't realize that they'd been working on making a case against Meacham for months."

Barney nodded. "Nobody did. Those guys work undercover, way undercover. Even Horowitz didn't know what they were doing. He was convinced Dora was the killer, and there was a lot of circumstantial evidence. But when Graves showed up with his story about Tamzin discovering the drugs, he contacted the task force and they set up the raid." He took a sip of brandy. "Meacham had quite an operation, bringing the stuff in from Mexico with the cocoa beans and using the factory to distribute it. It turned out that Chanticleer Chocolate's most popular flavors were heroin and OxyContin, along with pot, coke, and ecstasy. He had something for everyone, whatever their preference and budget."

"Who knew?" mused Marge, biting into a cookie. "He seemed so nice. I never would have guessed. And the scope—I couldn't believe the amount of drugs they found in his warehouse."

Lucy nodded, remembering the photo Ted ran in the *Pennysaver* showing huge bottles of pills and hundreds of plastic bags of marijuana and cocaine, laid out so they completely covered the big conference table at the police station. "Ted said Trey was going to be the Chamber of Commerce's Businessman of the Year."

"Some businessman," snorted Bill. "It was all a big lie."

"What's happening to all his drug customers?" asked Lucy. "They can't all be in rehab."

"They've found other dealers," said Barney, draining his glass. "Or they steal. There was a pharmacy break-in last night, over in Gilead."

Lucy shook her head. "What's the solution? How do we stop this?"

Barney set his empty glass on the mantel and stood studying the flames dancing in the fireplace. "I wish I knew," he said. "I wish I knew."

Spring has sprung in Tinker's Cove, and Lucy Stone has a mile-long to-do list. From painting eggs with her grandson, to preparing the perfect Easter feast, to reviving her garden after a long, cold winter, she hardly has time to search for a killer with a deadly case of spring fever . . .

Lucy has always loved covering the annual Easter egg hunt for the *Pennysaver*. Hosted by elderly socialite Vivian Van Vorst at Pine Point, her luxurious oceanfront estate, it's a swanky event where the grown-ups sip cocktails while their children search for eggs that are as likely to contain savings bonds as they are jelly beans. But when Lucy arrives with her three-year-old grandson, VV's normally welcoming gates are locked, and a man dressed as the Easter Bunny emerges to drop dead moments later . . .

Lucy discovers that the victim is Van Vorst Duff, VV's grandson, and soon learns that not all is as it seems at idyllic Pine Point, where the champagne and caviar seem to be running dry. Always a social butterfly, VV has been skipping lunch dates with friends, and her much-needed donations to local charities have stopped with no explanation. Maybe she's going senile, or maybe her heirs are getting a little too anxious to take over her estate . . .

As Lucy gathers a basketful of suspects, she's convinced that someone's been hunting for a lot more than eggs. And she'll have to chase the truth down a rabbit hole before the killer claims another victim . . .

Please turn the page for an exciting sneak peek of Leslie Meier's newest Lucy Stone mystery EASTER BUNNY MURDER coming next month!

Chapter One

It was not the sort of thing you expected on a beautiful April morning. The sun was pouring through the kitchen windows and, outside, long wands of yellow forsythia blooms were waving in a gentle breeze. The newly installed granite countertop gleamed expensively beneath two dozen Easter eggs, freshly dyed in a rainbow of colors. Lucy Stone was admiring her grandson Patrick's handiwork, which featured crayon scribbles and garish color combinations, when she heard the scream.

It was a truly ear-piercing, heart-stopping sound. What was happening? Had the just-turned-three-year-old poked a finger into an electric socket? Had he run with scissors and stumbled, gashing himself? A second scream, even louder than the first, sent her flying up the stairs.

"What's the matter?" she cried, racing into Patrick's sunny little room, which was decorated with trucks. There was a parade of red, blue, and yellow trucks on the curtains, on the wallpaper border, and on his bedding.

"Nothing at all," sighed Patrick's mother, Molly, who was sprawled on the blue rug. She was attempting to restrain her wiggly son in something resembling a wrestling hold, with one arm firmly clamped across his chest. In the other hand, she had a miniature necktie.

Lucy, an experienced mother, grasped the situation immediately. "Patrick, don't you want to wear a necktie, just like Daddy does?" Actually, this was a bit of a stretch. Lucy knew her son, Toby, Patrick's father, rarely wore a necktie and then only under protest. His current occupation as a college student only required casual clothing, and he donned sturdy work clothes when he snagged occasional employment as a carpenter's helper or landscaper.

"No!" Patrick kicked a small foot, clad in brand-new brown leather oxfords, sending his shoe flying across the room.

"Patrick! That's enough! Now sit still so we can finish getting you dressed!"

Molly's tone was firm and Patrick paused in his protestations long enough to allow his grandmother to scoop him up and set him on her lap, where he continued to show his displeasure by shoving his lower lip out in a resentful pout.

"Now, now," crooned Lucy. "That's no way to behave. We're going to see the Easter Bunny! And there will be treats for good little boys."

"I don't know," murmured Molly, struggling to shove Patrick's small foot into the stiff shoe. "Maybe this isn't such a good idea."

"But he looks so handsome," said Lucy, nuzzling the little boy's silky blond hair.

Patrick was indeed the very picture of a proper little gentleman. In addition to the new shoes, he was wearing a pair of kelly green pants, a blue, green, and white argyle vest, a white shirt, and—hopefully—the matching green necktie.

"What if he has a tantrum there?" fretted Molly, brushing a lock of hair out of her eyes and leaning back on her heels. "I'd be so embarrassed."

"Tantrums happen," said Lucy with a shrug. "If he blows, we'll just pick him up and take him home. But it would be a shame to miss the Easter egg hunt just because he might have a tantrum. He'll probably be fine."

"If you ask me, I think Patrick has a point," said Molly, handing the necktie to Lucy. "I don't see why the kids have to dress up when they'd be so much more comfortable in their play clothes."

Lucy bent down and buried her nose in Patrick's neck, giving him little kisses at the same time she deftly fastened the miniature clip-on tie to his collar. "VV is a generous hostess. She spares no expense on the Easter egg hunt and the refreshments afterward, and she expects her guests to show their appreciation by dressing up a bit." She tickled Patrick, who responded by giggling. "And by using their very best manners."

"It's a lot to expect of a three-year-old," said Molly, gathering up Patrick's T-shirt and jeans, stained with dye. "And eating candy sends him into the stratosphere."

"There's more than candy in those plastic eggs," said Lucy. As a part-time reporter for the local

weekly, she had covered Vivian Van Vorst's annual
Easter egg hunt at her magnificent private estate,
Pine Point, for many years. "Some of them have
gift certificates, savings bonds, even tuition vouch-
ers. Wouldn't you love to get a free month or two
of day care?"

"Actually, yes, I would," said Molly, getting to
her feet. "Come on, Patrick. This is going to be
fun."

When Patrick was firmly belted into his car seat,
Lucy and Molly resumed their conversation.

"You know, I don't remember going to the
Easter egg hunt when I was a kid," said Molly.

"No, you wouldn't," said Lucy, pausing at the
end of Prudence Path before turning onto Red
Top Road. "VV started it about twelve years ago,
and it's only for children eight and under. You
were too old by then."

Molly gazed out the car window as they drove
along, noticing the bright yellow forsythia bushes
and the green shoots of spring bulbs that had
popped up around the modest gray-shingled and
white clapboard houses that were dotted along the
road. "How did VV get all her money, anyway?"

"She did it the old-fashioned way; she married
it. She's a local girl. I heard she grew up on a poul-
try farm but it's long gone. Anyway, at some point
she left Tinker's Cove and met Horatio Van Vorst
and captured his heart. Or maybe something
else."

Molly chuckled.

"He was a big industrialist and was immensely
rich. I think they came here to Tinker's Cove
sometime in the 1950s and began buying up land,

accumulating some two hundred acres and building the house. It's enormous, but they only came in the summers while he was alive. He died some years ago, leaving VV very well off. She's in her nineties now and she lives here year-round."

"I've heard she's the richest person in town," said Molly.

"She sure is," said Lucy, making the turn onto Shore Road. "These houses are nothing compared to Pine Point," she said, pointing to the McMansions that had sprouted up on the rocky bluff overlooking the Atlantic Ocean. "But she's a very generous benefactor. She's given lots of money to the library and the hospital. The town wouldn't be the same without her."

Molly's expression hardened as they drove past one huge, empty house after another. "Look at them, nobody's home at most of them. Their owners only use them in the summer. It's enough to make you a communist! Toby and I are struggling to pay our bills and these people have houses they don't even use."

"You just had your kitchen remodeled," Lucy reminded her, thinking of all that gleaming granite and stainless steel.

"That was my dad. He said we had to upgrade or we'd never be able to sell the house—and he paid for it."

Lucy was immediately alarmed; she liked having Molly and Toby and Patrick living so close to her old farm house on Red Top Road. "Are you planning on selling?" she asked, braking well in advance for the sharp turn where Shore Road clung to the bluff and curved high above the tiny cove known as Lover's Leap. The view of the bay was spectacular but Lucy didn't notice; she kept her eyes on the road, fearful of plunging down into the roiling water below.

"No. I love that house; I don't want to sell. And, frankly, I was perfectly happy with the old kitchen. I would much rather have had the cash, what with Toby's tuition and all. But Dad said we had to have granite."

"Well, getting a new kitchen isn't exactly a hardship," said Lucy, joining the line of cars snaking down the drive to Pine Point. "I don't know if that disqualifies you from membership in the Communist Party."

Molly laughed. "You think I should count my blessings."

Lucy nodded. "Whenever I complained that my friends had nicer things than I did, my mother would say, 'Envy's a green-eyed monster that comes hissing hot from hell.' " She looked over her shoulder at Patrick, whose chin had dropped onto his chest. "Uh-oh. Guess who's asleep?"

"I thought he was awfully quiet," said Molly, as the car crept along.

In past years, Lucy remembered, parking had been allowed along one side of the long driveway and was supervised by young men hired for the day, equipped with whistles and red flags. There were no attendants on the job this year, but most people remembered the drill and pulled off to the right, lining up neatly on the gravel verge. A few others, however, parked any which way on the lawn, at which Lucy clucked her tongue in disapproval. "That lawn is VV's pride and joy," she said, pulling into the next available spot, "and those cars are going to leave tire marks."

"At least they're not blocking the drive," said Molly, who was busy unfastening the straps on Patrick's car seat. The little boy stirred, yawning adorably and stretching his little arms.

Lucy, meanwhile, got out of the car and unfolded the umbrella stroller and in a moment Patrick was settled and they joined the other families walking up the drive toward the house. There was a sense of happy anticipation. It had been a long, hard winter and everyone was enjoying the fine weather and looking forward to the afternoon's entertainment. The Easter egg hunt was always lots of fun; the kids were cute as they scrambled across the lawn, first racing to grab the obvious eggs scattered on the grass and, then, encouraged by shouts from their parents, searching for the more valuable eggs that had been hidden in the shrubbery, beneath flowers, and behind statuary.

Then, when all the eggs had been collected, VV would award prizes. She would stand on the front steps of the magnificent mansion, dressed in a lovely pastel suit topped with a flowery hat, beaming at the assembled children. There were always so many certificates and ribbons that everybody got one: most eggs, fastest collector, most polite collector, best blue outfit, best pink outfit, shiniest shoes, curliest hair, and on and on, until every child had been recognized for some special attribute.

Later, after all the prizes had been distributed, Willis, the butler, would open the massive front doors and everyone was invited to partake of refreshments in the hall. This was Lucy's favorite part, because the oval hall was always beautifully decorated with garlands of spring flowers. They were clustered on the crystal chandelier, they twined around the railing on the floating staircase, and they were looped on the overloaded buffet tables.

The food was always delicious, served up by uniformed caterers. There was something for everyone: fruit punch for the kids, tea for the tee-totalers, and wine punch for those who enjoyed a drop of something stronger. Of course, there were always tons of deviled eggs, as well as mountains of tiny sandwiches and platters of cookies and cup-cakes, all iced in pretty pastel colors. Most tempt-ing of all, perhaps, were the fruit tarts, each one heaped with a generous mound of glistening berries.

But before diving into the buffet, Lucy always took a moment to admire the priceless Karl Klaus sculpture that was VV's pride and joy. The sculp-ture, aptly titled *Jelly Beans*, was a group of four ovoid shapes clustered together—orange, pink, and lavender were on the bottom, yellow on top. The sculpture was always displayed on the round table in the center of the hall, but on the day of the Easter egg hunt, it was featured in an elabo-rate ice sculpture depicting the Easter Bunny with his nest of eggs.

All this was running through Lucy's mind as they walked along the drive, toward the curve and the final approach to the mansion, where budding Japanese cherry trees flanked the drive leading to the elaborate iron gates. Those gates were always thrown open for the Easter egg hunt, but today they were inexplicably closed, and a sizable crowd had gathered in front of them.

"I wonder what's going on," said Lucy.

"Are you sure this is the right day?" asked Molly.

"Absolutely. It's always the Saturday before Palm Sunday, a full week before Easter," said Lucy. "At noon. Precisely."

"They must have forgotten to open the gates," said Lydia Volpe, a retired kindergarten teacher who had brought her two grandchildren, twins, dressed identically in pink gingham jackets.

"I dunno," said a bearded and tattooed young man Lucy recognized from the Quik-Stop. "I don't see any eggs on the lawn."

"And the gate's not decorated," added his companion, a pasty-faced young woman who was bouncing a doughy baby on her hip.

"If you ask me, the garden looks a bit run down," whispered Rebecca Wardwell, an elderly woman who Lucy knew was a dedicated gardener. "That quince needs pruning and those daffodils are tired; most of them don't even have buds."

"I noticed that, too," said Lucy, who had always admired VV's impeccably tended grounds. "And there were no parking attendants. I'm beginning to think they decided not to have the egg hunt this year."

Her comment sparked a little buzz as people speculated whether or not the hunt was going to take place. Despite the disturbing evidence to the contrary, most people insisted it must be on, perhaps just delayed for some reason. After all, there was always an Easter egg hunt at Pine Point.

Then a sudden hush fell over the crowd as VV's

butler, Willis, was seen opening one of the French doors that opened onto a stone terrace. He carefully closed the door behind him, then began a stately walk across the terrace, down the stone steps and then proceeded along the paved walk to the oyster shell drive. As always, he was dressed in a black suit with a white shirt and striped tie and his gray hair was combed straight back from his lined face.

Reaching the gates, he paused and cleared his throat. He was about to speak when a collective gasp arose from the crowd. The Easter Bunny had appeared! Everyone could see him standing in the elaborate front doorway, where two double doors were now open behind a protective metal grille. He was a big bunny, at least seven feet tall, covered in white plush with a pink felt stomach and a huge round head, complete with big blue eyes, a pink nose, toothy smile, black whiskers, and enormous pointy ears, one of which flopped down over one eye. An absolutely huge basket filled with colorful plastic eggs was looped over one arm.

"There he is!" shrieked a little girl, whose black hair had been twisted into braids tied with crisp polka-dot bows.

"It's the Easter Bunny, it's really him," said a serious little boy wearing wire-rimmed eyeglasses.

Lucy scooped up Patrick, holding him up so he could see the Easter Bunny for himself. "See!" she said, pointing. "He's going to hop, hop, hop down the bunny trail."

Patrick chortled merrily. Like everyone else, his eyes were glued to the big bunny, who raised one paw in a wave to the crowd before he grabbed the metal grille to push it open. For a moment, he seemed to stagger, and everyone held their breath: Was something the matter with the Easter Bunny?

Then there was a collective sigh of relief as the bunny seemed to recover, shoving the grille open and leaping awkwardly down the steps to the lawn, where he began a clumsy gallop toward the gates, dropping a few plastic eggs on the way.

Patrick was getting heavy and Lucy was passing him to Molly when the bunny reached Willis, swayed on his feet, and suddenly collapsed, dropping the basket. The colorful eggs rolled every which way as the bunny convulsed and then was still.

The crowd stood in shocked silence, until the little girl with braids began to cry. "The Easter Bunny is dead," she sobbed.